# THREE
# MARID
# DJINNS

## An Unrequited Love

## JUAN BERRY

ARCHWAY
PUBLISHING

Archway Publishing books may be ordered through booksellers or by contacting:

Archway Publishing
1663 Liberty Drive
Bloomington, IN 47403
www.archwaypublishing.com
844-669-3957

ISBN: 978-1-6657-3766-1 (sc)
ISBN: 978-1-6657-3765-4 (e)

Library of Congress Control Number: 2023901328

Print information available on the last page.

Archway Publishing rev. date: 02/08/2023

# CONTENTS

# An Unrequited Love

Contrary to certain myths and legends, Jinns do not inhabit lamps to give three wishes. This particular type of Jinn inhabited humans and creatures. Since the first great war of the heavens, an iconic Jinn named Iblis sought to corrupt and oppress humanity. No Jinns were more feared and respected for the task than three Marid Djinns. Iblis had spawned the creatures within the magma, ash, and water vapors of an erupting volcano. Since the day of their creation, his selfish nature had kept their faces hidden from all creatures, and they were forced to cover their faces with black silk scarves.

Their proud, arrogant, and rebellious ways quickly moved them through the ranks of their father's army. They manipulated their human vessels by granting powers through seduction and increased strength for plots based on revenge. For this same reason, Iblis lost his Marid Djinns to a king. A deal forged by a practitioner of black magic forced him to barter the services of the Marid Djinns to soldiers in peril. They displayed their vengeful nature by refusing to bow down to any person or creature. They inspired characteristics that created legends for all cultures to follow. Many Greeks, Romans, and Scandinavians referred to them as Moirae, Parcae, and Norns—the *Fates!*

Every weapon they wield or create is designed for death and feared by all. They spawned legends within Spartan vessels, which led three hundred soldiers on a suicide mission against an unstoppable Persian army. Throughout history, they continued to weave fates in battle, such as when three Roman soldiers, inseparable and unmatched in skill, refused to surrender to an army on a bridge that crossed the Tiber River. In present times, their names are Gall, Sitoel, and Banter. I'll tell you their story. . .

After Sitoel discovered Hel's sordid affair with Banter, Iblis honored her victory in Ragnarok by granting her the request to return home. In the middle of the night, Sitoel slowly strolled through the shack-filled hills of El Carmel in the district of Horta Guinardo. In a secluded area that contained a caravan of gypsies, Sitoel approached a wooden carriage resting on the outskirts. She slowly walked up the creaking staircase, wondering why it was isolated from the others. A wooden sign posted on the door brought a smile to her face. She quickly recalled a childhood scolding from her grandmother as she touched the bold lettering. It read, "MADAME CARREA, FORTUNE TELLER AND SEER!"

Sitoel's grandmother dragged her into the carriage after a fight with the male teenagers in the tribe.

"Give me those escrima sticks!" shouted Madame Carrea.

"I earned it fair and square!" protested Sitoel.

Madame Carrea reached into her brassiere and removed the tribe's sacred bloodstone. "While you were plowing through the men of our tribe, did it ever occur to you that one of them would be your king someday?" shouted Madame Carrea.

"No, I was having too much fun. To stop and think would have ruined it for me," answered Sitoel.

Madame Carrea nodded with disappointment. She placed the stone in a small metal container and grabbed a deck of tarot cards from the shelf. "Well, I hope you enjoyed your workout. Your little adventure has cost us our place among the tribe."

"A little voice kept daring me to take it, and after a few nightmares it showed me how. I didn't want you to lose your place in the tribe. I'll do anything to make it up to you," said Sitoel.

"I always hoped you possessed a skill more favorable than the stick-fighting your father taught you. Now let's see if you really can make it up to me," replied Madame Carrea.

Madame Carrea sat at a large circular table centered in the caravan and gestured for Sitoel to remove a card from her tarot deck. Sitoel obediently complied and placed the card on the table. Madame Carrea's eyes broadened with amazement. She moved her hands over the upward-facing symbols. "The wheel of fortune! Your gift is true. Our Great Secret means things will come to hand," explained Madame Carrea. She stepped away from the table and walked back to the shelf. Sitoel curiously watched as she grabbed a can of paint and a paintbrush.

"What are you planning to do with that?" asked Sitoel.

"I've never been one to look a gift horse in the mouth, so I'm making you a part of my show," answered Madame Carrea. When she was done, the sign read as follows:

MADAME CARREA
FORTUNE TELLER AND SEER!
PERFORMING WITH THE GREAT SECRET
SITOEL CARREA!

A familiar voice interrupted Sitoel's daydream to bring her back from the past. "My child has returned to me. You may enter when you wish," said Madame Carrea. Sitoel opened the door and found her grandmother sitting at the table with a deck of tarot cards. Sitoel removed her mask and ran to her side to give a heartfelt hug. "I feel the same. You couldn't have picked a better time to return and redeem our name," said Madame Carrea.

"What do you mean by redeeming our name? Why are you isolated from the others?" asked Sitoel. She pulled out a chair to sit beside her grandmother as she explained.

"A lot of events have taken place during your absence. After your sister's death and your imprisonment, your parents were forced to leave the tribe."

"Forced? Who would dare?" interrupted Sitoel.

Madame Carrea debated on giving an answer as Sitoel's eyes lustered.

"Tell me!" demanded Sitoel.

"Our new king—he slowly bled them out of your small fortune," answered Madame Carrea. "When they could no longer provide, he claimed they were cursed and made them outcasts. They now reside in the rebuilt shacks of El Carmel."

"I'll have to find time to tend to our king," mumbled Sitoel.

Madame Carrea quickly changed the subject to keep Sitoel's anger from escalating. "Enough about me. Tell me what brings you home?" she asked.

Sitoel's eyes kept their luster as Banter and Hel came to mind. "I just needed to get away for a while," Sitoel shyly answered.

"I've seen those eyes before. Age is supposed to bring you wisdom. Why do you foolishly try to hide the truth from me?" asked Madame Carrea. She picked up her deck of tarot cards and gestured for Sitoel to remove one. Sitoel obediently complied and placed it on the table with her mask. A stunned expression crossed Madame Carrea's face as she looked over the reversed symbols of the lover's card. "You're here because of a man! I'm almost hesitant to ask if he or his mistress is still alive."

"You can put your worries at ease. He's still alive, but I can't determine how long the other one will be," answered Sitoel.

"Why trouble yourself over a man who makes you wear a mask?"

A smirk crossed Sitoel's face as she recalled the time Banter first asked her to wear it. "He also wanted me to dye my hair a color called Ruby Eruption."

"You refused?"

"He wanted me to match the ruby casing that almost killed me, and I didn't have to match to see that Hel's keys were also present."

Madame Carrea disappointedly shook her head. "You should learn a lesson about love," she replied. She then slowly stepped away from the table to retire for the evening.

"I never gave anything to anyone who didn't deserve it!" snapped Sitoel.

"This is true about you, but can you speak for him?" asked Madame Carrea.

The question stumped Sitoel as she stood from the table. She walked to the corner of the caravan and pulled back a curtain that covered the space she called a room.

Madame Carrea could hear the rings slide as though she were slamming a door closed. She gently rested her head on her pillow as the sound of escrima sticks banged against the wall. Madame Carrea closed her eyes and whispered, "You'll soon learn."

After the death of Jormungandr, Gall caught a ride on a barge that docked in England. A smile appeared on his face as he recalled an Abominable safe house in East Riding of Yorkshire. Kaleb purchased a pub and inn in the village of Tunstall to help launder his business earnings. Fortunately for Gall, a master fabricator was in his employ. A bald and burly middle-aged man named Moss Guiles worked as a bartender there. He was extremely useful in gathering passports. Gall boldly entered the crowded pub to greet his old friend. "Moss, fetch me a glass of old ale!" shouted Gall.

Moss could hardly contain his laughter as Gall approached the bar. "Bollocks to that! What would happen to the caliber of this establishment if I willingly served two Abominables?" joked Moss.

"Two Abominables?" Gall asked as he glanced through the bar.

"I guess you've forgotten Victor always makes his rounds this time of year," answered Moss. "He's checked in to a room upstairs if you care to visit." He wrote down the number of the room and gave it to Gall with a glass of old ale. "I'll stop and say hello, but first I need one of your special favors. My friend needs some help getting back to the states," whispered Gall.

"This friend of yours—will he be Seth Reno or Bronco Campos?"

"Seth Reno, and make sure it's your best work."

Moss responded with a nod and raised a glass to gesture a toast. Gall raised his glass and guzzled the ale like water. He slammed the empty glass on the bar and caught the stare of a waitress. Gall looked over the curvy frame hidden in a barmaid uniform with a devilish smirk. A long black ponytail and a pair of almond colored eyes under thick brows complemented her caramel complexion. "Moss, what can you tell me about the new girl?" asked Gall.

"A foreigner with a foreigner's attitude best describes that one. A bit sassy for me, but just right for the job. Her name is Pandora," answered Moss. He poured Gall another glass.

"Call her over here," said Gall.

"Pandora, this gentleman would like to have a word with you!" shouted Moss.

"My shift is over in five minutes. He'll have to come back to-morrow," replied Pandora.

"I tried to warn you," whispered Moss.

Gall chuckled as Moss made another attempt with a more serious tone. "If you value your job, you'll tend to one of the owners of this establishment," advised Moss.

A loud grunt disguised Pandora's purpose as she slowly approached Gall. "So what makes you so special?" she asked.

"Weren't you paying attention? A pub and inn," answered Gall.

"Is that the only influence you have to sum up an Abominable life?" quipped Pandora.

"I'll need you to spend the night and most of the following morning to answer that question," boasted Gall.

"Is that a challenge or an invitation?"

"I have a short stay, so you can take it as you wish."

A smirk appeared on Pandora's face while she twirled the ends of her ponytail around her fingers. A web of deceit was in place, and Gall had just landed in the center. "Let's see if your words are true to your appearance," replied Pandora. Gall grabbed Pandora's hand and escorted her to a reserved room in the Inn. Gall looked over her flawless features, filled with anticipation as she entered the bathroom to prepare herself.

Under her laced-up petticoat, Pandora removed a small jar filled with myriad illnesses that were burdensome to man. She coyly removed the lid and sorted out a malicious illness with her fingernail. A small black wisp of mist seeped from the jar and slid under the door to take hold of Gall.

The mist crept to the bed in a snakelike manner before an unexpected visitor barged through the door. "I can't believe you're here!" shouted Victor. Gall jumped out of bed and grabbed a robe to cover his bare frame. "Now that you have satisfied your curiosity, please leave!" pleaded Gall. He pointed to the bathroom door to inform Victor of his guest.

Victor turned away with laughter, and as he walked out the door, a black mist flooded his nostrils. "I'll kill all of you!" he shouted. He unexpectedly charged at Gall and tackled him to the floor. Gall looked into the eyes of his enraged brother. Delusions and paranoia caused Victor's veins and pupils to enlarge. Gall's Marid Djinn emerged, knowing there was only one way to end the madness Pandora had unleashed.

In a frenzied state, Victor reached for his sidearm, but Gall grabbed his wrists. The Marid Djinn that stirred within squeezed until they were permanently immobilized. Curses flooded the room as Victor's wrists became limp. Victor dropped the gun and struggled to get to his feet. Before he could run out the door, Gall took advantage of the opportunity to place him in a sleeper hold. A tear overlapped his cheek when the struggle was over.

The last time he could remember a tear falling was when he lost his younger brother Paul. Gall gently placed Victor on the bed and promised to heal the emotional scar in the same manner. He kicked open the bathroom door for answers but found no one inside. The empty room confirmed his suspicions, and Gall called Kaleb for assistance. After a tongue-lashing, Gall was given directions to an underground hospital.

That same night, at the end of the Styx River, an Olympian prepared himself for war. A small group of centaurs debated a drink while running for their lives. One mustered the nerve for a sip, and as he lowered his head, the axes of Fear and Terror pierced his hide. "The Fates, can you believe it!" shouted Ares. The Greek god of war boasted as he approached his prey with his twin son's. Deimus and Phobus cheered as they removed their axes from the centaur's hide. "To war with the Fates is a battle worthy of recognition. The victory will be heard throughout Mount Olympus!" boasted Ares. He briefly paused to quench his bloodlust on the centaur's wounds.

"Then allow us to deal with them, Father," Deimus eagerly requested. "Give us an opportunity to be favored by Zeus and earn a place with the Olympians."

"You have fought by my side in many wars, but this enemy is not like any other. Everything they create and wield is a design for death. They are not to be taken lightly," replied Ares.

"They should be more afraid of us. In war we bring fear and

terror to all we face. Give us this opportunity, and we will bring you victory," begged Deimus, "As well as earn a place among the Olympians."

"I will grant you this opportunity, but I must caution you, Zeus will not be merciful if you fail. Your punishment will be severe regardless of my stature," warned Ares.

"Have no fear, we will fill our glasses and quench our thirst with the blood from his vessel," replied Deimus.

The following day at the Styles Estate, Banter mulled over his loss to Hel by testing a new armor-piercing projectile for his Barrett rifle. "Target!" shouted Alexander. Banter fired a round that penetrated the bark of an oak tree with a slow buzz. The bullet successfully exited the opposite side as Bella approached with news of an unexpected visitor. "Master Styles, there's a gentleman by the name of Mr. Maxwell here to see you," said Bella. Banter looked as she pointed to the Abominable standing by the patio door.

"Kaleb?" blurted Banter. Banter rose to his feet and handed Bella his rifle. "See to Alexander while I tend to the matter," commanded Banter.

Banter approached the patio with uncertainty. The only thing he knew about Kaleb was that he was the eldest Abominable. He attempted to pay Gall to avenge the death of the youngest Abominable, and Gall had to pay for his assistance with Sitoel's escape. The first impression forced Banter to place a "For Services Rendered" label on the experience. When Kaleb removed a large stuffed envelope from his inner pocket, he knew this meeting wouldn't be much different. Banter extended his hand to greet Kaleb, and Kaleb responded by handing Banter the envelope.

"I need your services," said Kaleb.

"What's the job?"

"I need you to get Gall out of East Riding in Yorkshire."

"England? What is Gall doing in England, and why can't you get him yourself?"

"If I tend to the matter, it will only bring attention to a place I prefer to keep off the radar of public officials."

Banter handed Kaleb the envelope. "I accept the job, but you can keep your money. Gall is not just an employee. He's my friend."

Kaleb shook his head in disbelief. "You judge my actions? In my profession, being a boss is costly. In a world where a wife can cross you and have your best friend dispose of the corpse, you quickly learn ways to donate other people's plasma. I offered you the job because it's just that. Gall would want to stay at the pub and inn until he finds the one responsible for our problem. This puts us all at risk. Gall cannot roam around a place where he broke an inmate out of a highly secure mental facility."

Banter suddenly recalled the Rampton escape and nodded in agreement.

"I knew you would understand. I know you as well as your team," said Kaleb.

"My team? If you're referring to Sitoel, she returned to Spain after our last assignment," replied Banter.

"Then she'll be part of a gypsy caravan in El Carmel. She'll be staying with her grandmother, Madame Carrea. I make it my business to know all my brother's affiliates. I sent Matthew to inform her of the matter. You can use her assistance to find a barmaid that slipped away before we could deal with the problem."

"Suit yourself, but I meant what I said. You can keep your money," replied Banter. He handed Kaleb the envelope and prepared for the trip.

Before admitting Victor into a mental hospital, Gall and Moss took him to the underground facility. Surgeons on Kaleb's payroll that specialized in cosmetic and general surgery were waiting. Gall spent the entire day in a reclining chair, waiting for Victor to return from the operating room. While in a deep sleep, a beacon of light brought him a vision of Akantha. "Gall, you are in great danger!" warned Akantha.

"Do you know who is responsible for the mental state of my brother?" asked Gall.

"Hel has made the Fates an enemy to the Greek gods," answered Akantha. "Zeus sent Pandora and Ares to punish the actions you've taken against the Norse gods. My friends on Mount Olympus tell me Ares has granted his twin sons the opportunity to dispose of you. They wield hand axes that personify fear and terror. They used this power to help their father win numerous wars. You must be delicate with this matter."

"The only delicateness given will be the brittle breaking of bones throughout the torso!" snapped Gall.

"Do not be foolish!" advised Akantha. "You cannot go after Zeus bent on revenge. You will spend an eternity fighting the Greek gods, deities, and Olympians. A Marid Djinn may succeed in the task, but there is no guarantee for the vessel."

"What do you suggest?"

"I'm advising you to address the matter in a way they will respect. There will be no retaliation."

"In simpler terms?"

"A challenge—one that would lead you straight to Zeus. Iblis will negotiate the terms."

Akantha's light slowly began to fade.

"Wait! What about Deimus and Phobus?" asked Gall.

"It's too late to negotiate with them. You are their challenge, and they'll arrive shortly. To survive, you must listen to my warning. Before facing a great enemy, the twins will look for a place to drain a fresh corpse. There is a place where they can avoid suspicion."

Gall woke from his sleep as her light disappeared. "A place where they can discreetly drain a corpse?" mumbled Gall. His right eyebrow rose on his forehead as he raced to the morgue. He found a stretcher befitting his size and covered himself with a large sheet.

Underneath, he transformed into his lycan state and recited the verses to "A Warrior's Creed."

Just before midnight, Deimus and Phobus infiltrated the hospital. They discreetly made their way to the morgue disguised as surgeons. The twins entered the room and foolishly boasted a victory not yet obtained. "I can't wait to hear the screams of the vessel as I sever the limbs!" Deimus excitedly whispered. His eyes gazed over the stretcher that held Gall's large frame.

"Easy, brother. If we choose that one, we will be bloated before battle. Let us drink from the one in front of him and be on our way," advised Phobus. The twins removed the hand axes from the belts fastened on their waistlines and made incisions into the corpse.

As they lowered their heads to sip from the spring, a Marid Djinn emerged to weave a fate of general surgery. The possessed lycan crept from under his sheet and confronted the twins with a howl of reckoning. They turned to face their prey with a stunned expression as he spear-handed their abdominal cavities. Gall pushed his arms until he felt their gallbladders in the centers of his paws and extended his claws. Within seconds, Gall ended a reign of Fear and Terror, with an outpouring of blood and bile. Gall continued to push through their insides until he sat them down in their own puddle. Deimus and Phobus closed their eyes to embrace death as they returned to Hades with the sight of Gall holstering the axes on his waistline.

Gall returned to Victor's room and took a shower to remove the stench of battle. When he was done, he found Banter waiting on the reclinable chair. "Glad to see you made it out of Hel alive," Gall greeted with sarcasm.

"The loss will remain unforgettable," replied Banter. "You can only bury the dagger deeper if she's responsible for what happened to Victor."

Before Gall could answer, a nurse frantically screamed for a guard outside the door. Banter walked to the door to investigate as one came to her aid. "Two surgeons were murdered in the morgue!"

yelled the nurse. They ran into a stairwell as Banter suspiciously turned to Gall for an explanation. "They invited me down there to crack open a cold one. Imagine my surprise when I discovered they meant that literally!" explained Gall. He dressed himself and gestured for a quick departure.

On Mount Olympus, Zeus witnessed the failed attempt with the Greek gods. Whispers of doubt stirred as Deimus and Phobus descended the Styx River. "Never send boys to do a man's job," quipped Zeus.

"Is that all you can say? That insolent dung worm sent my sons to Hades covered in blood and bile!" snapped Ares.

"You have no one to blame but yourself," replied Hera.

"Himself and Zeus!" a voice interrupted from the surrounding pillars. A stream of smoke gathered in the center of the coliseum as the revving sound of a chopper motorcycle engine echoed. "You dare cross my borders and accuse me!" shouted Zeus. He reached for his staff while Iblis conjured himself a black hooded robe.

"You speak of borders when you violate the one made by my son," replied Iblis.

"Your borders are within the Norse realms. You have no authority beyond that point. I acted accordingly as a watcher to Hades and Poseidon's realms," corrected Zeus.

"I disagree, the Midgard serpent's ashes shadow all that is mine," protested Iblis.

"Your claim is an insult and threat of war!" interrupted Hera.

"An outburst I'll gladly put to an end to," said Zeus. He stood from his throne and extended his staff to form a lightning bolt.

In response, Iblis quickly took cover behind a pillar and issued a challenge. "You would be wise to ponder on your actions, great king. There is a more gratifying way to resolve our dispute."

"What can be more gratifying than striking you down at this very moment?" replied Zeus.

"What can you possibly offer?" heckled Hera.

A pair of red eyes glowed from under Iblis's hood as he returned to the center of the floor. "I offer what has brought amusement to the Greek gods for centuries: The entertainment of witnessing battles and pursuits of great heroes. A challenge to retrieve your most sacred treasures. I will send my Marid Djinns on a quest for the helm of Hades, Poseidon's trident, and your staff."

Zeus returned to his throne with the laughter of the Olympians. Whispers about the dangers that protected these items solidified his decision.

"What do I gain when they fail?"

"*If they fail*—their demise and the Norse realms."

A sinister smirk appeared on Zeus's face while he rubbed his hands like a miser. "I accept your challenge," replied Zeus. "I will grant your Marid Djinns permission to enter our borders and pursue our most sacred items. *As well as a certain death!*"

"To the victor go the spoils!" shouted Iblis. He returned to a mist of smoke and left the coliseum with laughter.

"This challenge will not settle my thirst for revenge!" Ares bellowed from his chair.

"I can" interrupted Hel.

Hel entered the coliseum in a black two-piece swimsuit designed to win competitions. Female goddesses sucked their teeth and hissed as she approached the center. The male gods watched in awe as her high heels tapped against the marble floor.

"Those feet are rumored to have crushed skulls. Why would a goddess wear something so primitive?" asked Hera.

"This war has forced me to walk amongst mortals," explained Hel. "Lord Treachery has taught the Lycan buccaneer Ninety-Six Nine many disguises. I narrowly escaped two assassination attempts to be here. Thanks to the hospitality of Zeus, I'm now a dancer in a tavern owned by your Furies. I'm in desperate need of extinguishing these vermin from my realm."

"Why are you here?" asked Zeus.

A flame ignited around the dragon tattoo that covered Hel's frame as she approached the throne in a seductive manner. "I have many talents to offer a king, but at this moment I share only the information given by my servant. One of the Fates is currently resting with her grandmother in the hills of El Carmel. A brother to the Fate that slaughtered Ares' siblings will join her. If they happen to meet an early demise, it will favor the Greek gods in the challenge."

A smirk appeared on the face of Zeus as he turned to Ares. "Do you accept the task?" he asked.

"I do!" answered Ares. Ares grabbed his broadsword for war and raced from the coliseum.

In El Carmel, Sitoel's past quickly caught up with her. Her king would not grant her an audience. He sent word that her only option to regain her family's place in the tribe was an escape act. Unfortunately for Sitoel, no man in the tribe would help her construct a stage for the show. Sitoel was forced to hire carpenters from the neighboring town. Her eyes darkened while she gave the details of an act she called "An Unrequited Love."

Madame Carrea quoted Abraham Cowley's "Emotion" in a Spanish dialect to promote it. "'A mighty pain to love it is, And tis' a pain that pains to miss. But of all pain's, the greatest pain is not to love, but love in vain.' This is the tragic affair of the Great Secret—a tragedy that she will depict through the dance of flamenco. I will stand on the top plank of a scaffold and throw daggers, blindfolded, while Sitoel expresses her pain. "But it pains me to repeat the pain that pains to miss!" If Sitoel avoids the daggers, she must repeat the song and dance blindfolded!"

They traveled the countryside until nightfall promoting it. When they returned to the caravan, they prepared for the act. "Don't forget to place two sharpened daggers to the side," said Sitoel. She parked the caravan and handed Madame Carrea a pouch filled with daggers.

"Must you be so dramatic?" replied Madame Carrea.

"I give shows that bring down the house. We'll make enough to return all that we have lost," promised Sitoel.

"I understand your determination, but how can we accomplish that when no man from the tribe will help? We couldn't find one to build a stage. Where will we find a guitarist? Or do you think you can avoid that obstacle too?" asked Madame Carrea.

She followed Sitoel into the caravan with a doubtful expression. "You worry too much, grandmother. You can't expect me to reveal all my secrets," replied Sitoel. She walked to the corner of the caravan and pulled back the curtain to her room. Sitoel knelt and opened a large trunk at the end of her cot. The excitement sparked the luster in her eyes as she removed a black spandex suit. A betta fish outlined in gold rested in the center. Sitoel anxiously grabbed her flamenco shoes and fan to complement the attire. She quickly changed clothes and modeled the outfit for her grandmother. "What do you think? "asked Sitoel.

"I can't believe my eyes. After all these years, it still fits your frame. A wrap-around skirt should help conceal the daggers. Now share your secret for maintaining your shape?" asked Madame Carrea.

"Prison fights," replied Sitoel.

Madame Carrea walked to a shelf and grabbed a sharpening stone for two daggers. She quickly turned to Sitoel as she opened the door. "Where do you think you're going at this time of night? Dressed like that?"

Sitoel's eyes lustered as an Abominable approached the caravan. "To handle my business," answered Sitoel.

Matthew removed a large envelope from the inner pocket of his suit to greet her. "The Great Secret, I presume?" asked Matthew. Sitoel answered with a nod as she walked down the staircase.

"My name is Matthew Maxwell. I would like to hire you for some business that concerns Gall."

"What type of business?"

"Abominable business." Matthew handed Sitoel the envelope and began to explain. "My employer offered Banter half that sum to bring Gall back from England, but he didn't accept it."

"The job or the money?" interrupted Sitoel.

"Just the money. He left yesterday to pick Gall up from an underground hospital. Two murders have taken place since then. You can understand my concern when I say this brings a lot of unwanted attention our way. An Abominable has many disguises, but he can't parade around the same town more than once—especially when he aided in the escape of a mental patient."

"I'm not a mental patient anymore!" snapped Sitoel. She inspected the contents of the envelope, and the mood suddenly changed. She sorted through the sum of a hundred thousand dollars and removed a résumé that bore a photo of Pandora. "I apologize for my outburst. I do understand your concern. Now tell me about this woman," replied Sitoel.

"She was the last one to be with Gall before he placed Victor in the hospital. The directions for the pub and inn are written on the back. Gall is our primary concern. The woman is a bonus. Should you happen to find her, just send word back to our employees at the pub and inn. They'll handle the rest from there."

Sitoel closed the envelope and extended her hand. "I accept the job, and feel free to stay for my performance."

Matthew accepted the invitation with a gracious stage bow as she made her way back into the caravan.

The following evening, a small area of El Carmel was flooded with townspeople and Sitoel's tribe. Matthew bullied his way to the rear of a scaffold fixture and found a quiet spot behind a hay filled cart. Everyone curiously watched as Madame Carrea climbed the staircase of the scaffold with a portable gramophone. When she was settled on the top plank, Madame Carrea announced the act in a

Spanish dialect. "The Great Secret welcomes you all to our performance. Below me, Sitoel will randomly pick a child and parent from
the audience to check the authenticity of the props. When they are
done, Sitoel will express her emotions through flamenco. Will the
tap, clap, and snap of her fingers aid her escape or scorn her like a
love lost? Wait no longer for an answer. I give you, "An Unrequited
Love!'"

The audience applauded as Sitoel walked onto the stage with a
pail full of daggers. She graced the center with a new Venetian mask
that displayed the same betta fish as the one on her outfit. Sitoel
pointed into the crowd for a father and son to join her. The father
that answered the call guided his toddler onto the stage. The boy
ran to Sitoel, and she tightly fastened a blindfold around his head.
After a slight push, the boy wandered the stage as if he couldn't find
a light switch in the dark. The father pulled him back by the collar
before he could fall over the edge. He dragged the boy back to Sitoel,
and she placed the blindfold in the pail. She raised it and gestured
for the father to remove a dagger. He threw it at the stage to test
the authenticity, and it stuck with precision. The father turned to
Sitoel with a concerned expression as the audience applauded, and
she escorted them off stage.

Sitoel carried the pail to the scaffold fixture and tied it to a
string. Madame Carrea pulled it to the top and wound up the
gramophone. The audience watched in awe as she put the needle to
Del Shannon's "Runaway." After she wrapped the blindfold around
her head, Sitoel began to express her emotions through flamenco.
The crowd gathered around the edge of the stage as Sitoel overcame
the first obstacle of her performance—a rhythm that matched the
unorthodox selection of her song.

When the song had reached the interlude, Sitoel put away her
fan and began the routine. After hearing two loud taps, a clap, and a
snap from her fingers, Madame Carrea threw a dagger. *Tap, tap, clap,
snap, thud!* repeatedly sounded from the stage as Sitoel maneuvered
the daggers. Madame Carrea followed the routine until the song

came to an end. When it was over, she heard the roar of the crowd. Madame Carrea removed her blindfold and had to shield her eyes from the stage lights that reflected off partial pieces of the blades.

Matthew cheered from the rear of the stage as Sitoel walked off to prepare for the second act. He worked up the nerve to climb into the hay-filled cart and a hand grabbed him from behind. Ares pulled the Abominable onto the tip of his broadsword and thrust it past his spine. He muffled Matthew's cries for help as he faded into a cold death. "If I could only be there when your brother hears of this," whispered Ares. Ares tossed the lifeless body into the cart and looked toward the stage with anticipation. He licked the blood off his sword while Madame Carrea announced the second act.

"Ladies and gentlemen," announced Madame Carrea, "behold the consequences of 'An Unrequited Love!' 'Tis a pain that pains to miss. Now Sitoel must repeat the song, dance, and danger blindfolded. Will she escape, or will she be scorned like her love lost? Wait no longer for an answer. I give you the second act of "An Unrequited Love!".

Sitoel returned to the stage with a blindfold and knelt at the edge. She pointed to a man from her tribe to check the authenticity of the cloth. He boldly approached the stage and snatched it from her hand. After he tied it around his head, he laughed. "You will die!" he shouted. He tossed the blindfold back on stage and returned to his tribe. Their children turned his words into a chant. Sitoel ignored the harsh cheers and put on her blindfold. Madame Carrea wound the gramophone and put the needle on the record. After she put on her blindfold, the audience stepped several paces away from the stage—a precautionary measure in case Sitoel didn't know where the edge was.

The song began, and Sitoel expressed her emotions through flamenco. At the interlude, Madame Carrea waited to repeat the routine, but Ares interfered. *Tap, tap, tap, tap, tap!* repeatedly sounded from the stage as Ares hit the scaffold fixture with his sword. He heckled as he circled Sitoel. "I wonder how many limbs I can hack off before your audience discovers the realism of your performance. Or maybe I'll take something close to you like I did your companion." He swung his broadsword above his head and ran to the scaffold fixture. He attacked the poles, and half the scaffold collapsed.

At that moment, a Marid Djinn emerged to weave a fate that required only two daggers and a passion. "Enough!" Sitoel shouted in a tone that carried a hiss. The bold response only provoked another attack from Ares. "Let's dance!" he shouted. Ares swung his sword overhead, and Madame Carrea emptied the pail of daggers over the rail for a line of defense. The rain forced Ares to stop and defend himself. He skillfully avoided the onslaught by tapping the daggers in Sitoel's direction. *Tap, tap, clap, snap, thud!* repeatedly sounded from the stage as Sitoel maneuvered the daggers. When it was over, Ares struck the remaining fixtures.

Madame Carrea unleashed a string of curses as she jumped into the hay-filled cart to escape the sag. A dust storm amassed around the stage and chased the crowd into the hills.

Ares parted the smoke screen and tiptoed around the daggers to finish his prey. "It's a pity that I have to waste such an alluring vessel. I hear your eyes possess the fire of emeralds," he complimented.

"And they can pierce into the soul," replied Sitoel. Ares raised his sword to Sitoel's shoulders to measure a clean swipe, and the glare of a green flame pierced beneath the edges of her blindfold. Her puzzle of death had come to an end as the luster of her eyes reflected off the blades that surrounded her.

The green light spectacle distracted Ares long enough for her to remove two daggers from her waistline. It also granted Sitoel the opportunity to plant a dagger in the mind and heart of her prey. *Tap, tap, clap, snap, thump!* sounded from the stage as Ares collapsed. Sitoel bowed to the corpse that lay at her feet with daggers planted in the forehead and coronary artery. "They love me!" boasted Sitoel. She removed her blindfold and caught the crowd running into the hills. "I told you I'd give a performance that would bring down the house!" shouted Sitoel. She ran to the pile of broken fixtures to check on her grandmother.

"When something seems too good to be true, that usually means it is!" grumbled Madame Carrea.

"That's the thanks I get for a hundred thousand dollars and a potato sack filled with euros. If I wanted that attitude, I would have stayed with Banter," replied Sitoel. She pulled her grandmother from the hay-filled cart and saw Matthew's body.

"You'll be joining Banter soon. I only hope it doesn't end like that," replied Madame Carrea.

"It will when the others find out. I'm sorry Grandmother, I was hired to do a job. I have to leave you," said Sitoel.

"Then go, my child. You did all you can here. I will tend to your friend and our affairs," replied Madame Carrea.

Sitoel packed only her mask and outfit for the trip. She left for England and arrived at the pub and inn the following evening. Moss met her at the door. "Nice to meet you, Miss Carrea. They're expecting you in the den," greeted Moss.

"Who?" Sitoel curiously asked while she looked over the bar.

"Gall and a few other men I care not to mention," answered Moss. He pointed to a room at the end of a hallway by the bar.

Sitoel slowly made her way to the door while contemplating a way to tell Gall about Matthew. When Sitoel reached for the doorknob, she discovered he had already heard the news. "I also need to know where you left Excalibur!" shouted Iblis.

"I'm in no mood. I have a brother in the hospital, another in the grave, and you want me to sail on a quest?" barked Gall.

Sitoel entered the room to console Gall. "If it makes you feel any better, Matthew didn't die alone," interrupted Sitoel.

"You put down the dog, but I really want the one who turned it loose in the first place," replied Gall. He gave Iblis a cold stare. Sitoel cautiously stepped back to Enemy and Banter. "I'm appalled! For you to think that I could construct such a plot is unbearable. Allow me to clear the air before the foolish notion to embrace me worm's its way into your simple mind. The Greek gods pursued you because of Hel. She reluctantly had the misfortune of living after the events of Ragnarök," Iblis defensively replied.

Iblis briefly paused to give Banter a cold stare. "Now that we've eliminated the motive for power, let's address the motive of greed. Your dear friend and companion received a large sum of money from your departed brother just to be here." He briefly paused to give Sitoel the same cold stare.

"You took the money!" shouted Banter.

"You dare judge me. We wouldn't be in this mess if you hadn't chosen to resolve matters on your back!" replied Sitoel. "I bet I can make you say that again with more feeling," threatened Banter. "Now you want to do battle. What position will you take?" replied Sitoel.

"Gypsy hag!"

"Spoiled punk!"

Banter and Sitoel approached each other with clenched fists as Akantha entered the room in a hooded black robe. "Doomed! Doomed are we all if you continue to go on this way! Do not underestimate your enemies. Myths depict great tales of heroism, but do not overlook the fact that they are fierce and cunning killers. Iblis has granted you an opportunity to avenge the wrong. This quest is not an insult, it is the perfect disguise for your motive" explained Akantha. She removed a Venetian bauta mask from the inner pocket of her robe. She handed it to Gall as he extended his claws. A quick swipe left three scratch marks that promised the fall of Zeus, Hades, and Poseidon.

Akantha turned to Banter and Sitoel to further address the matter. "As for you two, I suggest you find a way to resolve your issues—and fast. You will not succeed against the Olympians if you continue to doubt each other."

"Now that we've resolved the matter of my involvement, I have to ask. Which one of the gods will you pursue first?" asked Iblis.

Banter and Sitoel turned to Gall. He pondered on the question for a couple of minutes and decided the sea would be the best option. "Poseidon," answered Gall.

"I shall retrieve the coordinates and give them to Enemy before the time of departure," said Iblis. He merged into a fog of smoke and exited through the fireplace with the revving sound of a chopper motorcycle engine.

Akantha removed the hood to her robe and gave the Marid Djinns another warning. "I heard the only time Poseidon is without his trident is when he sleeps. During that time, it rests on a small island. Three of the most notorious sirens patrol it on hippocampus."

"Sirens! Did you say sirens guard the trident?" asked Enemy. Akantha responded with a nod as he extended his claws. "Would they be Parthenope, Aglaope and Peisione?"

"They are the ones I speak of."

"For Gall I would bite the cannon smoke, but if you mention those names to our crew, you'll be sailing without one."

Banter shook his head in disbelief. "The fierce Lycan buccaneers," he quipped. "I'll take no flak from you, scallywag! Their vocal abilities surpass the use of wax in the ears. My crew can attest to that firsthand. Bloody Bartholomew Smyte escaped with the booty from one of their islands. I couldn't speak of his facial features after that. The scars could not be healed, even with lycan abilities!" explained Enemy.

"What did he take?" asked Sitoel.

"I'll tell you the story. Before he was recruited by the Lycan buccaneers, we knew him as Bartholomew Smyte—a fearless buccaneer with the cold-heartedness of a rattlesnake. We had raided a Spanish galleon, and Bartholomew fell overboard during the attack. He was reported lost at sea. He drifted for several days. He was about to give up hope before three exotic ebony, red and blonde-haired songbirds surfaced from beneath the current, bareback on hippocampus. Bartholomew wouldn't have believed what he saw if he himself wasn't a lycan. They introduced themselves as Parthenope, Aglaope, and Peisione before taking him to a deserted island.

"At the time, Bartholomew felt it was safe. When he overheard them bickering about a wager on his life span, he discovered he was wrong. He immediately transformed into his lycan form for a final say in the matter. Before he could attack, they sang and played Pan's instruments. The music overwhelmed the savage beast, and Bartholomew fell into a trance. While in this trance, Bartholomew recollected the thoughts of all he had accomplished during his time as a Lycan buccaneer—a life he had desired since he was a boy. After enduring thoughts of plundering and raids, Bartholomew was left to face his true self. All of his rampages were personified through the one thing he discarded before he pledged to the Lycan buccaneers—his conscience! Bartholomew begged them to stop as he walked to a boulder and repeatedly hit his head against it. They responded with laughter as he continued to find ways to defile and hurt himself. The torture session lasted until the end of the day.

"By then the sirens had tired and fell asleep. Bartholomew rushed to the ocean for a mirror before the sun retired. The reflection told him he could never look at himself again. Neither could anyone else."

"Sounds like a one night stand to me," interrupted Banter.

"More like therapy," added Sitoel.

"We are already aware of the ways a friend can perish while in your company. Please allow me to finish!" pleaded Enemy. "Bartholomew took Pan's flute and lyre to compensate for the foul act. Then he sneaked into the sirens' lair and put a claw to Parthenope's throat. He demanded she return him to our ship, and she obeyed the request. Bartholomew climbed onto the deck and dared Parthenope to face our cannons. The siren simply blew a kiss in response. It carried an echo that ripped through the deck and knocked Bartholomew off his feet. When he came to his senses, *he was forever bloody.* Bloody Bartholomew Smyte."

Akantha walked to the fireplace to further explain the siren's new ability. She put her hands over the fire and clenched her fists to capture the crackle of the flames. "This ability is an echo of karma.

I saw it evolve during the time I served as a caretaker for the Greek gods. It began with a beautiful maiden named Echo. Her beauty eventually caught the eye of the god Pan. No matter how hard he tried, she refused every advance. This angered him to the point that he cast a spell over a group of shepherds. They relentlessly pursued and captured Echo under Pan's madness. The group ravaged and tore at the maiden until nothing was left but the spirit with a fragment of her voice.

"She spent some time wandering the hillside as a nymph before Zeus discovered her abilities. He used Echo as a warning system to keep Hera from discovering his acts of infidelity. Echo would repeat every word of her whereabouts to him. When Hera discovered the plot, she had Echo banished to the pits of the darkest sea caverns. For the second time, Echo had become the victim of a love gone bad. She molded her voice into a powerful weapon while in confinement. It could kill on a whim or through the course of time. Poseidon heard about her gift and wanted it for his arsenal. He also knew of Echo's hatred for the gods, so he devised a scheme with Pan.

"Pan gave Poseidon his flute and lyre to keep Echo from using her gift against him. Poseidon gave them to two of his sirens. Aglaope and Peisione played the instruments to guide Echo through the maze of her prison. She followed the tune, bent on revenge, but it led her only to a third siren. Parthenope was imprisoned in a sea cliff for her failure to entice Odysseus. Echo felt her strong hatred for man, and they developed a bond. She freed Parthenope and joined the sirens. Unfortunately for Echo, Poseidon had previously arranged the terms of Parthenope's freedom. Echo unknowingly serves the will of the Greek gods."

Sitoel's eyes lustered while she analyzed the deaths depicted to her. "Echo will be furious when she finds out!" she said.

While the Marid Djinns devised a scheme to deal with the sirens, the Olympians bickered with each other on Mount Olympus. The axes of Fear and Terror stirred, and the shadow of a broadsword for war hung over an empty seat. Zeus paced the coliseum floor until his brothers arrived. Poseidon was the first to enter the coliseum with disbelief. "Why do you summon me, brother? They will not prevail against my sirens. They have left sailors in peril for centuries," said Poseidon.

"We may have underestimated our opponent. I want you to increase the guard," demanded Zeus.

The charred scent of armor flooded the coliseum as Hades made his entrance. "Hail Zeus!" he greeted with sarcasm. He made an effortless attempt to hide a devious grin as he approached his king.

"What amuses you?" asked Zeus. "Allow me to explain in the manner of one of your prestigious daemons. I was on my throne and just happened to see an Olympian crossing the Styx River. Normally this wouldn't bother me, since he frequently visits my domain to quench his bloodlust, but this time he was riding coach," heckled Hades.

"You should be wary of the Fates and their challenge to retrieve our most sacred items. If I were you, I'd spend more time protecting the helm of invisibility than watching Tartarus," warned Zeus.

"Why should I fear a being on a quest for my helm? I allow heroes to borrow it, knowing they will either end the life of a great opponent or fail and return it themselves," replied Hades.

"If they retrieve these items, what realms do you think they'll lay claim to?" hinted Zeus.

Hades' dark red eyes ignited into a fiery flame. His bluish skin hardened like his armor. "Why haven't you sent agents to deal with this matter?" he snapped.

"That was the purpose of Ares," answered Hera.

"Then send another! We are not protected by the heavens. Our mightiest warriors were bestowed upon you during the Titanomachy," replied Hades.

"He has a point, my king. You have Nike, Zelos, Bia, and Kratos by your side. Hades will need assistance if he is to face our enemies," said Hera.

"Then I shall send Hermes to fetch Heracles and the Norse

goddess Hel. As for you, Poseidon, how do we increase your guard?" asked Zeus.

"Do not be troubled, my brother. There will be a beast waiting if the Fates succeed against the sirens, and he will surely make them wish they hadn't," promised Poseidon.

Early the following morning, the Marid Djinns met Iblis aboard the Skidbladnir. Enemy hoisted a Joli Rouge bearing two monstrous wolf heads as they gathered around him. "So what's our heading?" asked Banter.

"The Pitcairn Islands," whispered Iblis. He handed Enemy a scroll that gave the heading of the trident.

"Mutiny on the *Bounty*!" shouted Banter.

"If you don't silence that scallywag, I'll see to the task," threatened Enemy.

"I thought we only had to keep ourselves from mentioning the names of the sirens?" asked Sitoel.

"You do not see the message Poseidon has sent us! Pitcairn Island is where Fletcher Christian and his mutineers settled after he took command of the ship *Bounty*," replied Enemy.

The Marid Djinns followed Enemy to the ship's wheel as he explained. "John Norton was stoned to death in Murderer's Cove. While in Tahiti, Matthew Thompson shot Charles Churchill and was later stoned to death by Churchill's kin. After the mutineers settled on Pitcairn Island, the Polynesians began revolting against them. It led to the death of Jack Williams, Isaac Martin, John Mills, William Brown, and Fletcher Christian. The men involved were in turn killed by the widows and others of the crew. One widow died of respiratory illness, and another supposedly fell from a cliff while gathering eggs. Leadership fell into the hands of Ned Young and John Adams.

"They brought a moment of peace to the islanders until William McCoy, a man after my own heart, created an alcoholic beverage from a native plant. The mutineers' chronic drinking eventually took its toll, and the women protested. McCoy unexpectedly met his demise in a drunken fall. His fellow mutineer Quintal was hacked by John Adams and Ned Young's hatchet after he threatened to kill everyone. Acts that provoked those cold hearted savages to destroy the still! Ned Young eventually died of asthma. John Adams found religion and was pardoned from his actions."

"That's not so bad. A sailor and Captain Bligh escaped," interrupted Sitoel.

"Now that you've informed us that the memory of one's crewmates being extinguished means nothing to you, please allow me to finish!" said Enemy. "It's true Captain Bligh left unharmed from the mutiny and escaped cannibals, also the fear of being lost at sea. Only to return to civilization and face the same revolts and backstabbing during the rum rebellion. Now can you see Poseidon's message clearly? No one escapes!"

Gall walked over to a barrel of mead and filled the cup that rested on top. He handed it to Enemy to calm his nerves.

"I don't lack confidence in you," said Enemy. Before guzzling the mead, Enemy paused to give Banter a cold stare.

"I also share your concern," commented Iblis.

"If I ever see Hel again, it'll be tragic!" Banter defensively replied.

"I want one of your armor piercing bullets to put yourself and others at ease," replied Iblis. "Blackmarket Ginyel can make a special batch with a recipe he learned while living among the dwarves and dark elves. *It pierces the heart and clings to the soul!*"

It took only a couple of days for the Skidbladnir to reach the waters of Pitcairn Island. Before reaching the shore, Gall had a plan in place. Enemy complied with Gall's plan and anchored the ship a few miles from shore. Iblis played his part by placing the crew in a dormant state. The Lycan buccaneers stood upright and lifeless on deck as he dived into the sea to watch from a secluded location. When the reflection of the moon settled on the water, the sirens made their presence known. Enemy caught sight of a wave circling the ship and ducked behind a barrel of mead. "It's them!" he loudly whispered.

The Marid Djinns ran to the ship's rail for a look. "Let's introduce ourselves," said Gall. Sitoel's eyes gained the luster of an emerald flame as Banter aimed his rifle. "Hit a hippocampus in the hippocampus," mumbled Banter. He timed his mark on the current and fired two rounds at the sight of a hippocampus's head fin. The bullets pierced the neural structure and wedged themselves in the temporal lobes of the mythical seahorses. Two of them sank with the echo of a car riding on a blown tire as the sirens crashed into each other.

The last hippocampus gathered a large wave that carried the stranded sirens to the ship's deck. "Someone will pay dearly for that. Who is the captain of this vessel!" shouted Aglaope. Parthenope climbed over the ship's rail to join them as Enemy stepped out of hiding.

"No need to look about. I am he," answered Enemy.

"I've seen you before. You sailed with Bartholomew Smyte. Does he still bleed among you?" asked Parthenope.

"Bloody Bartholomew Smyte found peace in a watery grave not so long ago. He's far from the reach of you and your wenches," Enemy answered as he extended his claws.

"That matches my estimated year to date," said Peisione.

"I'll get your dress the next time we attend a party on shore. Now let's tend to the captain of this crew. I wonder if his tongue can do without the foulness," replied Aglaope.

Aglaope stepped forward and wrung the water out of her hair. Enemy wearily watched as the droplets echoed the sound of mead stirring in a barrel. When she was done, Aglaope stepped back from the puddle and Peisione stepped forward. Peisione seductively blew the droplets of water off her body and knelt to stir them into the puddle. The mixture matched the red color of her hair and echoed the sound of a vessel riding the waves of the sea. A sound that made Enemy long for land and the tavern that rested on its shores. When she was done, Peisione stepped back from the puddle, and Parthenope stepped forward.

Parthenope placed her big toe in the center of the puddle, and a ripple extended from the motion. It broke the floorboards of the deck and blew Enemy off his feet. He screamed in agony while he tossed and turned across the deck. His heartbeat rapidly increased while his body shook, and nausea took him over. "What poison have you wenches cursed me with?" asked Enemy.

"Mortals call it withdrawal," answered Parthenope.

"Sobriety? I'm to be sober. These wenches aim to kill us all!" shouted Enemy. He squirmed on deck and stabbed at the ankles of his closest crewmates. It was at that moment the Marid Djinns emerged to weave a scale of fates.

"Enough!" Gall shouted in a tone that carried a hiss.

A smile appeared on Parthenope's face as she stepped away from the puddle for the others to repeat the process. Aglaope stepped forward and wrung out her hair. Echo carried the sound to Gall and was greeted by his Marid Djinn. He escorted her through the memories and thoughts of correcting a hand raised against him. Aglaope stepped back from the puddle, and Peisione stepped forward. She seductively blew the water droplets off her body and into the puddle. The sound carried Echo to Banter's Marid Djinn. He escorted her through the thoughts and memories of a night in Hel. Echo relived the most tragic day of her life while the name Forgetful rang in her ear.

Peisione knelt and stirred her finger through the puddle to loosen more memories. The sound carried Echo to Sitoel's Marid Djinn. He escorted her through Akantha's tale of her past and a performance of "An Unrequited Love." When the show was over, as fate would have it, Echo befriended the Marid Djinns for an eternity. Gall's kusari-fundo chain slowly unraveled down his sleeve as Peisione stepped away from the puddle, and Parthenope stepped forward. Before she could strike, Gall whipped his chain around her neck and pulled her to him. He continued to pull on the links until droplets of blood fell to the deck. "Release your hold on Enemy and I'll spare your lives!" demanded Gall. He released Parthenope's corpse on the deck to express the seriousness of his words as they echoed with a hiss.

Peisione ran to Enemy and held his head to spew liquid seaweed into his mouth.

"What is the name of the beast that guards the trident?" asked Gall.

"How did you know?" asked Aglaope. She turned to Sitoel as her eyes beaconed an emerald flame. "So the rumors of your gift are true. The creature you've seen is an ichthyocentaur. Poseidon merged Bythos and Alphros into a creature that's half human at the waist. Beyond the waist they're rage matches a ferocious sea serpent. The combination of rage and hunger has no boundaries. He needs no other guard while that creature is chained to the prongs of his trident. If you value your lives, you'll end your quest here."

"I have a better idea. While Banter guards your friend, you can take me to him," demanded Gall.

"It will be my pleasure," replied Aglaope.

Aglaope walked to the ship's rail and whistled at a circling wave. Within seconds, a hippocampus rose to the surface and pressed against the ship for passengers. Aglaope and Gall jumped onto its back. Before Sitoel climbed over the rail, she gave a wink to Banter.

"I wonder what that was about?" mumbled Banter.

"You can ask me that question after you secure the prisoner, scallywag!" shouted Enemy. He grabbed a mug off a barrel of mead and knocked Peisione unconscious with it.

"I'd tend to the task myself but there's a void I need to fill, and it will take years to do so," said Enemy. Banter leaned his rifle against the mast to gather binding rope on deck. When he returned to Peisione, his rifle fell and discharged a round.

Banter tried to stop the sea-green fluid gushing out of her body as Hel climbed over the rail.

"You are as *careless* as you were *forgetful*, my love," greeted Hel. She grabbed Banter's rifle off the deck and walked to the opposite rail.

"You're responsible for this!" Banter shouted in a tone that carried a hiss. Hel's servant, Clumsy, quickly took hold of Enemy. Banter could hear a whimper as he forced the Lycan buccaneer to empty his mug.

"You should be made aware of my low tolerance for beautiful women in your presence—especially when all your attention should be focused on me," replied Hel. Enemy picked up the siren and fell overboard as he tossed her.

Hel propped the rifle on the rail and focused the optics on Sitoel. "Every breath she takes brings out the best in me," she whispered. Her trigger finger itched, but a laid plan held her at bay. "I was asked to deliver a message from Heracles."

"You don't need my rifle to deliver a message. Toss it back to me so we can finish what we started," replied Banter.

"Is that another request to put pleasure before business? Have you forgotten what happened the last time a rifle was between us?" heckled Hel. Banter's eyes darkened with a peculiar luster to the sudden outburst of laughter.

"Deliver the message!" demanded Banter.

"Heracles has challenged the Marid Djinns to a combat of their choice. If your friends leave the island alive, you are to give your terms to Hermes," replied Hel.

"He acts like this is a game or sport," said Banter. "Many of his battles were."

Hel turned to Banter with a saddened expression and a hint of danger. "After his mortal death, Zeus made Heracles an immortal. You will meet your own demise only if you choose to weave a fate like that of the creatures that still roam this realm. I would hate to have to seek you out of Tartarus." The sound of yawning and groggy moans quickly gained Hel's attention. The Lycan buccaneers were recovering from their dormant state.

"If you're lucky, we will finish this conversation in my realm!" shouted Hel. She tossed Banter's rifle into the air and dived over the ship's rail.

Banter raced for his weapon, but Sneaky took hold and tangled him with the rope he was holding. Clumsy released his hold on Enemy as Hel dived into the sea. He clawed his way back to the rails and found Banter on the deck.

"Why do I find you on the floor, scallywag?" barked Enemy.

"Hel escaped again!" cried Banter. A few loud splashes from the calm sea confirmed his story.

"Since you don't have a corpse, I suggest you don't brag about it," quipped Enemy.

"Brag?" shouted Banter.

The sound of arguing woke the Lycan buccaneers from their trance, and two fell to the deck from unexplained wounds.

"I'd know those claw marks anywhere!" shouted Unchained Gauge.

"Enemy?" blurted Obnoxious Koss.

"This is no quest for Excalibur. Enemy, explain yourself!" demanded Unchained Gauge.

"A thousand pardons, my crewmates. Brother Gall and I felt it would be best to face the sirens without you," replied Enemy.

"Sirens? You faced the sirens without us? What horrors did they unleash upon you?" asked Obnoxious Koss.

"You have sailed with me your entire life," whimpered Enemy. "You know my heart never raised past the roof of a tavern filled with mead and wenches. With one motion of her big toe, a siren sought to make my tongue a desert land. I was to lose the taste of alcohol forever!"

The Lycan buccaneers watched as he walked to a barrel of mead and spear-handed the center.

"A sober Enemy is an obnoxious cost," uttered Obnoxious Koss.

"Aye, they meant to kill us all," Unchained Gauge replied as Enemy raised the barrel over his head and emptied its contents.

When the second group reached the shores of Pitcairn Island, Gall removed his mask and jumped into the water. He slowly took sips from the sea while his Marid Djinn stirred within.

"You would find it suitable to drink from the well you polluted with the world serpent's ashes," Aglaope complained as she walked ashore.

"Gall killed a kappa a while back. He inherited the creature's abilities and the one Iblis bestowed upon him. When the time comes, it will serve us well," Sitoel explained as she walked ashore.

"The time is now!" shouted Aglaope. She pointed to a large wave as Bythos and Alphros emerged from the sea. Gall slyly dived underwater to locate the trident as they approached the shore for a quick meal. A strong kick from their front legs catapulted the hippocampus from the water. When it landed, Bythos displayed his rage with clenched fists and pounded the life out of the mythical seahorse. Alphros snatched the hippocampus from the sand. He bit into the flesh to tear the spine out. While he continued to appease his appetite on boneless limbs, Bythos picked up the bones and rudely tossed them in Sitoel's direction. Sitoel maneuvered around the falling pieces of cartilage and removed her mask to return a cold stare. The sight of flamed emeralds only stirred another charge from the sea serpent. Bythos clenched his fist and raised it over Sitoel's head for a lethal blow.

It was at that moment, a Marid Djinn emerged to weave a fate with a major arpeggio.

"*Doh!*" shouted the Marid Djinn. The sonic wave scissored the flesh from Bythos's hand and broke his wrist. He looked dumbfounded at the cartilage as it landed on the sand. Alphros attempted to avenge his brother with a quick meal. He reached out to grab Sitoel as she unleashed another note.

"*Mi!*" echoed over the sea serpent and rattled their heads. Their insides ruptured, and their spines erupted from their flesh.

Bythos and Alphros squirmed in agony and pounded small dust storms out of the sand as Sitoel unleashed another note.

"*Sol!*" echoed through the cartilage. The sonic wave severed man from fish as it shattered the rib cage into pieces. To end their suffering, Sitoel finished with a "*Doh*" in a high octave. It echoed over the shore and severed the heads from the bodies as Echo finished her song.

"You are truly a Fate," Aglaope uttered as she looked over the aftermath.

A large wave crept over the shore as Poseidon unexpectedly emerged from the sea. His merman form eclipsed half the island. "My pet! What have you done to my beautiful pet!" cried Poseidon. He clenched his fist and raised it over Aglaope. "The sirens have failed me for the last time. You will know the same prison as Parthenope!" His hand dropped with the force of a boulder and pounded Aglaope into a prison of sedimentary rocks beneath the sand.

Poseidon turned to Sitoel and entertained the thought of impaling her on his trident. He pulled on the chain that collared Bythos and Alphros in search of it. He stirred large waves, but only the broken links surfaced.

"I need no trident to avenge what you have taken from me!" threatened Poseidon. His fist bulged as he raised it over Sitoel's head. At that moment another Marid Djinn emerged from the sea. Gall now stood at a height worthy of a Saturday matinee for the King of Monsters marathon. His shadow overlapped Poseidon's as he pinned his tail to the trident. Poseidon screamed in pain as Gall embraced him from behind. Sitoel walked to the edge of the shore as the sound of a breaking rib cage followed her steps.

Sitoel tossed her mask into the sea to unleash an echo of karma. The smack against the water echoed as it sank, and a tidal wave amassed. It rose to the height of Poseidon's stomach as Gall forced his head down and pinned his nostrils on the high seas. The tidal wave formed a mask around Poseidon's face, and the silhouette of a betta fish carried Echo through his nostrils. She rattled inside Poseidon's cranium and disintegrated his brain to leave him lost at sea forever. A waterfall of blood poured from Poseidon's nostrils. The brain fragments shadowed the image of broken bars as Echo dived back into the foam. ✸

Gall picked up the lifeless corpse and tossed it into the deep end of the sea. The roar of a revving chopper motorcycle engine followed as Iblis leapt from the sea with the trident in hand.

"One might say you possess a new skill," complimented Iblis.

"In your service it will only become a vice," replied Sitoel. Iblis responded with laughter as he took a bite out of the sea serpent's tail. He placed the trident in the water and stirred a large wave to bring the Skidbladnir close to shore. The Lycan buccaneers gathered on deck as they anchored near Gall's feet.

Iblis stirred the trident and made a wave of steps that led to the ship's rail.

"At the beginning of this plan, we had agreed there would be a prisoner so I could gather intel about Excalibur," said Iblis. Enemy looked toward Banter as he made his way to the front of the crowd.

"The prisoner is dead. Hel was here and killed her before leaving," replied Banter.

"Then bring me Hel's corpse!" demanded Iblis. Banter shamefully lowered his head with a look of disgust.

"Is it too much to ask for you to be like me!" quipped Sitoel.

"These missed opportunities are quite annoying," added Iblis.

"Before she escaped my scope, Hel delivered a message from Heracles. He openly challenged us to a duel of our choice," explained Banter.

"Zeus's greatest enforcer and general has challenged my Marid Djinns" said Iblis. "Since the day of his birth, Zeus and Hera have set stages to breed Heracles into an awesome killing machine. His palms were stained with blood from the time of his infancy. He killed a teacher for correcting his mistakes. His superhuman strength is backed by his cleverness. There was a giant named Antaeus,who was an immortal while he walked the earth. Heracles overcame that obstacle by holding him above ground while strangling him to death.

He developed and improved his skills throughout his labors. He was a difficult kill during that time. Now he is an immortal!"

Everyone turned to Sitoel for an answer, but her eyes lacked luster. Surprisingly, the best idea was proposed by Banter. "In vino veritas! Heracles' record isn't flawless. He lost a drinking contest to the Greek god Dionysus. Gall now towers at a height that can easily put our troubles to rest."

"Did wine kill him?" asked Sitoel.

"Dionysus's wine selection can harbor many ingredients to seduce or drive a person mad, but Heracles' demise came through the hands of his wife, Deianira," explained Iblis. "She feared that she would one day lose their love to his philandering ways, so she took the advice of a dying centaur. He offered her his poisoned blood and said that if she ever found Heracles unfaithful, she was to spread it over one of his tunic's. He promised that the effects would forever solidify their love. Deianira applied the blood after Heracles had an affair, and the blood ate the flesh from the garment. Deianira unknowingly gave the centaur revenge from beyond the grave."

Enemy slowly approached the ship's steering column with more questions in mind. "So what will we use against him? Wine, woman, or tunic?"

"All of them!" blurted Sitoel. Her eyes suddenly began to luster in color. They raced back and forth as if she were speed-reading through passages.

"All of them?" replied Banter. "We don't even know where to find Deianira or the tunic. Not to mention all the wine we will need to win. Heracles and Dionysus were not mere beings. Their consumption of alcohol that day was an incredible feat." Enemy's eyes widened with thirst. He licked his lips and turned to Iblis with a facial expression that begged for an estimation.

"An amphora vase is approximately five feet in height, and the potency could put a bull to sleep," said Iblis. "You would have to fill the bow of the Skidbladnir and most of the deck to be successful.

Enemy repeatedly counted his fingers and mumbled numbers

while he compared the count to the height of the possessed lycans that had filled the bow during Ragnarök. "Dionysus is my idol!" shouted Enemy. He raced to a barrel of mead and poured a cup to honor the victory.

Banter looked over the Skidbladnir with skepticism. "There's no way we can make that much wine or match the potency."

"Banter speaks hastily," said Iblis. "Dionysus can fill that order within a day. He'd only want to be paid for his service. As for the tunic, it lies in Tartarus, under the trees of suicide. It is guarded by harpies. Deianira also resides in Tartarus. You will have trouble seeking her out. She remains fearful of the day when Heracles discovers her actions."

"Heracles doesn't know?" Sitoel asked as her eyes continued to race through unknown dangers.

"Heracles blamed and killed his servant Lichas for the act," answered Banter. "Deianira learned ways to donate other people's plasma, and the tunic of Nessus became a popular reference throughout history."

Shortly after devising a plan, Iblis placed his hand on the bow of the Skidbladnir to send Banter, Sitoel, and the Lycan buccaneers to Tartarus. Gall rested his giant frame on the island and monitored his consumption of water to maintain his height. Iblis departed for Ethiopia to place an order for wine. Above one of Ethiopia's highest peaks hovered a mass of red wine colored clouds. In the center stood the temple of Dionysus. Two centaurs escorted Iblis to a patch in a grape vineyard where Dionysus guzzled one of his finest wines on a cushioned cot.

"If you haven't already heard, you should pour a little on the ground for Poseidon," said Iblis.

"I will not spoil good wine for that matter. After the first war of the heavens, I learned that an uneasy head lies under a crown. I choose to live carefree in my realm," replied Dionysus. He took a sip from a tall wine glass, and a servant girl rushed to pass a cloth around the edges of his lips.

"Now tell me why you are here?" asked Dionysus.

"I would like to place an order for your finest wine."

"What is your payment and purpose?"

"Heracles challenged my Marid Djinns, and they chose a drinking contest. I want as much as you used to win. The payment is yours to decide."

Dionysus tumbled off the cot with uncontrollable laughter. His centaurs rushed to his aid and fought his sporadic movements as he rolled hysterically on the floor. When he paused to catch his breath, they gently placed him back on the cot.

"The idea is cunning, but I'm afraid they outsmarted themselves," warned Dionysus. "The wine I served that day was potent enough to overwhelm Heracles without having the slightest effect on me. Your Marid Djinns will not fare any better than he did on that day. And you underestimate Heracles. He's a sore loser."

"I'll take my chances. Now name your price," replied Iblis.

"Besides this ill fated idea, I heard a rumor that one of your minions has something in his or her possession that's worth risking my seat among the Olympians," hinted Dionysus.

Iblis took a moment to ponder on his words and sorted the meaning. "You seek the chemistry between wine and music. The effect would be overwhelming if both were made by gods. Pan's flute and lyre were successful in guiding Echo out of the labyrinth that imprisoned her, but that path was also laced with revenge."

"And my path will be laced with crushed grapes," said Dionysus. "Bring me the instruments as payment. I'll have your order filled by the end of the next day."

"I will return on that day with your payment," agreed Iblis.

In Hades, the *Skidbladnir* raced past the borders and sailed a river that circled the underworld nine times. At the end, a ferryman appeared and signaled Enemy to stop to collect his toll. Enemy boldly displayed his bird finger in response and pulled a lever to raise the sails of the Skidbladnir. It slowly levitated toward the dark ceiling of the cavern while the crew fastened pouches filled with stones around their waists. Enemy's ears pointed and rotated like radar dishes as the crew threw the stones to guide him through the darkness. He navigated the ship with the ease of a bat until he reached an abyss with the lure of an unmarked burial ground.

Large clouds of gray smoke funneled through the opening from the nostrils of the Titans imprisoned beneath Tartarus. Enemy ordered the anchors to be dropped as he navigated his way through it. The weight rapidly pulled the Skidbladnir to the waters that irrigated the land, and the open sails cradled the fall as Enemy steered the ship in for a landing. Only the cries from the Titans and grief of the inhabitants greeted the ramp that extended to shore. Sitoel suspiciously watched as the crew cursed and made obscene gestures to a group of women filling their water jugs.

"I'll have the lot of you flogged! Must you alert all of Tartarus to our presence? Keep your minds on returning to the ship if you want to survive the horrors of this place," warned Enemy.

"I only curse at the missed opportunity," joked Motley Yukyur Graves. "As a coroner, I would have earned a pretty penny back in their day—before and after I hid my coins."

"I also curse them," said Pryur Body. "A coroner has a coroner's dummy to enhance his skill. If I am judged and punished for my actions, my soul will be anchored in Tartarus."

Banter sadly watched as a stream of tears rolled off her cheek. "I never thought a Lycan buccaneer could be so emotional."

"Now you know how Pryur Body can capture an audience," said Enemy.

"You're an actress?" asked Banter.

"An actress is an obnoxious comparison," explained Obnoxious Koss. "Pryur Body has graced several stages without the assistance of an acting coach. When playing the role of victim or villain, she seeks out other habitats. This precautionary measure is taken because of the intensity of grief and fear birthed into her role. It can bring the presence of an unwanted character in the home. Her chemistry can match the emotions of a dying mother."

"We came across a dying mother when Lord Treachery and I discovered the Blast brothers. She accumulated enough grief and fear to summon a guardian angel," said Enemy.

"An obnoxious cost before discovering their guardians would be Lycan buccaneers," added Obnoxious Koss.

Enemy proudly looked back at the Blast brothers as they reflected on the day. "And what have you learned under the tutelage of the *Deaf Dum Dead*?"

"Grit Blast! Muzzle Blast!" the brothers simultaneously shouted.

Sitoel looked over the group of women as they walked ashore. "What's so horrible about fetching water?" she asked.

"Those women are the Danaides. They contested their matrimonial arrangement by decapitating their husbands on their wedding night. They have to carry those jugs to a bath and wash off their sins as punishment," explained Banter. Just as Sitoel was about to repeat the question, the Danaides lifted their jugs and water poured from the bottom. After taking two steps, they had to fill them again. "As you can see, they never make it to the tub."

The group continued down an unpaved road and came upon a man chained in the center of a wheel. It spun in place while in flames.

"What did he do?" asked Sitoel.

"That can only be Ixion," answered Banter. "Zeus invited him to his house and discovered his lust for Hera. Zeus spared his life and condemned him to the wheel for an eternity."

The group continued farther down the road and came upon a hill. After a boulder rolled to the bottom, a man slowly pushed it back to the top. Before Sitoel could ask, Banter shouted the explanation.

"His name is Sisyphus! He purposely killed travelers to display acts of power and was condemned to push that boulder back to the top."

A few miles past the hill, the group walked through a thicket of bushes and crept along the border of a forest. In the center stood the Trees of Suicide.

"Where are the harpies?" asked Sitoel.

"Lying in wait for anyone foolish enough to take an item from their nest," a delicate voice answered. Everyone turned to face a woman in a hooded robe, and she placed a knife at Banter's throat in defense.

"Who are you?" she asked.

"*Who are you?*" replied Enemy. The Lycan buccaneers extended their claws in defense. Sitoel's eyes reflected an emerald-green flame as she lowered her hands from her gun holsters.

"We mean you no harm. We've come to retrieve the tunic of Nessus," explained Sitoel.

The stranger removed her blade from Banter's throat and cautiously stepped back. "What purpose do you have for it?" she asked.

"That's none of your concern. We don't involve strangers in our affairs!" snapped Enemy.

"A foolish notion," replied the stranger. "Almost as foolish as the act you are about to commit. No one has ever succeeded in snatching an item from the harpies—especially the tunic of Nessus."

"Why do you know so much about the tunic?" asked Banter.

"My name is Deianira, and I've been condemned to retrieve the tunic from the Trees of Suicide—a task I've constantly repeated during my stay in Tartarus," answered Deianira. She pulled back her hood and revealed the beauty and sincerity of her face.

Enemy quickly took advantage of the opportunity and placed a claw to her throat. "Luck has shined upon us today. Brother Gall also requests your presence."

"Do as you wish," Deianira said with tearful eyes. "I'm condemned to this place. All my hopes to return to my love are lost. There are rules that the inhabitants of the underworld and gods must obey. The gods cannot consume our dead, and we cannot consume anything from the underworld if we intend to leave. I gave in to my hunger a century ago. Even if I find a way to break the laws that border these realms, I risk condemning Heracles to another fate if he were to have me."

Hel unexpectedly appeared and placed a blade at Banter's throat. "Do you honestly expect these men to have any compassion or sentiment for love? This one tried to kill me before he bedded me!"

"You stayed long enough to see the picture of Jesus that hangs over my bed. If you come to my house, I'll show you what happens to women after that" said Banter.

"I would love to take you up on that offer, but you're so forgetful that you might misinterpret the meaning," replied Hel.

While Sitoel fought her instincts to reach for her pistols, two of Hel's servants raced from the Trees of Suicide. Within seconds, Depression and Loss of Control overwhelmed Deianira's vessel. She violently struggled out of Enemy's hold and raced for the tunic.

Hel amusingly whispered in Banter's ear as Deianira snatched the tunic from the roots. "Watch carefully my love."

Having no regard for her life, and overwhelmed with depression, Deianira wrapped herself in the tunic as a trio of harpies attacked her. Deianira pulled her knife, and they snatched it from her. She stopped to throw stones, but they snatched them in the air.

Before Deianira could make another run, the sharp talons and fangs of the harpies were on the tunic. The struggle was relentless and without meaning. An unearthly scream ended it all as the harpies took flight with two detached arms clinging to the tunic. Sitoel ran to Deianira as she collapsed on the ground.

Hel spoke up. "A poet named Otomo said, 'It was better never to have met you in my dream, than to wake and reach for hands that are not there.' Next time, send Sitoel!" With that, she pushed Banter into Enemy and ran deeper into the forest. The Lycan buccaneers gave chase while Banter and Enemy regained their bearings.

"There's too much suffering in this place," said Banter.

"Aye, this will be a strange tale to tell over a cold brew," replied Enemy.

"Who was the cuckold, and who the cuckoo bird?" asked Banter.

"We're not in a place to joke about her actions," warned Enemy.

"I didn't intend for it to be a joke," said Banter. "A cuckold is another name for a husband with an unfaithful wife. The word is derived from the Old French word for 'cuckoo.' It pertains to cuckoo birds, which lay their eggs in other birds' nests to avoid the responsibility of nursing the eggs before they hatch."

Sitoel knelt at Deianira's scarred and battered body.

"I can't tell which one hurts the most," uttered Deianira, "These torn limbs or the life I wasted trying to keep what never belonged to me. Was it all in vain?"

Sitoel removed her mask and pressed her lips to Deianira's cheek as a tear trickled down.

"No," Sitoel answered in a tone that echoed a hiss. Echo circled the tear and encased it in the center like a marble. When she was done, Sitoel safely tucked it under her tongue and returned with self determination.

"Take everyone back to the ship and keep it elevated over the water. I'll be there shortly," instructed Sitoel.

"Don't be foolish. Hel is expecting you to go after the tunic by yourself," warned Banter.

"Trust me!" Sitoel shouted as she raced for the Trees of Suicide.

Enemy unleashed a howl to summon the Lycan buccaneers. They gave up the chase for Hel and quickly returned to his side.

"I'm afraid that whatever plan you had in mind has changed, and so has the meaning of 'cuckoo,'" quipped Enemy. The pack raced back to the Skidbladnir while Sitoel cautiously watched the trees. The harpies propped the tunic on the aerating roots and flew to the strongest branch. In a thicket of leaves, they waited for Deianira's punishment to begin again. It was at that moment, a Marid Djinn emerged to weave a fate that synchronized with the mechanics of a pendulum-driven cuckoo clock.

Sitoel raced from the cover of the bushes with increased speed and snatched the tunic from the tree. The dense forest and a trail of dust clouds were all she left behind. She thought it was an ample start before the sound of talons clipping behind her grew louder. The pursuit took another dramatic turn when a boulder appeared at the end of her path. Sitoel was at the top of Sisyphus Hill. Before today the boulder had always waited for Sisyphus to return to the base before rolling down, but today Sitoel was in Tartarus. She charged at the boulder, and the impact pushed it back down the hill. Stunned expressions appeared on the faces of the harpies as Sitoel jumped on top and backpedaled over Sisyphus.

Sitoel drew her pistols and switched to rapid fire to buy more time. She turned and fired at the harpies while the boulder stormed into Ixion's plain.

"How many punishments must I endure!" bellowed Ixion. The boulder knocked the wheel out of place and sent it rolling in the direction of the Deianades. Sitoel's sporadic gunfire briefly stalled the harpies. They dropped the shells over the boulder to taunt her as she continued to backpedal to the Skidbladnir. The Deianades ran for cover as the wheel and boulder stampeded into their plain like wild buffalo. They crushed the tub and rolled into the waters that irrigated Tartarus.

Ixion's wheel generated a steam cloud as the water began to evaporate. Unchained Gauge unraveled a rope ladder from the ship's rails, and Sitoel grabbed the links as the boulder passed.

"Give the cuckoo bird cover!" shouted Enemy.

"An obnoxious cost! The steam cloud beneath the ship has stirred a dense fog," replied Obnoxious Koss. The steam cloud erupted over the sides and blanketed the ship.

"Pull me in!" shouted Sitoel. The crew quickly responded, and so did the harpies.

Banter grabbed his rifle and changed the clip as the crew reeled Sitoel to the rails. When a pair of flamed emeralds bounced on the deck, Banter fired a round. Just seconds before grabbing the tunic, a harpy stopped to catch the bullet. It shook its talon to release the shell as a slow buzz pushed a fist-shaped hole through the harpy and the one that followed. Their carcasses whistled back to Tartarus and provoked a charge from the one that remained. Sitoel stood on deck to face the harpy on her own. When it closed in, she fired Deianira's tear like a spitball in a straw. It unleashed an echo of karma as the harpy snatched it from the air.

"No!" echoed with a sonic blast.

The harpy collapsed on deck with a shattered heart as Echo tightened her blanket on the tear.

"A souvenir!" shouted Motley Yukyur Graves. He ran to the carcass and cradled it while the talons still twitched. Echo rolled the tear back to Sitoel's feet like a marble.

"I told you to trust me," boasted Sitoel. She snatched the tear off the deck and brushed it off before placing it under her tongue.

"I trust you to be you," Banter replied as the steam pushed the Skidbladnir out of Tartarus.

The following day, Iblis returned to the temple of Dionysus with Pan's flute and lyre. He quickly made his presence known as he entered the dining hall with the roar of a revving chopper motorcycle engine. The sight of Zeus and Hera at the table immediately raised his suspicion.

"What's the meaning of this?" asked Iblis.

"A small celebration of your defeat to mull over the loss of Poseidon," answered Zeus. A centaur retrieved the flute and lyre as Iblis looked to Dionysus for an explanation.

"Can I tell him, my king?" whispered Hera. Zeus nodded in approval. "You are bold and cunning, but there is one flaw in your plan. The amount of wine you ordered slightly outweighs the amount Dionysus consumed to beat Heracles, but it will not defeat him."

"Slightly?" Iblis replied as his eyes darkened.

"Do not blame me," answered Dionysus. "I honored our agreement for the flute and lyre. You requested the amount of wine it took for me to win that day. I also warned you about Heracles being a sore loser."

Hera strolled to a window behind Dionysus's chair with a sinister smile. She pulled back the curtain to unveil the sight of centaurs loading wine into three Greek merchant ships. "As you can see, we are also here to fill a wine request. After his loss, Heracles trained himself to consume twice as much." She returned to the table with spurts of laughter.

"No need to trouble yourself any further," said Zeus. "We will deliver the wine and host the event on Mount Olympus. You just bring the skulls."

"Skulls? What skulls?" asked Iblis.

"Heracles desires the skulls of the Marid Djinns vessels," explained Zeus. "He will mount one on his olive club, mount another on the collar of Cerberus, and turn the last one into a wine cup. He will call it Gall."

A dark cloud circled beneath the feet of Iblis as Zeus extended his staff. Zeus hurled it and shattered the ground beneath Iblis's feet to cast him out of the sky. Iblis withdrew the trident and summoned a large wave to cushion his fall. It carried him back to Pitcairn Island, where he joined the others.

"How dare he cast me from the sky! He rests only on the doormat of the heavens," sniveled Iblis. He holstered the trident in a pouch on his back as everyone gathered around him.

"Dionysus has deceived me. He agreed to make the amount of wine he needed to defeat Heracles, but failed to mention that Heracles conditioned himself to consume twice as much since then. The potency remains a factor as well. Gall's giant size will not be as beneficial as we thought," explained Iblis.

Enemy removed a sharpening stone from his pocket and filed his claws with grief. "You are not the only bearer of bad news. We found Deianira at the Trees of Suicide. Zeus condemned her to retrieve the tunic from the harpies. We attempted to bring both back, but Hel interfered. We only have the tunic."

"That obstacle cannot be overlooked," replied Iblis. "We cannot weaken Heracles without the woman. She could've lured Heracles into a tunic with ease. He is unaware of her betrayal and would have doubted Cerberus's barks of warning."

"I have something that can serve as the equivalent. I brought back one of Deianira's tears," said Sitoel.

"You managed to leave the underworld with a tear? My faith in you is increasing more and more. Now all we have to do is find a way for Heracles to consume it," replied Iblis.

"Why should that be difficult? We can easily slip it into his wine," said Banter.

Iblis's eyes darkened. "I told you, Heracles was bred for a purpose since the day of his birth. Zeus sent daemons to help guide Heracles through his life and twelve labors. They thought of everything—even the weaknesses of the underworld. The capture of that three headed mongrel served that purpose. Cerberus is at the side of Heracles because it can detect anything from the underworld. Nothing alive or dead passed the gates when he was the guard. Now he guards Heracles in the same manner. He'll sniff out the poison with ease and find the person that handled it. I'm afraid Heracles will get the trophies he requested."

"What trophies?" asked Banter.

"Heracles wants your skulls," answered Iblis. "He'll put one on his club, put another on the collar of Cerberus, and the last skull will become a wine cup that he will call Gall."

Gall's ear's rotated like radar dishes in their lycan form as he unleashed a howl of reckoning. "Bring my war chest!" demanded Gall. Enemy hurried below deck to retrieve what would be the base of Gall's scheme as the others gathered around to hear his plan.

While the Marid Djinns prepared for the contest, the Olympians prepared the coliseum for the event. A large wooden table rested in the center for Heracles. Every wall between the pillars was stacked to the balcony with wine. Outside, servants stacked carts to bring in more wine on command. A crowd gathered from the skies to the underworld to be the first ones through the door. At sunrise, the spilled wine created a fiery red horizon, and Zeus muffled the cheering of the crowd with thunder. A band of flutes and trumpets opened the doors as the Olympians walked to their seats.

After everyone was seated, Hermes flew to the center of the coliseum to announce Heracles. "Gods, goddesses, deities, and creatures of realms foreign and mine. Stand and applaud the immortal that has slain kings, giants, and creatures without fear. Outsmarted and cunningly defeated countless enemies in combat and competition. The hero of the twelve labors ... Heracles!"

The rampant chanting of his name could not muffle the sound of his presence. The ground paid a penalty to hold his bulky frame. Every footstep carried the sound of a body collapsing on the floor. The oil coating on his chest and abs made his skin shine like armor. The short curly hair cropped close to his crown highlighted the royal grooming of his beard. Cerberus viciously growled, and whipped his serpent tail at every servant that stood close to Heracles. The control over Cerberus as he obediently knelt at the chair boosted his strength. He patted the mongrel's head as he sat and rested his olive club on the table.

"I will teach these Marid Djinns the same respect. Now bring me my skulls!" demanded Heracles. The boast ignited the crowd and brought a proud smirk to the face of Zeus.

The sudden roar of a revving chopper motorcycle engine ended the cheers. A large fog amassed and overshadowed the coliseum. It generated a wave of fear as Gall appeared with Iblis resting on his shoulder. Banter led the Lycan buccaneers into the coliseum with an ecstatic cheer from an opposing crowd. Cerberus's nose flared, and he barked in the direction of the potential threat.

"My king, that cheer comes from the Danaides!" said Hera.

Zeus made a gesture for Hermes to come to his side. "I want this matter investigated immediately," commanded Zeus.

"But my king, the competition is about to start," pleaded Hermes. Zeus angrily gripped his staff to provoke a sudden departure.

The presence of the Danaides wasn't the only thing that brought anger to the Greek gods. Gall removed the tunic of Nessus from the center of his palm and dropped it on the table. The sight ignited a series of thoughts and spurts of rage from the immortal Heracles.

"This one has no regard for his own life. Did you not hear what happened to the last man that brought that tunic before me?" threatened Heracles.

"I did not come to hear another tale of your strength and feats. *I am here for your fate!*" replied Gall.

"Then drink long and heavily, because you will never see the day. I am immortal in this realm and yours," boasted Heracles. The crowd cheered as Heracles picked up his first wine vase and guzzled.

Gall followed by picking up an entire wine cart with two fingers. The wine flowed like a small waterfall as he tipped it over and guzzled the contents. They kept pace with each other throughout the day. Servants rushed wine into the coliseum, and the crowd cheered as the empty vases were taken away. When the sun had started to set, Gall finished a cart of wine and sat in an upright position. His head swayed as his vision started to blur.

"The bigger they are, the harder they fall," said Heracles. "By now you must be seeing three vases, and this one I'm about to finish leaves me one ahead of you. I know because I was in that position when I lost." Heracles grabbed his club as he stood from the table. He walked to the center and poked at the tunic. "What was your plan for this? Did you think I would lose focus when you brought this before me? Fortunately for you, the thirst for wine mollified my anger. I was going to split your head open without the patience of a blissful state. Now I can make you one of my fonder memories."

"Tell me about those memories," said Gall.

Heracles gestured for a servant to bring him another vase as a smile appeared on his face. "I wore that tunic when I toured my vineyards. My harvest was the most profitable in all the land!"

A servant brought another vase, and Heracles paused to consume it. When he was done, he handed it back and gestured for another. "I also wore that tunic when I sought the affections of my wife, Deianira. I remember her beauty and love. That night, I entangled my fingers in long strands of ebony hair. We mixed oils and perfumes with sweat. For many nights and occasions, our lust knew no borders. Now that you've managed to bring her to mind, I will seek her out," said Heracles.

Gall leaned over the coliseum wall and picked up another cart of wine to regain the lead. "Yes, Deianira's beauty and love are unforgettable," replied Gall.

Heracles slammed the empty vaser on the ground and gestured for another. He turned to Gall and asked in a harsh tone, "You act as if it is something we both shared?"

"It is, but only because she now stands before me," answered Gall. It was at that moment, a Marid Djinn emerged to conjure a sop for Cerberus. Gall pointed to the entrance of the coliseum, and Heracles turned to face the woman he desired.

Everyone in the coliseum cheered as an object they desired entered. Sitoel had applied the lotion the Lycan buccaneers stole from Freyr during the events of Ragnarök, and this quickly gained the attention of Heracles.

"Deianira, come to me. I will commemorate this occasion with another vase of wine, and dedicate the fatal blow to your return!" said Heracles.

Iblis jumped off Gall's shoulder and glided to the Lycan buccaneers. The reunion had stirred tension in Cerberus. Sitoel slowly approached Heracles while the mongrel growled at his side.

"I know better than to doubt Brother Gall, but the suspense is unbearable. The effects of the lotion we stole from the Norse god during the events of Ragnarök are successful. We all see what we desire, but what does Cerberus see?" asked Pryur Body. She reached out and extended her claws to the illusion of a cowering victim as Sitoel approached Heracles.

"An obnoxious cost!" replied Obnoxious Koss. "You have been a canine long enough to know that a dog doesn't see. He smells what we all fear. We are doomed!"

Iblis's eyes darkened as he looked at the world through Cerberus's eyes. He whispered a depiction while Cerberus's nostrils flared.

"He detects the scent of Tartarus—his place in the underworld—and the duty to watch over it," explained Iblis. "He also remembers the fight with Heracles and being paraded through the streets after the loss. The celebration represented Heracles' victory over all earthly desires—Heracles conquering the three heads of human strife by nature, cause, and accident."

Cerberus turned his nose to the table and sniffed the tunic.

"Now the confusion, because the tunic is proof that Heracles failed at all three," added Iblis. The sight of a serpent's tail wagging caught everyone by surprise.

"So what does he see?" asked Enemy.

"*Heracles!*" snickered Iblis.

"Why would he desire Heracles?" asked Unchained Gauge.

"Imagine being tied down by someone that never made it over the hump," answered Banter. Cerberus stepped back and allowed Heracles to welcome death. In response, Heracles ran to Sitoel and greeted her with a long kiss.

During his display of affection, Sitoel discreetly maneuvered the tear from under her tongue and unleashed an echo of karma. Echo pushed the tear through Heracles' digestive system and manifested the effects of water intoxication. Within seconds, Heracles was suffering from confusion, nausea, and vomiting. A broad smile appeared on Gall's face as he picked up another wine cart. He gestured a toast and tipped it over as Heracles became human. While Gall enjoyed his victory, Heracles endured a seizure, fell into a coma, and died. Cerberus drooled from the mouth as he sunk his teeth into Heracles' flesh, dragging the body through puddles of spilled wine.

"They call him Gall!" cheered Iblis.

Zeus angrily gripped his staff as Cerberus dragged the corpse back through a portal that led to the underworld.

"Every time I think I'm dealing with a thrill seeker, Gall comes up with a plan that proves me wrong," mumbled Banter. A black fog circled beneath Gall and the pack.

"We've outlasted our welcome. Prepare yourselves," warned Iblis. He turned to Zeus as he stretched his staff into a lightning bolt and fired.

"I'll see you in Hades!" shouted Iblis.

"Not if Existere sees you first!" replied Zeus.

Gall's large frame collapsed on the ground and stirred a small tremor in the earth. He opened his hands to cradle the pack.

Iblis glided to the ground, mumbling threats about the second offense.

"This is an outrage!" shouted Iblis.

"Who is Existere?" asked Sitoel.

"In your tongue, her name is Existence. She is the offspring of Heracles and the serpentine queen Echidna," answered Iblis.

"Heracles had a daughter?" Sitoel asked as her eyes lustered.

"Unbeknownst to your realm, her birth was kept in secrecy. Echidna spoke only of three sons after she laid with Heracles. He predicted that one would succeed him and rule a powerful army, *if he could gird his bow.* As predicted, Echidna gave birth to three sons and unexpectedly had a daughter. Echidna tested her sons when they had reached manhood. Two of the eldest failed and were cast out of her kingdom. Echidna proudly looked to the youngest and handed him the bow with the expectation of him achieving Heracles' prediction, *but he failed!* This troubled Echidna until Existere boldly left her cave and accomplished the task. Echidna saw great things within the child, but she knew a woman could not rule in peace. She kept Existere a secret and claimed that the youngest child fulfilled Heracles' prediction. That lie fueled a rage and ambition in Existere. She refused to be denied her title and her existence. In the pit of a cave, she assembled a band of rebels with her brothers that were cast out. The surprise attack conquered Echidna's lie and Heracles' youngest heir. Existere united their forces, and under her command they created an army of superior archers.

"Unfortunately for Existere, her actions brought about her mother's concern. She had to maintain the respect of her men and hold a title for her enemies. So she stormed the gates to Hades' domain. She fought her way into the throne room, and Hades tumbled over with laughter.

"'Did you think the gods would be any different when it comes to power? Not even my throne is safe when it comes to the thirst for power. Zeus will descend upon you himself before you become acquainted with it,' warned Hades. His words rang true to her ears. For her to exist as a ruler, she would have to become a queen. At that point, her only option was to offer herself to Hades.

"This was another act that caused him to tumble over with laughter. It stirred a rage in Existere, and since hell hath no fury like a woman scorned, she closed the borders to the underworld. She vowed that if Hades would not let her in, no one would be allowed to leave. Her army successfully guarded the gates while Heracles paraded around with Cerberus. Time after time, Hades has put the helm of invisibility to great use. He willingly offered it to heroes who placed themselves in his service. After doing so, he sent them out to exterminate Existere.

"They quickly learned the prey was more than an arrogant female. She possessed the thermal and binocular vision of a predatory snake, as well as its sense of smell and sensitivity to vibration. Along with herculean strength and arrows laced with a venom as powerful as her mother's, Existere erased the opposition from existence. A courageous creature would have an arrow in every vital organ of its body before her fang tasted blood, or body felt blade fatigue. Oddly, she became the best defense for his domain. I'll have to summon Lord Treachery's legions to retrieve my helm when she hears about the death of her father."

Iblis paced back and forth while trying to come up with a solution that would avoid another war. As his thoughts circled, a strange mist appeared with Akantha in the center.

"You've already won the helm of invisibility," said Akantha. "The next course of action should not be Hades. It should be Zeus! He'll never expect an attack at the festival" She stepped out of the mist wearing a white silk gown that sparkled like the sun's rays on the sea. Her hair was straightened to luster silver while it flowed over a red pashmina shawl.

"His festival for wolves! I almost forgot about the event. Zeus is always in attendance," replied Iblis.

"Zeus was hoping to be done with the Marid Djinns by now, but he will appear. I brought Gall something to return him to normal," said Akantha. She removed a vial with an orange solution from a white pouch on her waistline. Gall lowered his head, and she poured it into his mouth.

"What is this festival about?" asked Sitoel.

Enemy's ears perked as he climbed out of Gall's palm, and he began to explain. "The Lycan buccaneers were invited to this festival nearly a century ago. A young man in his twenties said it was part of his military training. Every nine years, in the ash heap of a forbidden precinct that casts no shadows, a clan of ephebes perform a ritual. On the tallest peak in Arcadia, the ephebes entangle a human entrail with that of a wolf. After they feast, they turn into wolves. They run rampant through the night and search for victims, because feasting on humans is the only way they can regain their form."

"You ran with a pack of ephebes. They'll let us in with no problem," said Banter.

"An obnoxious cost!" replied Obnoxious Koss. "We were invited but never accepted the invitation. Enemy was always partial to wolves outside the monstrous wolf bloodline."

Akantha raised her nose in a presumptuous manner at the remark. "Did the captain forget that Gall is a wolf by the fetter?" she said.

The effects of Akantha's solution spread through Gall's insides like a wildfire and soaked his glands. After a loud belch, Gall returned to his normal size.

"In my book, that's tolerable. The fetter never made Gall my brother. First feed the face, then tell me right from wrong," quipped Enemy.

"Smart ass," Akantha blurted as they huddled together to plot another scheme.

After Hermes returned with news from Tartarus, Zeus sought to avenge his loss. Word of Tartarus falling to the Marid Djinns and the death of Heracles forced his hand. He summoned his personal guard to retrieve the closest kin of the Marid Djinns.

"There's never a Marid Djinn around when you need one!" grumbled Kaleb. He loaded his XM8 assault rifle while he watched his security monitor. The guards posted outside the house mysteriously collapsed from a whirlwind of unmeasurable speed. Kaleb's eyes widened with fear at the sight of Nike snapping necks outside his window.

Nike politely stepped aside after breaking the door for Kratos. He stepped through the doorway and welcomed a hailstorm of bullets. He walked through a small band of guards, bare-chested and without armor, to get to Kaleb's office. While the guards were distracted, Nike stirred another lethal whirlwind of neck-snapping. Kratos broke through the office door, and Kaleb opened fire. He emptied and reloaded his weapon with just a tap of his finger, but a gift from the gods made Kratos impenetrable. His skin hardened with every attack and personified his strength.

Kratos brushed off the shells and snatched the rifle from Kaleb's hands. In response, Kaleb removed two knuckle braces from his suit pocket and took a defensive stance.

"Suit yourself, ogre. I cannot lose!" Nike boasted as she entered the office. She clenched her fists and rushed her opponent. A flurry of lightning-fast punches rendered Kaleb unconscious before he could swing.

"Another victory brought forth by my hands!" shouted Nike.

"Save your cheers for when we face the Fates," replied Kratos. He picked Kaleb off the floor and tossed him over his shoulder with ease.

"Why worry about the Fates? Existere is a formidable opponent. Zeus's wolf pack will be feasting on the entrails of their loved ones before they make it out of Hades' realm."

At the Styles estate, Bella helplessly screamed with despair as Bia stormed into the mansion. She waved her hand to induce a gravitational pull that placed Bella in a motionless state.

"Run, Alexander!" shouted Bella.

"I'm not afraid of some warrior princess," replied Alexander. He stepped from behind Bella and took a defensive stance.

"Such brave words for a young pup, but I'm afraid your bark is bigger than your bite," said Bia. Her dark red eyes pierced the darkness of a gold Corinthian helmet. She motioned her free hand, and a gust of wind quickly placed Alexander in her grasp.

Bia tossed him over her shoulder and turned to Bella. "As of today, your services are rendered. Your masters will not return," said Bia. Bella teared in her frozen state as Bia motioned for a gust of wind and took flight with Alexander.

In the hills of El Carmel, Zelos stepped out of Madame Carrea's caravan with her lying unconscious over his shoulder. He briefly paused at the bottom of the steps while his nostrils flared. His height and strength increased as he fed off a rivalry.

"The air is riddled with the scent of jealousy and envy," said

Zelos. "It's so thick I can almost taste it. Do not bother to hide yourself from me. I have been aware of your rivalry since it began."

Hel boldly stepped out of the darkness and pulled back Madame Carrea's head to observe a wound. "As much as I hate her, I still knew better than to touch this one."

"That is why you are without a realm," said Zelos. "Zeus knows no boundaries when it comes to his enemies. Your rivalry is coming to an end. Now you'll have to prepare for another."

"Another?"

"After Existere rids us of the Fates, Zeus will reward her by granting a pick of one of your realms. Are you surprised?"

Hel returned to the cover of night. "I expected as much. The reward is just a cover for his own desires. He would eventually want all my realms. One tyrant is the same as another."

To keep the illusion of the Marid Djinns presence in Hades, Iblis ordered Lord Treachery to move his legion of lycans to the Styx River. He also allowed the Marid Djinns to secretly return to their loved ones. The visit would serve as their final moments in case the sneak attack failed. Sitoel was the first to return. After finding her caravan in shambles and a patch of blood on the last step, she stormed the gypsy king's home. He sank into the relaxing cushions of his throne as the sound of Sitoel battling his bodyguards filled the room. Outside the door were two of the tribe's best stick fighters. They were twice her size and had spent half their years training for the fight. It lasted until Sitoel broke her sticks.

In the end, Sitoel threw them through the door like two pebbles. She boldly entered the throne room to lay siege on an artery and crown.

"Your pockets weigh heavy and are lined with my money. How dare you take someone dear to me!" Sitoel shouted in a tone that carried a hiss. She charged at the king sitting on the throne before he could escape. Sitoel jumped in his lap and unsheathed her dagger. His bald head pushed out a stream of sweat while she curled her blade in his long gray beard. His skin clung to the bone, and the diamond studs in his ears—a decoration to keep the attention off the scars of misaligned bones, which had been left behind when Sitoel retrieved the tribe's sacred bloodstone. It was a hopeless effect for the large nose that overlapped his top lip.

"She wasn't abducted by my hand!" uttered the gypsy king.

"Speak swiftly. You'll learn I'm not like the victims you've extorted over the years," warned Sitoel. Her blade began to flicker as she removed pieces of his beard.

"Someone saw who took her. He said the man wore old Greek armor. His muscles became bulkier, and his skin turned serpent-like when his accomplice appeared—a beautiful woman with a dragon tattoo trailing from head to toe."

"Hel!" snapped Sitoel. She turned from her king and started for the door. He quickly took advantage of the moment and removed a pocket-sized glock from under the cushion.

"You were always the type to ask forgiveness before asking permission," said the gypsy king. "Now it's finally caught up to you. You will learn to respect your king!"

"*I am your king!*" replied the Marid Djinn.

Sitoel's eyes beaconed like flaming emeralds while Echo watched her back. She unleashed an echo of karma when the gypsy king cocked his gun. It rattled his hand, and he grabbed his chest as he suffered from the effects of a cardiac arrest. Sitoel's tribe rushed through the door as their king trembled on the floor. They watched until he lay lifeless. Sitoel cut the diamonds from his ears and handed them to the tribe's blacksmith. He diligently watched as she knelt to carve a design on the floor.

"They're called the Judges' Pens. You will make me two sets. Have them ready before my departure," instructed Sitoel.

In response, the entire tribe knelt before her and replied, "As you wish, my king."

Shortly afterward, Banter walked through the crumbled entrance of his mansion. He found Bella standing as stiff as a statue, her eyeshadow running from tears. Banter lightly tapped her face so she could wake from her dormant state.

"Master Styles, I have been standing here for an entire day!" said Bella. Banter slowly moved her joints to ease the stiffness.

"Where's Alexander?" asked Banter.

"A woman took the young Master Styles. She said my masters would not return, and rudely commanded me to retire," explained Bella.

"Maybe you should take her advice," said Banter.

"I beg your pardon!"

"It'll only be for a short while. Just until I bring back Alexander."

Bella pushed Banter out of her way and stumbled to the closet door. She opened it and removed Banter's first sniper rifle.

"I haven't seen the old Remington since I was a teenager," said Banter.

"And how quickly you've forgotten who brought it to your interest. I didn't cower when I served your father and the unnatural horrors kept in the vaults at Styles Corporate. I don't plan to run now," replied Bella.

"I can't take you with me," said Banter.

"We can mull it over during target practice!" she shouted.

Banter reached into his pocket and removed the clip Iblis handed him before he left the pack. He remembered the conversation they had shared before leaving.

"They look like the same bullets I gave you," said Banter.

"On the outside, *but inside they pierce the heart and cling to the soul!*" Iblis explained.

At the Abominable estate, Gall and Enemy cautiously made their way into Kaleb's office. Gall walked to the desk and played back the footage on the security monitor. The outside camera showed Kaleb jumping out of his limo while a whirlwind broke off parts of the vehicle. A band of armed guards swarmed around Kaleb and opened fire with XM8 assault rifles as a large toned man appeared. A barrage of bullets sparkled over his chest. The wounds disappeared like scratch marks as the muscle tissue hardened and pushed the slugs out of his skin.

"They're the children of Styx," explained Enemy. "They helped rid Zeus of the Titans and now serve as his personal guard. The woman is Nike, she is victorious in battle and competition. The man is Kratos, his body can strengthen to a point where it becomes impenetrable."

Footage of Kratos brushing off the flattened bullets on his chest, and Nike following with an attack that couldn't be seen by the normal speed of the camera, confirmed his words. Out of anger, Gall pounded his fist on the desk and unleashed his lycan form. A howl of reckoning followed and rattled the fixtures in the mansion. In response, Enemy tightened the straps on his protective vest and removed a sharpening stone from his pocket.

"Another hunt begins!" he barked as they returned to the darkness of night.

On the day of the festival, everything appeared to be a normal Olympic event. After the head priestess recited a victory ode, an athlete carried a torch into the stadium and lit the wick to begin the games. Throughout the course of the day, spectators and residents cheered their favorite athletes. Ephebes, who were wolves in their previous years, now supervised the event in hooded black sweat suits. They stood guard with the heightened senses and agility of their counterparts. Zeus watched from the cave of Rhea with his staff mounted over his throne. An army of wolves slowly gathered around him for the meal that would return them to their human forms.

The cave was the safest place on earth for the Greek god. Inside, history stirred echoes in the mind—a parallel of ideas, styles, and feelings for the event that came to be. As an infant, Zeus was brought to the cave by his mother, Rhea. In a desperate attempt to save her child from the prophecy that one day her child would overthrow his father. Out of fear, Cronos devoured every child Rhea gave birth to. To protect Zeus, Rhea wrapped a stone in a newborn's garment and fed it to Cronos. Zeus grew up in the cave in secrecy and fulfilled the prophecy when he became of age. In later years, history attempted to repeat itself.

Zeus was invited to a dinner given by the king of Arcadia. King Lycaon plotted to serve Zeus the flesh of his dead son to weaken him, and then strip the Greek god of his powers. Daemons warned Zeus of his treachery, and he punished the savage act by turning the king into a wolf. When Zeus discovered another purpose for a half-man, half-wolf, a festival was made. It helped raise an army for his immortal son. They were to conquer realms and bring about victory in the second war of the heavens.

When the closing ceremony was over, Zeus ordered Kratos and Nike to retrieve the new ephebes. He commanded Bia to retrieve their prisoners while Zelos prepared the sacred ritual. When Nike and Kratos arrived at the festival, they gathered the ephebes and hunted for more victims for the sacred ritual. Within a short while, the audience uncovered the horrific purpose of the event. Two small armies waited for people to stray from the crowd to feed their wolves. When their cages were full, Nike departed with half their numbers. Kratos watched the other half and suspiciously waited for the last pack to return.

As the pack made their way back to the event, a drunken and debauched lycan in a hooded black sweat suit gained their attention.

Enemy groggily sang as he fell to the ground. "Now if you lost your inheritance or he left his common sense. You're not too picky of the crowd you keep or the mattress where you sleep. Behind every window ... behind every door ... the apple is gone, but there's always the core."

An athlete cautiously flared his nostrils and noticed the familiar scent of a wolf. "This man is one of us!" he said.

"He probably thought he'd have a couple of brews before attending the ritual. Let's give him a hand," he commanded. Two athlete's raced to Enemy's aid. One felt the presence of a vest as they raised him to his feet.

"Why do you wear a *vesssh!*" he uttered as Enemy swiped a claw across his larynx.

"Why don't you?" answered Enemy. He finished the other with a devastating punch.

Before the other athlete's could react, the Lycan buccaneers raced from the cover of darkness and attacked. They quickly snapped the necks of their opponents to avoid the spilling of blood.

"There aren't enough suits here to fit us all," complained Unchained Gauge.

"Haven't we wasted enough time here already!" snapped Banter. He stepped from behind a tree and snatched a sweat suit from Morbid Medley's hand.

"It would've taken longer if we didn't outnumber them," explained Enemy. "Take the advice of a Lycan buccaneer that has been pursued, tortured, and imprisoned over the centuries. You do not want to rush these things. Everything we have planned will be in vain if their guards smell blood on these clothes."

Enemy disrobed the athlete that had suffered his punch while Banter looked over the torn larynx of the other.

"If that's the case, why make a mess of this one?" asked Banter.

"He questioned my love," answered Enemy.

"Then allow me to question your strength!" interrupted Kratos. He charged at the Lycan buccaneers with a small army of athlete's. He pushed Enemy into three Lycan buccaneers, and the impact uprooted several trees. Kratos turned to Banter, and Banter removed his sniper rifle from the pouch strapped to his back. He chuckled as Banter loaded the clip Iblis gave him.

"You are as foolish as the last mortal that brought a weapon before me. Discharge as many fiery metals as you desire. I like the sparkle on my chest when they bounce. You'll soon learn I am—"

"A target!"

At that moment, a Marid Djinn emerged to weave a transparent fate. Banter fired three rounds into Kratos. They drilled holes through his heart, upper left chest, and navel. The wounds leaked blood as Kratos's skin hardened. Before it pushed out the slugs, they turned into a liquid that stayed in the bloodstream of his body. Inside, the liquid trail hardened a few seconds after the skin. An arm with a clenched fist over the heart was imprinted on the chest. When Kratos collapsed to the ground, his fallen body gave the impression of Banter's Marid Djinn symbol.

While the battle continued with the athlete's, Gall and Sitoel waited on the road that led to the forbidden precinct. They stepped out of the darkness to face Nike as she approached with her small army.

"I know you told me not to ask, but how do you beat something that doesn't lose?" asked Gall.

Sitoel's eyes lustered as she grabbed her stomach. "I'm going to be sick," she uttered.

"Is it because I used the shotgun or the knuckle braces?" asked Gall.

Sitoel knelt on the ground and vomited.

"If you want to beat someone that can't lose, *cheat!*" said Hel. She stepped out of the cover of darkness as Jealousy, Envy, Hate, Hunger, Clumsy, and Reckless attacked. Within seconds, Nike's army turned against each other and engaged in a bloody battle. Nike attempted to escape as Clumsy and Reckless took hold. She took flight, and they toyed with her in midair. They forced her to crash into a tree next to Gall. Three Judges' Pens that had been wedged into the branches impaled her arms and back.

"Knuckle braces!" blurted Gall. He removed them from the pocket of his coveralls as he approached Nike. At that moment, a Marid Djinn emerged to weave a fate that cast a shadow.

"Your skills were impressive on camera, but now I have a riddle for you. How do you cast a shadow in a precinct that does not cast shadows?" Gall asked in a tone that carried a hiss. His blows pounded into Nike's flesh without mercy. They were brutal and severe. When it was over, Nike lay lifeless with a large puddle of blood and vomit at her feet. Clumsy and Reckless fell into it as they staggered out of the body. Their imprints left shadows as they crawled away.

Above him, Gall could hear a cannon fire from the Skidbladnir as it passed.

"I told you to wait for my signal!" shouted Gall. The Skidbladnir hovered over the sacred ritual site, and Bia took flight. She confronted the attack head on. She grabbed the mast to force the cannons to roll back. The ammunition exploded as she swung it into the base of the mountain. The explosion rendered Gall and Sitoel unconscious. Shattered pieces of wood and a fire killed all the passengers that remained. Zeus and Zelos raced to the edge of the ritual site to look down on the aftermath.

"It appears our enemies have detoured from the realm of Hades to attend your sacred ritual, mighty Zeus," said Zelos.

"Thanks to Bia, the attempt was in vain. Search the wreckage and make sure there are no more disturbances before the priests arrive," commanded Zeus.

Zelos inhaled the smoke that rose from the crash. The scent of the ashes fueled his body and gave him the height of a giant as he raced down the mountainside to inspect.

When Zelos reached the base of the mountainside, Bia greeted him with the corpse of a Lycan buccaneer.

"Zeus wanted proof," said Zelos.

"There's only ashes," said Bia. "The explosion blew this corpse out of the ship. I was barely able to pry it from the wooden spears that pinned her to the ground."

"Here are two more survivors," said Hel. She dragged Gall and Sitoel to Zelos.

"You never cease to amaze me. Here I was preparing myself for steak, and you brought me lobster!" quipped Zelos. He threw Gall and Sitoel over his shoulder. "You'll finally have the opportunity to put an end to your rival. Zeus will organize a battle for his entertainment after the ritual," he said as he climbed back to the ritual site.

When Gall and Sitoel regained their senses, they found themselves chained to stone slabs. They looked around and found their closest kin in the same position. Kaleb was propped on a stage with a group of priests chanting in hooded black robes. Bloodthirsty wolves kept an audience with the new ephebes for their expected meal.

Iblis crept from under Gall's stone slab and whispered into his ear, "You've finally awakened."

Gall looked at his brother and pulled on his chains with desperation. "Now you can free me!"

"He will do no such thing," explained Zeus. "He cannot interfere with a ritual by a god of my stature. This is a moment in time that can change or repeat itself." He made his way to the stage with Zelos and Bia by his side.

"Your position will be questioned when this is over," replied Iblis.

"Yes, but it will no longer matter. I care little about concealing my intentions after the damage your Marid Djinns created," said Zeus.

Zeus approached Kaleb's stone slab and grabbed two surgical knives propped on the table. "The realms of the underworld have proven to be more valuable than I could imagine. I would never have allowed Hades to rule over it if I'd known it's worth. It has become a place undisturbed by mortals and a gateway to other realms worthy of my stature. I slowly discovered the secrets of the underworld and the keys that are centered in all living things. I needed to regain control without causing alarm or sibling rivalry. So I molded a conqueror to achieve the task. Time and time again, he proved his worth to me. Unfortunately he had one flaw. He could not control his lust for women. You discovered that when you took him away from him. For a nail, he lost the kingdom!"

The priests surrounded the sacred ritual site while Zeus prepared to cut into Kaleb's flesh.

"Even when he endured his twelve labors," Zeus went on, "he found time to spawn another nuisance that's been a thorn in my side. Existere advanced on Hades with an army of elite archers. She took control while Cerberus served at Heracles' side. After granting immortality to Heracles, I had to create an army to help him rid me of my problems. The events that took place today finalized the ritual that gave me that army. They can strategically hunt down any prey I command. To make the wolves elite, I returned them to their mortal form with animal instincts. Now that my army is complete, I lack a general. I'm forced to form a pact with Existere. She will gain Hel's realms and a seat at my table of Olympians."

Zeus made an incision mark for the removal of Kaleb's entrails. The priests took advantage of the opportunity to fill the surrounding ash bins with gunpowder.

"We will meet again. In another time or place," threatened Kaleb.

"Save your last cries for death," replied Zeus.

"You should heed a brother's warning!" interrupted Enemy. The head priest removed his hood to reveal a drunken and debauched Lycan buccaneer.

"You told me they were ashes!" shouted Zeus. Dumbfounded expressions crossed the face of Zelos and Bia as the Lycan buccaneers removed their hoods.

Enemy removed a mug filled with mead from his robe as he explained. "That wasn't far from the truth. A moment of silence for our dear departed Pryur Body—a Lycan buccaneer that possessed the madness of a wild boar. Always in search of the scene that mesmerizes the audience and immortalizes a career. After the scallywag ruined our ticket for entry with bloodstained clothes, *we found religion*. A group of priests increased our faith. Pryur Body volunteered to charge into battle headfirst to clear our path."

"An obnoxious cost! It's time to ante up for the loss of our ship and mate!" demanded Obnoxious Koss.

"No sudden moves from anyone. We have filled the surrounding bins with gunpowder," warned Unchained Gauge. He removed a Molotov cocktail from his robe, lit the wick, and handed it to Enemy.

"Fool, you'd kill all of them," said Zeus.

"Cheers to letting them know!" answered Enemy. He gestured a toast and threw the Molotov cocktail at a neighboring ash bin.

"Bia!" shouted Zeus. Bia motioned a gust of wind to hold the bottle in midair. The act served as a signal for the Lycan buccaneers. They removed their robes and raced to free the prisoners.

"It was only a distraction. Continue with the ritual!" shouted Bia. Zeus cut through Kaleb's chest and maneuvered through bone to remove the entrails. He entangled them with the entrails of a wolf as a Marid Djinn emerged for an Abominable fate.

Gall pulled on his chains until they broke and left an imprint on his skin. He charged after Zeus as Banter fired rounds from a secluded location. One round shattered the Molotov cocktail Bia held in the air. The flames rained over the ash bin and ignited an explosion. In response, the Lycan buccaneers quickly tossed the prisoners back onto the stone slabs. They grabbed the chains to steer as half the mountain started to crumble in a landslide. To avoid being crushed under the rubble, Zeus extended his lightning staff and threw it at the base of the mountain. Zelos helplessly watched as the landslide carried everyone into the realm of Hades. He knelt in failure and prayed for Zeus's survival as Hel approached from behind.

"My dear Zelos, you won't be having any steak or lobster," said Hel. "Then again, you should've been warned. A goddess of my stature does not serve any Greek god. They will serve me, *and both meats are on the table!*"

Zelos rose to his feet and turned to face Hel. His height and muscles started to bulk as she manifested hellfire. Hel spewed the red flame that outlined her dragon tattoo and stunned Zelos's growth.

A fire stronger than lava smothered his frame and reduced him to a pile of ashes.

Hel brushed the edges of her mouth as though she had just finished a meal, and she opened her folding fan. She knocked over the pile of ashes at her feet and watched with a smile as it fell to Hades.

The portal Zeus opened led to Existere's camp. Her jungle was flooded with burgundy and green trees. Bloodstains that accumulated from decades of hunting. The battles generated an overwhelming appeal for the occupants and challengers that dared to enter Existere's habitat. It was a place of seclusion and escape for Zeus, and he hoped to rid himself of the Marid Djinns that pursued him. They followed on stone slabs through several layers of the earth's crust.

The wave of rubble placed them on Existere's doorstep. Zeus quickly regained his bearings as a stench circled his nostrils. In front of Existere's stronghold was the last delivery for his army. They were pinned to a stone wall with arrows made of bone and laced with poison.

"My army! How could she have known?" uttered Zeus. The doors of Existere's stronghold opened, and three carved bone arrows flew through them. They knocked the staff out of his hand and pinned Zeus to a wall.

"Do my eyes deceive me? The mighty Zeus has come to grace me with his presence," greeted Existere. She boldly walked out the entrance with her army. The creatures that occupied the forest bowed to the woman that kept them at bay. Her sleek frame and pale face carried an awkward form of beauty. Small portions of snakeskin crossed the bridge of her nose and circled her eyes like a mask. Holstered on her back were carved bone arrows that were bent to resemble wings.

The long hair that rested on her shoulders matched the color of the forest. The armor she wore was the perfect camouflage for a serpentine strike.

"You dare attack me!" shouted Zeus.

"You dare plot against me!" replied Existere. "Hades warned

me about your lust for power. He knew his throne wouldn't be safe even if I sat on it. In time you would've turned on me. I learned the secret behind the wolves you sent here for my father, and I waited for my opportunity. I prepared myself for a little target practice today, but I see you've encountered another turn of events." She turned her attention to the Marid Djinns and Lycan buccaneers. "Which one killed my father?"

Sitoel's eyes flashed like emeralds in response.

The Lycan buccaneers extended their claws as her archers took aim.

"The female is the one that killed Heracles," answered Zeus.

Existere turned away from the pack and walked into the center of her army. They formed a protective wall around her as she removed an arrow from the quiver. "To appease your hunger for combative entertainment, you can watch me avenge my father. It will be the last thing you see while your body consumes the dead, and the poison of my arrows," said Existere. With that, she fired.

Everyone ran behind a stone slab for cover, but Sitoel held her position. The impact pinned her to the trunk of an uprooted tree.

"You'll soon learn that the poison of my arrow is as potent as wine. Kill the others!" commanded Existere.

The loss of another loved one provoked Gall into a monstrous wolf state. He charged after Existere with an uncontrollable rage. He leapt into the crowd of soldiers to take away the use of a bow, and in doing so, he forced close combat. He mauled and killed soldiers before a sword could be drawn. As he battled, Sitoel endured the effects of the poison. Her vision started to blur as a voice called out to her.

"Don't give up, victory is just a few feet away!" whispered her Marid Djinn.

At that moment, Sitoel unraveled a fate for Existence. The name "Victory" echoed through her body. It caused her arteries to pulsate and pushed a cold chill over her spine. Sitoel looked within the branches of the tree and found Nike. She removed a Judges' Pen from her waistline and pried herself from the arrow. She crawled to Nike's leg and opened a wound to drink. In a matter of seconds, the blood engaged in a battle with the poison. Sitoel's wounds and scars disappeared like scratch marks. She continued to drink until the gifts of Victory were embedded into her bloodstream, and then she took flight.

On land, Gall fought to get to Existere. His ears perked like radar dishes to the sound of arrows clacking against one another before a shot. When the sound stopped, Gall locked his jaws on an archer and threw them into the line of fire. His maulings and Existere's arrows rivaled each other in battle. They generated a river of blood as Zelos's ashes rained over them and brought victory from above.

"Enough!" shouted Sitoel. An echo of karma roared through the forest and stirred a series of clicks. Existere screamed in agony as the arrows holstered on her back snapped together and penetrated her hide. The metal tips of her arrows pushed out through her rib cage as Sitoel landed on her feet. Gall disappointedly pushed his way through the archers that watched the death of their general.

"You took the vent for my rage!" complained Gall.

"I put down the dog. You really want the one that turned him loose in the first place," hinted Sitoel.

Gall's tongue hung out of his mouth as he raced to Zeus. At the entrance of Existere's stronghold, Iblis slowly approached the wall where Zeus was pinned.

"My, how quickly the tides change. Just the other day someone of your stature threw me from the heavens, not once, *but twice!*" shouted Iblis. He removed his knife and pried open Zeus's mouth with the blade.

"Today I found him a level beneath me," quipped Iblis. He pulled on Zeus's tongue, and removed it with one swipe as Gall approached.

"You're a bit late for petty conversation," said Iblis.

"You took the vent for my rage!" barked Gall. Iblis placed the tongue of Zeus in the center of his palm.

"I know a place where we can quench our bloodlust," mimicked

Iblis. "It's undisturbed by mortals and a gateway to realms worthy of my stature. Hades owes me a helm!"

Everyone gathered around Iblis as he grabbed Zeus's staff. He extended it into a lightning bolt, and a cloud formed beneath their feet. Iblis fired the bolt into the center and brought everyone to Hades' lair. The gates slowly opened as Iblis eagerly raced into the throne room with everyone close behind. They cautiously crossed the threshold as Sitoel's eyes took on the luster of emeralds.

"What's wrong?" asked Banter.

"Echo is circling the throne with a warning," answered Sitoel.

Iblis's eyes beaconed with a bright red color. The sight of Hades slumping over the armrest provoked him to extend his staff.

"What is she warning us about?" Banter asked.

"The existence of Hel!" shouted Iblis. Hel's laughter filled the room as she removed the helm of invisibility. "The helm belongs to me now. Give it to me or feel my wrath!" threatened Iblis.

"You know what I've learned about bullies," said Hel. "In time you eventually find one bigger than the last. So I've decided to give the name to my new servant."

Hel's servants amassed behind the throne. They parted a lane for Zelos as he became the biggest one in the room.

"*Bully,* remove this bile from my throne and escort these worthless creatures to the border of my new realms!" commanded Hel. Zelos obediently responded to his new name and complied with the command. Hades' head fell off his shoulders as Bully snatched him from the throne. He threw the carcass out of the room and held the head up high until Hel sat on the throne.

"*The gall!*" shouted Iblis.

"No, the Abominable," replied Hel. Gall slowly approached the throne as Hel's next surprise stepped into the light. "These are my realms now, and my laws apply. May I ask why you did not mourn your brother?"

"He would've considered it a bad business practice," answered Gall.

A devious smile appeared on Hel's face as she recited, "'If all things alive or dead weep for him, then he will be allowed to return to the Aesir. If anyone speaks against him or refuses to cry, then he will remain with Hel.'"

Gall's eyes widened with surprise as Hel's servants made a lane for Kaleb. He backed away from the throne as Kaleb positioned himself at the right hand of Hel. Kaleb stretched his muscles in his Abominable vessel. After the shale structure hardened, he opened his eyelids and could not see.

"The missing pupils are its only flaw. I'll tend to that matter after they leave," boasted Hel.

"Kaleb?" blurted Gall.

"You should've peeled a couple of layers from an onion," replied Kaleb.

"There's not a lot of difference between his underworld and ours. He will make a fine general for my army of elite archers," boasted Hel.

"Enjoy it for as long as you can," said Sitoel.

Hel's eyes darkened, and a small string of steam funneled from her nostrils. "Do not let our brief alliance encourage your tongue to speak your mind freely around me. You will never be mine, because someone alive and dead will mourn for you. In time you will find the answer to that secret like I did. In the meantime, if I ever find you in my realms again, I'll tie your vocal cords to that glittering orb that hangs over your bed."

"That glittering orb is called a disco ball. If I find one hair longer than mine around it, you'll find karma to be too much for you to handle!" warned Sitoel.

"Bully, did I stutter?" said Hel. A dark cloud formed around everyone's feet as Bully approached. Iblis raised his staff and threw it in the center before he could claim a victim.

Everyone returned to the Styles Corporate Building in a flash. They hugged and embraced each other, but cheer eluded Gall. He watched as Iblis stepped away from the crowd and raised his staff.

"Lycan buccaneers, say your farewells and come to my side," commanded Iblis. "Hel has increased her muscle and we must prepare our lycans on the border." Enemy walked to Gall and gently patted him on the shoulder.

"I tried to save him before Hel made her claim," said Enemy.

"I know. He'll be a handful if Hel has her way," replied Gall.

"No need to worry. This war won't last long. We'll be swapping tales over several barrels of mead before Hel has the opportunity to give him a name."

"How can you be so confident?"

Enemy joined the Lycan buccaneers and answered as a cloud formed around their feet. "Hel may have more soldiers and gained more territory, but Iblis has better weapons. He's been collecting them since time began!"

The roar of a revving chopper motorcycle engine followed his words as Iblis threw the lightning bolt into the center. All of them shielded their eyes as they disappeared in a flash. They would soon discover that the only thing left behind was another tale.

# A Marid Kiss

As part of the punishment for Prometheus's theft of the secret of fire, Zeus ordered Hephaestus to mold Pandora out of earth. Upon her arrival, many gifts were bestowed upon her, including a deceitful nature. Among these gifts were a jar, and its evil contents contained many sicknesses, toils, and pains familiar to humankind. However, beneath all these evils lay the hope to master them all.

The Marid Djinns returned to face a reality scarred by the gods. Banter returned to his estate with Alexander, and within a few days an adjustment was made to enhance security. Bodyguards and a secret underground bunker gave the mansion an Abominable appeal. Gall returned to the Abominable estate to tend to their affairs. He thought about putting the place up for sale, but the sight of Kaleb returning from hell guaranteed another visit. Sitoel returned her grandmother to their tribe. She also tended to the responsibilities of the king. Her parents returned under her rule and solidified their bond. She continued to judge the affairs of her tribe while Hel's riddle ate away at her.

"Someone alive and dead mourns for you," mumbled Sitoel. It piqued her curiosity to the point where she needed to see Akantha.

After the demise of Zeus, Akantha put another plan in place— one that would contain Gall long enough to explain her involvement in the fates of the Marid Djinns. She got dressed and raced to a corner diner where Detective Rodriguez regularly bought a cup of coffee. His foot had just stepped on the curb when Akantha unexpectedly called out to him.

"Detective, I found him!" shouted Akantha.

"Does this look like a precinct to you? Today is Sunday, I'm off duty until tomorrow. How did you even find me?" asked Detective Rodriguez.

"It's a unique skill. The scent of your favorite coffee is like a window dressing for that diner. I also served it to you when you were a guest in my home," explained Akantha.

The detective looked over Akantha with skepticism, and pulled her under the shingles of a newspaper stand. "That's some skill. If I didn't know any better, I'd say you were one of them," said Detective Rodriguez.

"My origin is of no concern to you. I can't explain without the approval of my peers. Now, the subject we discussed during the events of Ragnarök is in play," replied Akantha.

"Are you sure you want to put that plan in play? Gall isn't going to be happy when I issue a warrant for his arrest," said Detective Rodriguez.

"It's the only way." Akantha handed the detective a piece of paper bearing a name and address.

"Are you sure this is the man that was there the night Gall killed three men in your home?" asked Detective Rodriguez.

"Yes, he is one of Mr. Styles's henchmen, and the only survivor. I spoke with him, and he's agreed to help us," answered Akantha.

"I'm not making any promises," replied the detective. "His testimony will be shaky without knowing where the bodies are buried. His credibility will also be a factor. If a good lawyer gets a hold of this, we won't be able to hold Gall long enough to make him break a sweat."

"I don't want Gall prosecuted. Just detained," pleaded Akantha.

"I'll try to prolong things as much as possible. Now you must fulfill your part of the bargain. You said the Jinn I want is prone to war and battles. What makes you think he'll come to me?"

"Hel has played her hand beautifully," explained Akantha. "She was able to maintain her realms, and she gained the underworld that belonged to Hades. She also made an Abominable one of her generals. A war is looming, and many battles will take place."

Detective Rodriguez briefly paused to look at his watch before Akantha unexpectedly disappeared. He walked into the corner diner and slid into his favorite booth as a waitress brought him coffee.

"I know, Brenda. I'll work it out later," said Detective Rodriguez.

"You live right across the street. How can you be late? Thank goodness she decided to wait until you got home to argue," replied Brenda. She placed the cup on the table and walked away with a rapid switch of her hips. Detective Rodriguez kept a smile on his face as he deeply inhaled the steam of his coffee. Nothing was going to spoil his mood for revenge. He took a sip and began to reflect on the events that had brought him to this day.

# The Vaults in the Styles Corporate Building

etective Rodriguez moved into an apartment across the street after his promotion into the Homicide Division. He never knew his father, and it was a fresh start after the passing of his mother. She spent her entire life working two jobs as a maid in Manhattan. From Monday to Friday, she worked for the corporate executive of an airline company. On the weekends, she cooked and cleaned for the orphaned son of a rock star. Since she was a devout Catholic, he always allowed his mother to attend Mass before coming to work on Sundays. Detective Rodriguez inherited her devotion and applied it to the career of a police officer. He quickly achieved his goal of becoming a homicide detective. On his first day, he woke up two hours early and entered the corner diner for a cup of coffee. He slid into the corner booth as his waitress approached with a menu.

"My name is Brenda, and I'll be your waitress," she greeted.

"Just a cup of coffee," replied Detective Rodriguez. Brenda tucked the menu back into her apron and walked away with a rapid switch of her hips. Shortly afterward, the detective's life would change forever.

A beautiful brunette with a pale complexion entered the diner in a pair of shiny black penny loafers. Every man in the diner turned to the sound of them tapping into a booth. Her toned body gave the impression of a soldier or fitness instructor. She revealed parts of her personality with a pair of black suede leggings and a red muscle shirt that read, "Graphic Details." The attire brought a smirk to the detective's face. Several charms highlighted the curves of her frame. They sparkled on her belly chain, bracelets, and anklets. They emitted a melodic jingle as she slid into the booth next to his. They exchanged looks, and the detective fell into a pair of dark brown pupils. They carried the same mystery as her charms. He was going to ask for her name before Brenda asked for her order.

"What will it be today, Risk?"

"The usual. And Virgil will be joining me today."

A bald middle-aged man entered the diner. A black striped suit covered his bulky frame. His eyes and complexion matched those of the woman sitting in the booth. His facial features were slightly similar, so the detective made the assumption that they were kin. To be certain, he switched to the opposite end of the table and eavesdropped on the conversation. Brenda handed Virgil a menu as he slid into the booth.

"We're getting a lot of new faces in here," said Brenda.

"You'll be seeing more of me. I moved into the building across the street," replied Risk.

Risk ordered a hot chocolate, and Virgil ordered a steak with two scrambled eggs.

"How do you want your steak—alive or dead?" asked Brenda.

"Alive!" answered Virgil. Detective Rodriguez leaned back into his seat to learn more as Brenda walked away.

"I spoke to him today. He said he'll hire you. Just come in for some training before you start tomorrow," said Virgil.

"I knew I could count on you. Thanks again for helping me move my stuff last night," replied Risk.

"It's not a problem when you pay for breakfast. If I were you, I'd reconsider my choice of bed sets. You're not going to fit in when your friends see half a bunk bed"

"My friends won't judge me. Besides, I like sleeping close to the ceiling," replied Risk.

"Who do you think you're fooling? You bought it because you like to walk on the ceiling."

"Some habits are hard to break."

Detective Rodriguez took the name *Risk* and the conversation to work with him. He walked into the office of his division with a smile and some buttered bagels for his partner, a detective by the name of Okinu Kelsin.

"No coffee?" asked Detective Kelsin.

"They serve coffee here," replied Detective Rodriguez.

"We won't be eating here. We got three bodies on the docks," said Detective Kelsin. He stood from his chair and grabbed the black sports jacket that hung on the back. "It's time to earn your pay," he added.

The drive to the harbor gave the detective time to take a closer look at his new partner. He asked around for friendly advice to break the ice. People that knew Detective Kelsin said he had just been through a bad divorce, spent a lot of time at the pool hall, and had a knack for catching a perp in a lie. A low fade, slicked back by hair gel gave him the image of a soldier in average street clothing. He kept everything in line like his trim beard and mustache.

Detective Rodriguez also piqued his partner's curiosity.

"What's the story behind your jacket?" he asked. "I got mine off the rack for thirty. I saw yours in a window for three hundred. If you're not careful, Internal Affairs will be knocking on your door."

"My mom worked as a maid for the son of a rock star that killed himself. I hardly knew the teen. In my opinion, he was just the spoiled brat my mother had to watch every weekend. I always thought he'd blow his father's fortune, but he managed to maintain. He showed up on my doorstep after my mother's funeral and handed me a check. He told me how much he loved my mom, and said that if I needed someone to talk to, I could look him up," explained Detective Rodriguez.

"How much?"

"A lot. I bought some new clothes and moved into a new apartment close to my elementary school."

"An unexpected inheritance also grants you the opportunity to wager on pool games."

"Sure, but you have to teach me your secret for catching a liar first."

Detective Kelsin responded with a nod as he drove onto the docks.

"Watch closely, this will be your first lesson," said Detective Kelsin. They stepped out of their vehicle and approached the commanding officer. The crime scene looked like a playground full of children trading toys every second. A handful of policemen struggled to hold back a crowd while setting a barricade.

"Why are you having so much trouble sealing this place off?" asked Detective Kelsin.

"The CSIs are still trying to determine how much of the area is part of the crime scene. They found a blood trail to a dumpster a mile from the dock, a couple of pieces on the dock, and the bloodbath in the freight compartment of the ship with the logo of a dragon," explained the officer.

The detectives made their way to the ship with the logo. It was named, " *Sacred Order of the Dragon*." On deck, an officer was collecting a statement from the Captain.

"You can check the ship's manifest. We do not have animals! We do not deliver animals!" he shouted with a foreign accent. Detective Kelsin tapped the officer on the shoulder and made a gesture for him to leave. Detective Rodriguez removed a small notepad from his pocket and approached the crew members that stood behind their Captain.

"Everyone form a single line. We'll ask you a few questions, and you can go on your way. Please do not leave the city without permission," instructed Detective Rodriguez.

As the crew fell in line, several of them conversed about a man they feared. Detective Rodriguez discreetly jotted down the name they uttered—"Peter Stubbe."

"Give me your name and tell me what happened here," said Detective Kelsin.

"I am Captain Amal Mihai. My crew and I were delivering a crate. We were supposed to hold it until a security team arrived, but all hell broke loose before their arrival. The crate was gone when I got here, and three murders had taken place."

Detective Kelsin removed a small notepad from his pocket and asked, "Who was supposed to get the crate?"

A cold sweat ran down the forehead of Captain Mihai. He removed the knitted black hat that rested on his head to wipe the puddle under it. "The crate was supposed to be delivered to Morgan Styles," he answered.

Detective Rodriguez looked at his partner and picked up the same expression of grief he knew he must be showing. He removed two small packets of Alka-Seltzer from his pocket.

"Where can I get a glass of water?" asked Detective Kelsin.

"Down below. First door on the right," answered Captain Mihai.

"Are you going to be alright?" asked Detective Rodriguez.

"Just give me a minute. You can finish up," replied Detective Kelsin.

Detective Rodriguez turned his attention to the Captain. "I need you to point out a man in your crew."

"What's his name?"

"Peter Stubbe."

The Captain used his hat to wipe away another trickle of sweat.

"That man is not in my crew. He's not even alive—just a ghost attached to the crate we delivered," he defensively replied.

"Do you know what was inside the crate?" asked Detective Rodriguez.

"A rare antique. A wolf fetter," answered Captain Mihai.

The detective wrote the information down and questioned the crew until his partner returned. On the way back to the station, he said to Detective Kelsin, "You walk through a grisly crime scene without a hitch. You hear the name Morgan Styles, and you need Alka-Seltzer. What's the story behind that?" asked Detective Rodriguez.

"What's the best way to put it? If you ask that question in the military, they'll tell you it's a problem way above your pay grade. Every brick in Styles Corporate Building holds a cold-case file. The Captain might as well have been delivering that crate to the devil himself. A couple of us almost lost our pensions going after him, but I'll save that story for another time."

"I'll find out for myself tomorrow," said Detective Rodriguez. "I'll stop by the Styles building after breakfast."

"You can go by yourself. I'll see what I can get on the crew while you're there. The Captain was lying, he saw who took that crate. Someone scared him into not talking. That animal attack was convincing enough."

"Do me a favor and run a check on the name Peter Stubbe," said Detective Rodriguez. "He might be the animal we're looking for."

The following morning, Detective Rodriguez went into the

corner diner for a cup of coffee and Risk Fenton. Virgil was the first one to walk through the door after the detective arrived. Brenda handed him a menu and purposely escorted him to the table next to his. A smirk appeared on the detective's face as Brenda winked, and walked away with a rapid switch of her hips. Shortly afterwards, Risk Fenton walked in dressed for her new job. The heels on her shoes were stiletto thin, and the taps attracted attention. A short and tight black suede skirt, with a small slit over the right thigh broadened wandering eyes. A tight white blouse suppressed the charms of her belly chain. He could still hear the jingling of the anklets and bracelets. They played a tune as she slid into the booth next to his.

"So how was training yesterday?" asked Virgil.

"That man is a megalomaniac!"

"Don't toy with him. Just do your job and leave. The woman that held the job before you disappeared without a trace."

"They were scraping the letters off the door before I could see the name. When the Governor assigned us the task, he had no idea how hard this job would be."

Brenda returned to the table and handed Risk a menu.

"Just a hot chocolate for me," said Risk.

"I'll have the steak and eggs. *Still alive*," said Virgil. Detective Rodriguez leaned back into the booth as Brenda walked away.

"You'd think the Governor would be a better judge of character. The vaults are filled with artifacts from the war," said Risk.

"*Our war?*"

"Yes, and you'd swear the Governor sold his soul to buy the piece they delivered. And get this—*it's not for him*. Vlad is the one that ordered it," replied Risk.

Detective Rodriguez glanced at his watch and realized he could no longer stay. He locked away his suspicions about their boss to face Morgan Styles with a clear head.

The crime scene and his partner's advice gave Styles Corporate building a chilling allure. High-tech security devices covered the entire perimeter of the block. He could feel eyes watching him as he drove down the main street and parked in the lot. After he parked his car, three armed guards ran to his vehicle.

"You can't park here without an appointment!" one guard shouted.

"I didn't have time to make one," replied Detective Rodriguez. He slowly removed his badge and began to explain. "I'm investigating the crime that took place on the dock last night. Can you show me where your shipping and receiving department is?"

"We'll escort you to the lobby," said the guard.

Detective Rodriguez walked through several doors with keypad locks before reaching the front desk. As they approached, the guard sitting in front of him immediately placed a booklet on the counter. The cover page read, "Disclosure Agreements."

"This book has enough pages to knock *Remembrance of Things Past* out of the *Guinness Book of World Records*," cried Detective Rodriguez.

"It's my duty to advise you that you can't go any further without a warrant," advised the guard. He pushed back the thick frame on his glasses and gave a cold stare.

"Tell the head of your shipping department to meet me here."

"You're a little early. She doesn't come in until … *now?*"

The familiar tapping of high-heeled shoes sent a chill down the detective's spine. He could see a lustful stare as he looked for a reflection in the guard's glasses.

*What are the chances? The probability that she works here?* he asked himself. After the tapping stopped, a jingle erased all his doubts.

"Miss Fenton, this detective would like to ask you some questions," said the guard.

Detective Rodriguez turned around to introduce himself.

"Detective Enicio Rodriguez," said Risk.

A dumbfounded expression appeared on his face as he extended his hand.

"Virgil is their top investigator," explained Risk. "You piqued his curiosity when he noticed you eavesdropping in the diner. You should also be advised about Mr. Styles's disclosure agreement. If you want more, you'll have to get the green light from Mr. Styles."

"I think you've helped me enough. I'll see you around," replied Detective Rodriguez. He lowered the hand he had extended and accepted the cold greeting. It came with the reassurance of another at their apartment building.

Detective Rodriguez returned to the precinct with a buttered bagel, and Detective Kelsin gladly accepted with a smirk.

"You knew I wouldn't make it past the lobby," said Detective Rodriguez.

"I knew, but you needed the experience. Were you tempted to sign every page in that book at the desk?"

"No."

"Then you're a better man than me. Halfway through you'll find a page that says, 'We still won't let you in—even with the warrant that you'll never get.' So, let me tell you what I found out."

Detective Kelsin removed two small packets of Alka-Seltzer from his shirt pocket and dropped them on the desk. He picked up a small notepad and read through the pages.

"The crew and the Captain are clean," said Detective Kelsin. "I placed a patrol unit outside their hotel and received some interesting news. Someone paid the Captain a visit. The receptionists said a muscled man in a suit roughed him up. The footage from the hotel security camera gave a detailed description, but the Captain refused to press charges. I told the patrol unit to keep a closer watch on him. I ran the muscle man through the system. He had some misdemeanors, but nothing serious. His name is Virgil Price, he's one of Morgan Styles's top investigators." He handed Detective Rodriguez a photo image from the hotel camera. Detective Rodriguez attempted to hide a troubled expression from his partner.

"I thought you didn't get in the building?"

"Virgil Price has a relative that works for Morgan Styles. She lives in my building. Her name is Risk Fenton, and I plan on seeing her tonight."

Detective Kelsin opened the packets of Alka-Seltzer and dumped the tablets into a glass of water sitting on the desk.

"Your conditioning is about to get all screwed up," said Detective Kelsin.

"I don't get what you're trying to say," replied Detective Rodriguez.

"You said your mother was a devout Catholic. That means she raised you to be a certain way. You gotta go from *Love thy neighbor* to *Even the person calling you for help should be considered a suspect*," explained Detective Kelsin.

"You don't have to worry about my conditioning. It's all blue," Detective Rodriguez defensively replied.

"I looked up the other guy you told me about. Peter Stubbe was a serial killer many years ago. He committed his murders under the disguise of a wolf. He claimed the devil gave him a belt to help him do it. That matches the report we got back from the Crime Scene Unit. Several strands of wolf hair were found around the scene, and the bite marks match the mauling of an animal. Unfortunately for us, no animals were reported missing from the zoo. There were no reports of any animals missing from the docks. If Peter Stubbe lived in our time, I'd be bringing him in for questioning. Instead, I find myself waiting on the Captain and Virgil Price. A hunch tells me they found out the belt is worth a pretty penny—enough to kill three people and stage a ghost story for a crime scene. So you should be careful about what you say and do with Risk."

That night, Detective Rodriguez entered his building and looked over the mailboxes in the lobby. Fenton's was next to the superintendent's.

He remembered that there had been an apartment for rent in the basement. They had offered it to him, but he'd thought, "Who'd be crazy enough to live in the basement?" Suddenly someone crazy enough to buy only the top half of a bunk bed set entered the building. A smirk crossed his face when her high heels approached with a jingle.

"I guess eavesdropping at the diner wasn't enough for you. You had to come to my job," said Risk.

"What did you expect? The trail from the docks led right to Morgan's door," replied Detective Rodriguez. Risk nervously looked around as a couple of tenants entered the building.

"It's not safe to talk in the open. I'll come to your apartment after midnight."

"I'll see you then."

Detective Rodriguez walked to the elevator with the conditioning his mother gave him. 'Make sure your room is clean. We're about to have company,' she'd say. When he entered his apartment, he quickly tossed scattered pieces of clothing into a hamper bag and removed two strawberry-scented candles from the bathroom cabinet. He planted the candles in the center of the living room table and opened a window next to the fire escape. A nice breeze brought the smell of rain. As the droplets hit the windowpane, it stirred up a chemistry with the police sirens that passed in the night. He thought a good movie would seal the mood, but the only thing of interest on TV was a *Manimal* marathon. He watched several episodes until he fell asleep.

Shortly after midnight, the detective woke to a jingle. He found Risk sitting beside him in a suit that looked like a cat burglar costume. He sat up, and Risk began to rub his shoulders as though they had been friends for years. He quickly poked holes into that fantasy as he slowly regained his senses.

"How did you get in here without a key?" he asked.

"Keep it down. You'll wake up the guy in the hallway if you talk too loud," warned Risk.

Detective Rodriguez jumped off the couch to look through the peephole in the door.

"What's so special about the vagrant lying in the middle of the hallway?" asked Detective Rodriguez.

"He works for Mr. Styles's lapdog—a guy named Brimm," answered Risk.

"Listen closely to me," said Detective Rodriguez. "I would like to participate in the fantasy of you being here, but I'm having trouble finding where to begin. Try to work with me as I go. You put some guy twice your size to sleep in the hallway. Then you break into my apartment and sit on the couch like nothing ever happened."

Risk leaned back into the cushions on the sofa. "It's not a fantasy. I'm here because I need your help. When I moved into the building, the superintendent told me a detective lived upstairs. When I saw you go into the diner, I figured it would be a good idea to leave you clues."

"The woman that you replaced is missing," replied Detective Rodriguez. "You don't work for Morgan Styles. You really work for a Governor. Three people were killed delivering an antique that never made it to its intended destination, *but you knew what was in the crate.* You also knew the value of the wolf fetter, because your Governor purchased it."

"The fetter was being shipped out, not delivered," corrected Risk.

"So why would the Captain lie?"

"Virgil is trying to find that out."

"Or Virgil was making sure he stuck to the story. Captain Mihai didn't press charges after he roughed him up."

Risk sat up and gave Detective Rodriguez a cold stare. "You think we're responsible for the theft of the wolf fetter?" she loudly whispered.

"Is there a reason to think otherwise? I'm a detective, I have to consider that even the person asking for help can be a suspect."

"I didn't replace the missing woman because I wanted her job.

It was given to me to avoid a war. The Governor and Morgan Styles have a joint venture. Morgan has the unlimited resources to acquire the antiques the Governor needs. Unfortunately for Morgan, a few of the Governor's requested items didn't make delivery. There was a lot of finger-pointing, so the Governor assigned me and Virgil to look over the next delivery."

"You were the security detail the Captain was talking about," said Detective Rodriguez.

"The crate was delivered, and we checked the authenticity of it in the Styles Corporate Building. When we were done, the Captain returned the crate to the ship for delivery. We stayed until the ship departed. Virgil is trying to find out what brought it back. He suspected the Captain of using the wolf fetter, so he started a fight to provoke the beast."

"Provoke the beast? You believe the wolf fetter can change a man into a wolf?" asked Detective Rodriguez.

Risk stood up from the couch and walked to the window. "I believe in the transmigration of souls. A soul can pass from body to body, animal, *or wolf fetter.*"

"Like a demonic possession. You think the Captain is possessed by Peter Stubbe?"

"No, he's possessed by the same beast that took Peter Stubbe. For a span of twenty-five years, Peter smiled in the faces of his neighbors while committing evil acts. No one suspected the man before they started looking for the traits of the beast. Peter Stubbe would chase his female victims and ravage them like a wolf on a hunt. The wolf is also territorial, it will exact revenge on all those that bothered Peter Stubbe. It will hunt and devour tormentors until it bathes in their blood." Risk walked back to the couch and collapsed on the cushions.

"What about the missing woman?"

"The Captain made several deliveries before we were sent here. The missing woman was the head of the shipping department.

She must have refused his advances or offended him before she disappeared."

Detective Rodriguez took a moment to ponder on the events that had taken place. Suddenly his partner's warning came to mind. "My mother had a strong faith. 'You can't be a true believer and over-look the fact that evil exists,' she told me. I even heard about a report being filed because a few deputies had trouble restraining a man that suffered from the demonic possession of a wolf. They said he fought like a beast as they tried to subdue him. Funny thing, though—I never heard or saw a case that involved a woman—one that took down a man twice her size and entered my apartment through the window." He pointed out a trail of footprints from the rain that led behind the couch, as well as the one Risk had made when walking back from the window.

"Explain this to me, why bother with the guy at the door? You came through the window," asked Detective Rodriguez.

"You can ask the guy in the alley," answered Risk. "I had to put them all to sleep because of the telecommunicators. Four total. There are two more in the car parked in front. They always travel in packs."

"I've heard enough. Let me see the wolf fetter!" demanded Detective Rodriguez. Risk tumbled over with laughter.

"I can't believe you still see me as a suspect. I do not have the wolf fetter." She stood up from the couch and started to unbutton her jumpsuit.

"I guess there's only one way to prove it. After you get an eyeful, you owe me a gift. It's customary where I come from," said Risk. She peeled off the jumpsuit, and there were several jingles as it fell to the floor.

"Are you happy now? No wolf fetter."

"My apologies."

Detective Rodriguez tried to avoid the beauty of her structure. He also tried to find a way to explain it's supernatural allure. She left footprints, but her body remained dry. The chorus of her charms and the rare gems they encased piqued his senses. They also heightened his guard as Risk got dressed and walked back to the window.

"Don't forget my gift," she loudly whispered. She climbed over the windowsill and jumped from the fire escape with ease. Detective Rodriguez ran to the window and suspiciously watched as she made her way down. When she landed, Risk stepped over the man she had talked about. She looked back at the car parked on the street before she entered the basement stairwell.

"No one would believe me if I did," mumbled Detective Rodriguez.

The following morning, Detective Rodriguez skipped the routine stop at the diner. Detective Kelsin curiously watched as he entered the office and poured a cup of coffee from the pot.

"No buttered bagel today? What did I do wrong?" Detective Kelsin asked with sarcasm.

"I had a long night. I would've been late if I stopped at the diner," explained Detective Rodriguez.

"Things must have gone well?"

"She practically handed me the case. They suspect the Captain of foul play," answered Detective Rodriguez.

"*Just the Captain?*"

"Yeah."

Detective Kelsin reached into his pocket and removed a packet of Alka-Seltzer. He dropped it on the desk and picked up a small notepad. "Three of the crew members didn't return to their hotel room last night. I posted an all-points bulletin an hour ago. The Captain returned, but a patrol unit caught him snooping around Virgil's apartment earlier. My case work usually ends around the time when people that knew or worked with Morgan Styles start disappearing. Some add to the load when we dig them up later. Others, like Morgan, lie back on an island, laughing at the ones we dug up later. Risk might be that same mastermind."

"Risk is not a mastermind. She's more of the soldier type."

"Funny ... you say that like you fell for her."

"No, it just looks bad."

Detective Kelsin stood up from the desk and walked to the water cooler. He poured himself a cup of water and dropped the Alka-Seltzer tablets inside. As it fizzed, he better explained the point he was trying to make. "For sometime I dated a woman that made me feel the chemistry between stockings and high heels were a timeless classic. *Then,* she put on a choker and told me I could have whatever I wanted. They're so much better at that than us." Detective Rodriguez nodded in agreement. "I'm going to tail the Captain tonight, and you keep a close eye on Risk. If we're lucky, we'll meet in the same place."

"What if Risk stays with me the whole night?" asked Detective Rodriguez.

"I said *if* we are lucky," answered Detective Kelsin.

After work, Detective Kelsin and Rodriguez went into a pool hall to wager on a few games. After Detective Kelsin collected his winnings, they prepared themselves for the biggest gamble of the night.

"I'll see you later," said Detective Kelsin. He walked to his car, and Detective Rodriguez made his way into a jewelry store next door. "My Parents' Jewelry Box" was painted in big gold letters on the door. When he entered, an elderly albino man walked from behind the display case to greet him.

"I hope you know what you want. We're about to close," said the jeweler.

"I was hoping you could help me with a gift. It's for a female friend," replied Detective Rodriguez.

"What can you tell me about her?" asked the jeweler.

"She has a body that stands out in plain clothes. Her bracelets, anklets, and belly chains have charms with rare gems encased in them. They make a subtle jingle, like wind chimes."

"Ornamental. Embellished. What else can you tell me about her?"

"She's the type that likes to walk on the ceiling."

"A sumptuous gingerbread."

"*Maybe a mastermind?*"

"Catch me if you can!"

The jeweler walked behind the display case and opened a safe underneath.

"I don't want anything that's too flashy. I might have to handcuff her later," said Detective Rodriguez.

"I understand, you're trying to save a buck before the big move. Well, you're in luck.I just made a chain and pendant for a man's anniversary gift. He received divorce papers instead of a gift from the other party. I don't want my time and work to go to waste. I'll give you a great deal for it."

He removed a gold chain with a diamond-studded combination lock for a pendant. As he gently placed it on the counter, Detective Rodriguez blurted, "I'll take it!"

The detective returned to his apartment building. He raced down the stairwell leading to the basement and hung the jewelry bag on the handle of Risk's door. He could hear his mother's voice as he made his way back to his apartment, "Clean up your room, we're about to have company." He followed the same routine the night Risk came into his apartment. He opened the window and saw Risk walking into the building with Virgil. Fifteen minutes later, the detective received a phone call.

"Hello."

"Do you have any idea what a chain and lock mean where I come from? It doesn't matter how pretty you make it. It becomes a trigger for depression."

"How did you get my number?"

"I told you, Virgil is their top investigator. Don't try to change the subject. I refuse to wear this. You'll have to get me another gift."

"I'll call you back later. I'm picking up a lot of static right now. I'm driving through a tunnel."

"Good try, but I know this is your home phone number. I'll be there in a few minutes."

Detective Rodriguez raced to the window to surprise Risk, but this time there was a knock on the door. He walked to the door and glanced through the peephole. On the opposite side was a muscle shirt that read, "Graphic Details." He opened the door and found Virgil standing behind Risk.

"You can't put a price on the things I share with you!" protested Risk.

"I can't believe you said that with a straight face. Every charm on your body holds a gem."

"I wear them for a reason that's vital to my existence."

Virgil reached for his sidearm and pushed his way through the door. "Quiet!" he shouted. He stared out the window. There was a shadow of a person standing on the roof of an adjacent building.

"*Praetorian!*" shouted the shadow. Before the detective could react, the charms on Risk's body jingled without movement. They rang like chimes and placed him in a dreamlike state. He stood motionless as Risk approached the window. He eavesdropped on the conversation and heard his partner in the alley.

"Freeze!" shouted Detective Kelsin. Virgil stepped behind the curtain while he placed Captain Mihai under arrest. He looked up to Risk as he locked the handcuffs on his wrist.

"You must be Risk. My partner told me so much about you!" shouted Detective Kelsin.

"I'm flattered," replied Risk.

"I hope I didn't disturb your evening," said Detective Kelsin. "I caught this guy snooping around the alley. I'm going to take him back to the station to find out why. You can tell my partner to meet us there. He should bring you with him!" There was a long pause of silence before Virgil spoke again.

"Something's wrong. He would not have been able to apprehend him if he'd had the wolf fetter," whispered Virgil.

The sound of jingling followed the question, and the song gave Risk an answer.

"You're right. The wolf fetter is still near," said Risk.

"Who, or what, is the Praetorian?" asked Virgil. The sound of jingles followed the question, and the song gave Risk the answer.

"*He is?*" said Risk. She walked back to Detective Rodriguez and gently rubbed his shoulders.

"Is there a secluded place you like to go to? Somewhere close by?" she asked.

The detective answered against his will. "I moved here because my elementary school is close to a cemetery. It always piqued my attention when my mother walked me to school. She's there, and I wanted to be close by."

"You are going to go there. I want you to do what comes natural to you. Don't worry about anything. We'll be close by," instructed Risk. Detective Rodriguez responded with a nod as he grabbed his jacket and walked out the door.

The cemetery was only three blocks away, but to Detective Rodriguez it seemed like several miles. His body was moving against his will. He didn't want to answer Risk or obey her instructions, but he still complied. His muscles ached as he walked through the gates of the cemetery. He walked a paved road until he reached a weeping willow tree. The roots were uprooted in the far corner of the cemetery. His mother would always stop to admire the tree while walking him to school. It was uprooted, and she told him that because of a rapid growth rate, its longevity was less than thirty years.

Detective Rodriguez stopped to admire the roots. It was something he normally did at the cemetery. The roots have a network that spread through the ground in all directions. They give a person the privilege to see the fight for life above and below the dirt.

After the small break, Detective Rodriguez proceeded to a plot a few feet away from the tree. He knelt and wiped the residue off a tombstone that read, "Deciembre Rodriguez." In the place of the year and date was the word "Forever." A smile appeared on his face as he began to complain.

That was something Detective Rodriguez normally did at the cemetery. He complained about not having enough time, work, and stressful relationships. At that moment, Detective Kelsin unexpectedly parked his car on the paved road. He paused to check whether the Captain was still safely handcuffed in the backseat. Afterward, he slowly approached the detective to put his fears to rest.

"I thought something was wrong when you didn't come to the window, so I waited for a minute," explained Detective Kelsin. Detective Rodriguez tried to speak but couldn't move his tongue. He was still under Risk's control. "I'll give you a minute. When you're done, you can come with me to the station. I bet the Captain has a lot to tell us." Detective Kelsin started back toward the car and noticed that the backseat was empty. He withdrew his revolver and cautiously looked for a fleeing suspect.

Nothing moved through the shadows of the tombstones as he raced to the car. There he found Captain Mihai lying on the backseat.

"You nearly gave me a heart attack. Sit up and enjoy the ride," quipped Detective Kelsin. The Captain sat up and smiled as a lycan crept from behind. She threw Detective Kelsin against the car with the force of an enraged bull. The car alarm sounded as he dropped his revolver and turned to face his assailant. She extended her claws as her paws glided over his body. Blood poured, and the broken pieces of a bulletproof vest fell to the ground. Inside, the Captain tumbled over with laughter.

"Hurry and free me," begged Captain Mihai. When it was over, the woman returned to her normal state and complied with his wishes. Captain Mihai picked up Detective Kelsin's gun and gave her a kiss. He looked toward the entrance of the cemetery as Risk and Virgil drove in. "I'll hold them off. You take care of the Praetorian," he said. The woman's eyelids trembled as the beast once again took over her body. She raced from the paved road to the grave as Detective Rodriguez knelt in front of the tombstone. The last thing he did before leaving the cemetery was recite a prayer.

"*Praetorian!*" shouted the lycan.

Detective Rodriguez turned to face his attacker as she delivered a hard blow. The impact tossed him a couple of feet in the air. He collapsed over the tombstone and felt a small barrier protecting him from the pain. Unfortunately, the state of paralysis Risk had placed him in kept him conscious. He looked to the sky while the possessed lycan dragged him to the weeping willow. She pulled him over the exposed roots and up the trunk of the tree like a cat after a pigeon. In the branches overlapped with lance-shaped leaves, she began his torture session.

"Praetorian!" shouted the lycan. She made several painful incisions over his body. Her paws twiddled under the flesh to generate an excruciating amount of pain. Stabs from every direction gave him the impression his suffering entertained the beast. Several words followed the lycan's actions, but "Praetorian" was the only word he could understand. Every word after "Praetorian" was babble. The pain increased while the story his mother told him came to mind. It was called "The Tower of Babel."

His mother said there was a time when everyone spoke the same language, even the animals. During this time, humans gathered to build a tower high enough to reach the heavens. His mother told him this structure didn't please God, who felt it would only push his people further away from him, so he confused the language. The construction on the tower had to stop, because no one knew what the others were saying.

At a point where he felt as if his skin was barely hanging on the bone, a shot ended the suffering. Detective Rodriguez fell from the branches, and his attacker fell on top of him. He could see Captain Mihai in Virgil's custody as Risk turned him over.

The Captain pushed Virgil away and ran to the woman lying next to him. His curses were slurred as he tearfully knelt over the body.

"This isn't over. He'll be back for the Praetorian," threatened Captain Mihai.

Virgil grabbed him by the collar and raised him to his feet.

"Who is she?" asked Risk.

"She's the woman you replaced," answered Virgil.

"Why didn't I see this coming?" A jingle followed, and a song gave Risk the answer. "I apologize, Enicio!" cried Risk. Emergency services arrived on the scene as Detective Rodriguez closed his eyes.

The sound of surgical tools being tossed on a tray woke Detective Rodriguez from a deep sleep. He opened his eyes, but his vision was blurry. He took the pillar of a green blur for a surgeon. His eyes widened in fear at another presence crouched in the corner of the ceiling. This pillar was black, and as his vision began to clear, the blur turned into a hooded black robe. Detective Rodriguez saw it as an angel of death. It prompted him to give his final words to his surgeon.

"No need to trouble yourself any further, doc," the detective mumbled. "It's almost time for me to check out. You can do me a favor and give the precinct my statement. The perp spoke a strange language. The only word I could identify was *Praetorian*. One of them threatened he'd return to finish the job."

The detective suddenly regained his sight. He gripped the rails in fear as the green blur became a hooded green robe. The man wearing it spoke to the black-robed figure crouched in the corner. Another chill ran down his spine when he heard the same babel from his torture session. Detective Rodriguez frantically looked for an object to defend himself, but he couldn't move his limbs. The wounds were fresh, and his muscles were still sore from fighting through a dreamlike state. He began to relax as the green-robed figure began to speak. His tone resonated with the same subtle chimes as Risk's charms.

"There's no need to fear us," explained the figure in the green robe. "I am Raphael. My brother Azrael came to collect your soul and found several disturbing things. Your wounds will heal. Right now they're just sore from tension."

"You healed me?" asked Detective Rodriguez.

"No, I am he who presides over every suffering and every wound of the sons of man. It is God who heals," explained Raphael.

A knock suddenly gained his attention as his visitors mysteriously disappeared from the room. Risk opened the door and cautiously peeked inside.

"So you came back to finish the job," quipped Detective Rodriguez.

"I deserve that, but you have to hear me out. You cannot depict the details of the events that took place last night. It will end badly for you." She entered the room and stared out the window.

"You came all the way down here to tell me that?" replied Detective Rodriguez. "You could have saved your breath. No one would believe the story of a werewolf. I'd get locked in a padded cell if I tried to explain it. You'll have to use your talking charms on my partner."

"Your partner was also attacked. He didn't make it, and there's no need to explain to your Captain. You should know that the Sacred Order of the Dragon has several agents that are high-ranking officials. The wolf fetter has been returned to its rightful owner. My talking charms convinced Captain Mahai to give a proper confession. You'll receive an award for your heroic service and the apprehension of a dangerous criminal."

"You wrapped this case up just as neat as it was when you handed it to me. I guess that's what you needed all along—someone to do the footwork."

Risk walked to the head of the bed and massaged his shoulders. "Unfortunately for you, I still need someone for that job. My Governor and Morgan Styles still have trust issues. You've been a valuable resource to me and Virgil. We'd like to know if we still have a friend that we can depend on while we're in town."

"You do if you can answer my questions."

"I'll try to answer them to the best of my ability."

Detective Rodriguez reached for a button that adjusted the bed to an upright position. He stared at Risk while the taste of Alka-Seltzer flowed across his glands.

"What is a Praetorian?" asked Detective Rodriguez.

"A Praetorian is an elite guard. They served in the Imperial Roman Army and protected the emperor. He also used their services to gather intelligence. I discovered you were one in a previous life."

"Captain Mahai said that thing would be back. Is he right?" asked the detective.

"That thing you speak of is a Jinn. Virgil is sure of his return. My charms are scared to speak of Jinn, but I also believe it will be back."

"That Jinn killed my partner. The hypnotic state you placed me in might have saved my life, but a world of pain was left behind. I have never felt so much hatred in my life. I want him. I want revenge!"

"That's a fair trade, but use caution. My resources are limited in the area of Jinn," advised Risk. She then turned to walk to the door and cautiously shied away from more questioning.

"One more thing. Do you believe in Archangels?" asked the detective.

"*Why would you mess with them!*" Risk stopped and walked back to the neighboring window.

Detective Rodriguez peeked out the corner of his eye while her head rose toward the sky. "And you wondered why you ever made my list of suspects. Are you one of them?"

"I can't tell you my origin without judgment from my peers. There is one way to explain, but in your case it'll be like giving a television to an Amish community."

"What's that supposed to mean?"

"You'll just have to wait until your time," answered Risk.

From that day on, Detective Rodriguez engaged in a private war with the Jinn. Risk and Virgil aided him in his search, and in return he helped with problems that escaped the boundaries of the Styles Corporate Building. He also learned how to identify the Archangels that visited his room. Despite their words of wisdom and warnings, he still craved revenge. As his thoughts returned to the present day, he realized he was about to get it.

Across town, Akantha returned home and unexpectedly found a gypsy king on her doorstep.

"I would've prepared a feast if I had known royalty would be stopping by," greeted Akantha.

"I'm still the same Sitoel to you. *Maybe more?*" replied Sitoel.

"This visit is not a formal one. Something is troubling you. Come inside and we will speak," said Akantha. She opened the door and escorted Sitoel to the living room.

"Hel said something before we left Hades, and it's been troubling me. She said she couldn't have me because someone alive and dead will mourn me. I returned to my tribe and felt closer to my grandmother than my parents," said Sitoel.

"Because they are not your natural parents," said Akantha.

"My grandmother?" asked Sitoel.

"She is closer to you than you think," answered Akantha.

"You know who my real parents are?"

"I do, but I cannot explain without judgment from my peers." Akantha walked to the bookshelf and removed her diary. "If you want answers, you must finish the job the Abominable hired you to do."

"Pandora? How do I find her?" asked Sitoel.

Akantha opened her diary and turned to the chapter titled "The Household of Zeus." "You will find Pandora in Greece. She frequently visits the Temple of Athena at the Acropolis of Athens. She has a bond with Athena."

"What type of bond?"

Akantha turned to a page that outlined a passage about Hephaestus and Pandora. "Pandora harbors a secret. She was made without a soul. When she discovered this, she approached

Hephaestus for an explanation. 'How could a blacksmith of your stature overlook such a thing?' asked Pandora. Hephaestus answered, 'I practiced alchemy with your soul.' Pandora had no idea what that meant. She continued to cater to the will of the gods without a will of her own. When she couldn't find an answer, she went to the Temple of Athena and cried on the steps. They shared their stories and discovered a bond.

"Zeus always had a fear of being overthrown. After he slept with Metis, he was told she would have two children and the son would overthrow him. So he tricked Metis into transforming herself into a fly and swallowed her. Unfortunately for Zeus, Metis was already with child. She gave birth to Athena and crafted a helmet for her inside Zeus. Her growth gave Zeus an unbearable headache, and Hephaestus was forced to remove her with an ax. Athena was born into the world knowing only the fear of her father. She took her first steps fully grown and with armor. Pandora was created in the same manner. Do not do this assignment on your own. I'm working with Gall, but you can take Banter with you."

Sitoel grabbed the diary and raced from the house, filled with anticipation.

By noon the following day, Sitoel and Banter had arrived in Greece. An hour before midnight, Sitoel was sitting on a step of the Acropolis with Akantha's diary. Banter discreetly made his way to a position adjacent to her with his rifle case. When he found a spot at a good range from the Temple of Athena, he tested the telecommunicators.

"King to a tribe of gypsies, and the men wanted you dead," joked Banter.

"I didn't volunteer for the position. The present king was trying to kill me," replied Sitoel.

"So you drank the Kool-Aid. Then you found out you don't

belong to the tribe. Killing Pandora is supposed to give you the answer to that, but there's a riddle."

Banter looked over the area with theater binoculars and noticed a woman with flawless features. In her hands was a small jar. "Pandora is here. Put on your gas mask," he said.

Pandora opened the jar and unleashed a small wisp of mist. It expanded into a black cloud and dispersed small hairlike strands that flooded the nostrils of the people occupying the area. They raced from the Parthenon filled with anxiety as Pandora climbed the steps to the Temple of Athena. Banter carefully watched as she entered the temple, and shortly thereafter, exited with the jar Hephaestus had made for her. She again removed the lid, and the cloud returned to its habitat.

"You can always return home. Why do I feel like I'm without one?" Pandora asked herself. Her cries to Zeus had not been answered, and no one had informed her of the cause. For the first time in her life, Pandora was alone and without guidance. Her eyes began to well with tears as she collapsed on the steps. She embraced the jar and mustered the strength to make one last attempt to communicate with her gods.

Pandora raised the jar to the sky, and Banter fired a round from behind. It shattered Pandora's frame, and the jar fell onto the steps.

"Confirm the kill," said Banter.

Sitoel raced to the steps of the temple with the speed of Victory, her guns drawn. She looked over Pandora's body as it slowly dissolved into a shimmering muddy substance.

"Nothing? There's nothing here but mud!" said Sitoel.

"You're still worried about Pandora's secret? Check the jar! Make sure it's sealed and intact!" shouted Banter.

Sitoel picked up the jar and carefully looked it over. "Hephaestus's precious jar is still intact. The hell they made remains in a jar," replied Sitoel.

A look of relief crossed Banter's face while an educated guess echoed through his mind. "Wait a minute, repeat what you just said?" asked Banter.

"Hephaestus's precious jar is still intact. The hell they made remains in a jar."

A smile appeared on Banter's face as he tucked away his rifle. "We overlooked the obvious, and so did Pandora."

"Stop talking in riddles. Just give me the answer!" demanded Sitoel.

"Pandora was carrying her soul the whole time. It was evolving in the jar Hephaestus made. Open the jar and pour the contents over the mud," instructed Banter.

"Open the jar? Are you sure?" asked Sitoel.

"No, but if you really want answers, you'll have to take a chance," said Banter.

Sitoel cautiously opened the jar and poured the contents over the mud. A large black cloud funneled from the opening and rained over the mud until it beaconed a small light in the center. Sitoel cautiously stepped back as it swirled into another form.

"The mud is transforming into another shape," said Sitoel.

Banter recited the riddle of Pandora's secret while it created another woman. "Zeus ordered Hephaestus to mold Pandora out of Earth. Upon her arrival, many gifts were bestowed upon her, including a deceitful nature. Among these gifts was also a jar that harbors many evils, toils, and pains familiar to humankind. However, beneath all these evils lies the hope to master them all".

Sitoel drew her guns as the mud returned Pandora's flawless features. "Pandora?" blurted Sitoel.

"Do not fear me," stated the new creation. "I mean you no harm. I am the opposite of Pandora in creation. I am Anesidora, and I harbor Hope inside me."

"Wrap it up and bring it home," said Banter.

In a crowded and busy police precinct, Detective Rodriguez entered his Captain's office with a cup of coffee in hand. A bald and broad-figured man in a uniform with stripes beside him immediately gained the detective's attention. A ray of sunlight reflected off his head and shadowed the face of his Captain. It gave a clue that both men belonged to the Sacred Order of the Dragon.

"I would have brought more if you'd told me we were having company," said Detective Rodriguez. He extended his hand, and the soldier reached out.

"Save your sarcasm for someone having a good day. Telly Montross is a member of JTF2 and just lost a member of his unit. He called in a special favor with the mayor to be here today," explained the Captain.

"My condolences, but what does that have to do with me?" asked Detective Rodriguez.

"I heard you filed paperwork to bring in Tibbigall Maxwell. He should be in a holding cell by the end of the day?" asked Montross.

"Yes, but why would that concern you?" Detective Rodriguez asked.

"Facta Non Verba. It's our motto. Deeds, not words, bring me here today. A soldier from my unit was found hanging outside his family home with a slit from his sternum to his throat. That sight was the first thing his children saw when his wife opened the door that morning. I'm not leaving here before I catch my man, and Tibbigall Maxwell will help me do it!" He slammed a folder containing investigative files on three women on the desk.

"I'm still confused. What does this have to do with Gall?" asked Detective Rodriguez.

Montross opened the folder and removed a file containing a mug shot of a blonde with short hair in the corner. A purple sickle-shaped curl rested in the center of her forehead. It highlighted her pale complexion and purple lipstick.

"They're triplets," Montross replied. "They call themselves Furies, and they run an underground network for exceptional

fighters. Mitten Masten is the eldest and boss. Every member of
their organization wears purple and black clothing. They invite
wealthy and notorious men from all over the world to gamble on
their fighters. We sent an operative in to investigate when one of
her fighters made our radar. He was my best man, exceptional in all
his training. We accumulated enough evidence to raid a warehouse
disguised as a bathroom surplus store. It was scheduled to happen
on the same night my operative was to face a fighter named Gutter
Ash. Unfortunately, the operation was a bust from the moment we
arrived on the scene. My operative was missing, and the only thing
Mitten left behind was purple-colored urinals. The following morning, I got a call from the wife of my operative. Well, I already told
you that part." He lowered his head as Detective Rodriguez looked
at the other files.

"Tell me about the other two?" he asked.

Montross removed Mitten's file and pointed to a mugshot of a
woman with a honey-colored complexion. Her hair was dyed purple
and pinned into two long ponytails. Her eyes bore the same alluring
color in the photo.

"Her name is Otava Masten. She is the Furies' top enforcer.
She has a short temper, and she parades around as a stripper in her
sister's club to help recruit fighters." Montross slid the file out like a
dealer would a card at a poker game. "We don't have a mugshot for
this one. We never caught her working on a street level. Her name
is Glimpse Masten. She's their lawyer and chief accountant." He slid
out a full-length picture of a woman with an olive complexion and
gold undertones. Her long black hair flowed over the right side of
her face as she removed a piece of lint from a purple fitted Cavalli
suit. "Fortunately for us, Otava does, and she's currently sitting in
one of your holding cells. She got into a fight with the club's disc
jockey last night."

Detective Rodriguez leaned back into his chair with uncertainty.
"I'm beginning to see where all of this is going. To think Gall will
partake in an undercover investigation is absurd. He'll never roll

with what we have on him. A sneeze could tear his case apart. I don't mean to deter you in any way, but the idea is senseless."

"The only senseless thing here is the time I'm spending with you," Montross replied. "Otava will invite Gall to participate in the circuit. All you have to do is bring him in and let nature take its course. You can do that much."

"We can and will. I'll see to the arrangements myself," said the Captain. He looked to Detective Rodriguez with an expression that demanded an immediate departure, and he began to make arrangements for Gall's cell placement.

Events continued to unravel through the morning as Gall roamed the rooms in the Abominable mansion. He attended to Kaleb's affairs in anticipation of a return. He paused to admire a family portrait as a black fog of smoke unexpectedly emerged from the fireplace. It carried the roar of a revving chopper motorcycle engine as it wrapped a hooded robe around Iblis.

"We have a problem!" shouted Iblis.

"What are you talking about?" asked Gall.

"I returned to Hades to collect Existere's bow and arrows, but your brother beat me to it. He also took her eyes," replied Iblis.

"Why is that my problem?"

"Hel is strengthening her army. She dug up a band of Scythians to train and increase the skill of her archers. There's also word of her seeking out the souls of Victor and Matthew. Their souls will inhabit the bodies of Existere's generals. If she succeeds, I'll have to face the Abominables." Iblis's eyes darkened as a smirk appeared on Gall's face. He couldn't hide the excitement of reuniting with his brothers. "This amuses you?" asked Iblis.

"What did you expect? I'm an Abominable. You're crying on the wrong shoulder here," replied Gall.

"I thought you'd be more sympathetic to our problem. Just the other day you saw how I removed the tongue from such a problem. I will not show favoritism to your brother. Lord Treachery, Enemy, and Rottenvein are about to attack the stronghold of Hel's archers with an army of lycans. They'll capture and burn the bodies of her generals to destroy the base for these unwanted souls. When your brother returns, he'll receive a proper and painless burial for his troubles. *Then again,* they can learn the flames of my rage and the abilities of my blade. It can torment a soul beyond the borders of Hel's realms and allow you the privilege to hear their cries."

Gall's mood and facial expression suddenly changed. "What do you want from me?" he asked.

"I can arrange a peaceful and proper burial for your brothers. All you have to do is retrieve Cronus's sickle."

"Where can I find him?" asked Gall.

"Where can you find *her!*" shouted Iblis. "After Zeus imprisoned Cronus, he placed the sickle in the care of the eldest Fury. She now roams your realm with her sisters, and they've earned a reputation. Many mortals in your profession call them Gutter Ash."

"I never heard of them."

"Do not be troubled. You will gain an audience with one Fury after your arrest."

"*Arrest?*" Gall turned from the conversation and raced to the Abominable safe.

"What are you doing?" Iblis annoyedly asked.

"After I disappear, you can put your tongue in your hand and answer that question when the police get here," replied Gall. He opened the safe and removed a small duffel bag filled with money. Iblis's eyes also caught the glare of the sacred bloodstone that belonged to Sitoel's tribe.

"Do not be foolish. The crime they seek you out for will not have a penalty. A man has bared false witness against you," said Iblis.

"I don't leave witnesses!" snapped Gall.

"Then there's no need for me to explain further. The authorities have no case," replied Iblis.

"You really expect me to sit behind bars while some maggot gives a false testimony? That's like asking me to trust the devil!" shouted Gall.

"You will abide by these terms if you want your brothers to rest in peace. While you're awaiting the end of this foolish search, I'll arrange your entry fee into the Furies' fighting circuit."

Iblis snatched the duffel bag from Gall's hand and tossed it on the floor. He waved his hand over it and increased its size while adding a couple more.

"Ten million will grant you entry without question. It will be here after your release from prison," said Iblis.

"Ten mil is a steep price for an entry fee," replied Gall.

"It was made to be. It's a precautionary measure to keep foolish mortals from entering, and at the same time make a vengeful punishment from the Furies more profitable. They thrive on their gladiatorial games as much as their gods. The supernatural gifts you bring will not only increase your chances but gain their favor."

The doorbell rang, and Gall peeked out of a neighboring window. He saw three patrol cars parked in the driveway. "You'd better be right about this," he mumbled.

"The money will be here when you return," said Iblis. He dived into the flames of the fireplace with the roar of a revving chopper motorcycle engine as Gall prepared for the ride.

Shortly afterward, two policemen escorted Gall into a holding cell next to Otava Masten. They purposely left the restraints that shackled his wrists to his waistline, and pushed him into the cell.

"Detective Rodriguez will be down to speak to you after he picks up his witness, so just relax and watch your luck run out" heckled the officer.

Gall kicked off his shoes in response and walked to the cot for a quick nap.

"As for you, your sister is posting bail as we speak. You'll be leaving us in a couple of hours. Try and learn a lesson this time and better yourself on the outside," the officer joked.

"*Outta here!*" blurted Otava.

Gall peeked into the cell next to his and caught the stare of a beast. The purple color of her eyes clashed into the black pupils of

the Marid Djinn that hid beneath his frame. Otava unzipped the
purple jacket of her jumpsuit and pressed her chest against the bars
of Gall's cell. Her black T-shirt pulsated as she curved around them
like a threatened puff adder.

"*Xiongqui Juren!*" whispered Otava.

Gall sat up and gave Otava a closer look. "Do I know you?" he
asked.

"No," said Otava. "While I was in Chinatown, I overheard the
name coughed out the windpipe of a dying man's lungs. That night,
you also solved a problem for me. One might say I owe you a favor."
She gathered the loose ends of her hair and pinned them into two
purple ponytails.

Gall shrugged at the introduction and laid back. "I don't know
what you're talking about. I spent my time in Chinatown washing
dishes."

"You don't know me, and I never heard of you leaving a witness
behind, but here we are. My sister's looking for people with your skill
and experience," offered Otava.

"I don't need a job right now. I already got that covered."

"I wasn't offering you a position in our organization. I merely
placed a bug in your ear about our fighting circuit. You can win a
lot of money fighting against our fighters. Gutter Ash is the best.
You might have heard the name."

Gall's right eyebrow rose into his forehead as an expression of
interest. "I never heard the name Gutter Ash before today."

"My sister got it from a novel titled *Reign or Rain*. It had a story
about a timid antique dealer and his wife. She had an affair and
mustered the strength to tell her husband about it. Her jealous lover
suggested they do it in a way that demeaned the antique owner's
sexual prowess. So they entered the antique store and started a
conversation about minutemen. The antique owner overheard this
conversation and quickly corrected their poor choice of words. 'I am
a minute man because it only takes a minute to load!' he shouted.
The antique dealer ran to a crate and loaded a musket into a colonial

rifle. After it was loaded, he chased the couple out of his shop and fired a shot. The musket hit the unfaithful wife in the foot, removing a toe. She limped to a gutter and calmly lit a cigarette. After two long pulls, she tapped the ashes into the blood that had spilled over into the gutter. At that moment, she discovered that the timid man she had fallen in love with wasn't the man she knew at all. That story moved my sister. She puts on a mask and enters the ring with the same advantage as in the story. You can look us up when you get out and say thanks."

"Thanks for what?"

"You'll know when I get *Outta Here!*"

The following afternoon, Detective Rodriguez walked into the holding pen and opened Gall's cell.

"What took you so long? No phone call, and a crackpot witness. My lawyer would've had me released yesterday," said Gall.

"I would be keeping you longer with a signed statement," answered Detective Rodriguez, "My witness was too paranoid. Every place I went to had a note to find him in another. When I finally caught up with him, he was facedown in a stack of pancakes with a hole in the back of his head. The forensics report said that he was shot by a musket. They have an evidence bag with the weapon in it. I'm assuming you had to add insult to injury."

"When you assume, you only make an ass out of you and me. No witness, no case, and a night in jail. What other tricks do you have up your sleeve?" asked Gall.

"I'm out of tricks. You're free to go," said Detective Rodriguez. He politely stepped aside and gestured for Gall to leave his cell.

Before leaving the precinct, Gall caught the stare of another predator. Telly Montross stood outside, looking at ease and wearing an iniquitous smirk.

Gall returned to the Abominable mansion and packed a small suitcase. He placed it on the front step with the bags Iblis had left as a purple limo pulled up to the door. Two toned Native Americans wearing the same purple jumpsuits as Otava jumped out of the front seat, and opened the passenger door. Gall cautiously watched as a pair of long, tanned legs stepped out of the dark interior. Glimpse brushed a piece of lint off her suit as she looked over Gall's bags.

"Which Abominable are you?" asked Glimpse.

"The worst one," answered Gall.

"Pardon my manners. My name is Glimpse Masten. You already know my sister Otava. She sent me here to give you an invitation to her show." Glimpse briefly paused to wrap her hair into a ponytail. The edges were dyed purple, and the tight wrap made it look like a paintbrush that had been dipped in purple paint.

"I'm kind of pressed for time. Things get a little weary after the death of a witness. I'm about to start my vacation," replied Gall.

"Then start it with us. We have a great investment plan for the ten million dollars in your possession," offered Glimpse.

"How did you know how much was in there?" asked Gall.

"I'm also an accountant. It doesn't matter what the wrapping is, I've seen ten million enough times to know," boasted Glimpse.

Gall looked over Glimpse's bodyguards, and a peculiar object piqued his interest. Their braid wraps looked like lollipops bound in leather.

"Why are you using lollipops for braid wraps?" asked Gall.

"They're not lollipops. They're drumsticks. We call them *rounds*," one answered.

A dumbfounded expression crossed Gall's face. Before he could ask them why, the other answered, "Pray you never find out."

"I might be able to spare some time. What type of performance is she giving?" asked Gall.

"She's an exotic dancer. You can use your imagination to figure out the rest," answered Glimpse.

"I just realized there's an opening in my schedule," replied Gall. Glimpse politely stepped aside and gestured for Gall to board while her bodyguards grabbed his bags.

The repetitious click of a camera taking pictures followed as they exited.

"I told you so," said Montross. "They'll have him wearing purple before the end of the week. I'd bet my stripes on it!"

"I still don't think he had anything to do with the death of my witness. What about Glimpse's muscle?" asked Detective Rodriguez.

"They're half of Otava's war party. She knew her temper would always get her in trouble, so she raised quadruplets to protect her sisters in case she ever had to serve time."

"She raised her muscle?"

"In her sick, twisted mind, it was the only way they could understand the bond she shared with her sisters. John Stormcloud and John Hawk look after Glimpse. John Bear and John Bullhorns look after Mitten."

Detective Rodriguez followed Gall with a puzzled expression. "How can you tell them apart?" he asked.

"The rounds in their braid wraps display their hierarchy," answered Montross. Detective Rodriguez checked for the pocket-sized Bible in his shirt pocket as he pursued monsters bigger than Gall.

At the rear doors of an uptown strip club called Purple Flames, Hel was knocking. John Bear and John Bullhorns escorted her to Mitten's office, while Bully pulled the collar chain of a prisoner. Otava suspiciously watched as he entered the office with a hood over his head.

"Well, look what the cat dragged in," said Mitten. "Just yesterday this little mouse was hiding in our basement and sliding from our poles. Now she's a Hel queen. What's that expression the mortals around here like to use?"

"'If you can make it here, you can make it anywhere,'" answered Otava.

"State your business, Hel queen!" demanded Mitten.

"You should know my new position comes with benefits. I have something you want, and you can get me something I need," said Hel.

THREE MARID DJINNS: THE VAULTS IN THE          115
STYLES CORPORATE BUILDING

"What can you offer me from a world I left long ago?" asked Mitten.

"Your father," answered Hel. She removed the hood of her prisoner and allowed the Furies to look upon Cronus.

Cold chills rattled Mitten's frame as she removed the sickle fastened on her back. She quickly tossed it under her desk before Cronus could see it.

"Don't be alarmed," explained Hel. "He is currently occupied by my servant Forgetful. The sight of you means nothing to him, nor does the castration."

"What do you want for him?" asked Mitten.

"The blood sport you host harbors a valuable weapon to my cause. It's called Gram, and it's wielded by William the Blacksmith," answered Hel.

"You want us to get a sword from the Corpse Candle!" yelled Otava.

Glimpse entered the room while Mitten pondered on the exchange. "Sorry to break up this little meeting, but Tibbigall Maxwell is waiting outside for a performance." Glimpse pulled back the curtain to expose a hidden mirror and pointed out Gall.

"*Xiongqui Juren!*" blurted Otava.

"It's unlike you to gawk over any man," said Mitten.

"Gall is no ordinary man. Death curls inside him. You can say the words to bend and fold steel, but Gall gives you the experience of a blacksmith," replied Otava.

A wicked smile appeared on Hel's face as she approached the window. Her eyes darkened as she took advantage of another opportunity. "Gall is not an ordinary man when Sitoel stands behind him."

Otava's eyes lustered as she removed her jumpsuit and revealed a purple leather bikini beneath. "Who is this Sitoel?" she demanded.

"A very possessive admirer. She snapped at me a few times because I looked at Gall," warned Hel.

"We'll see how possessive she is when I get *Outta Here!*" replied

Otava. Otava slipped into a pair of black stiletto shoes and raced for the stage. A Fury reeling from hearing the name Sitoel followed.

"You are truly gifted with a sickle in your hand, but I'm afraid your skill will be outmatched if this Sitoel meets her Fury. Now tell me about this prisoner that carries the stench of Hades," said Glimpse. Glimpse approached the prisoner for a closer look and shuddered at the sight of Cronus. "Forgive me, Father. I did not recognize you." She knelt before the Titan while Bully pulled him to the floor.

"Fortune has truly shone upon us this evening," boasted Hel.

"Fortune? I would have to kill William the Blacksmith to retrieve your sword. The circuit will suffer from the loss!" said Mitten.

"Look past that sentimental moment and see the Titan kneeling at your feet. You also have a Fate sitting in your club," replied Hel.

"A Fate?"

"Gall is one of the three Marid Djinns responsible for the death of Zeus."

A rapacious expression smeared Mitten's face, and the repetitious clicks of a money-counting machine rang in the ears of Glimpse.

"Otava was right," said Mitten. "Gall isn't an ordinary man. Contact everyone in our organization to spread word around the underworld. We have two new fighters entering the circuit. Make sure the bets placed are heavy."

Glimpse returned to her feet and raced to her office to make the necessary calls.

"I'll leave your father in your care. My servant will assist you in detaining him and notify me when you have my sword. It's been a pleasure doing business with you," said Hel.

Bully handed the chain to Mitten, and she dropped it.

"Take the collar off of him, and rest him in the same basement room we gave the mouse," commanded Mitten.

"Hel queen!" Hel corrected as she walked out the door.

At the stage area of the club, Gall cautiously looked over his environment. Nearly every patron was armed and wore purple. Then suddenly the music stopped, and a wire fence rolled down to curtain the stage.

"Now, for your viewing pleasure, we bring you *Outta Here!*" introduced the DJ. Gall's right eyebrow rose into his forehead as Otava danced onto the stage. Her seductive figure maneuvered around three poles centered on the platform. She wrapped her frame around the corner pole like a snake and inched her way to the top with ease. When Otava reached the ceiling, she leapt to the center pole with a purple aura. The aura formed into an enormous pair of bat wings as Otava removed her top. She gracefully spiraled down with her legs in a split position. A call for an encore roared through the club as every member stood and applauded.

Gall joined in, and after the crowd settled down, all of them drew their guns.

"I thought cheering was the thing to do?" mumbled Gall. He slowly unraveled the kusari-fundo chain hidden in the sleeve of his shirt as Mitten made her way through the crowd. She boldly confronted Gall with the sickle fastened on her back and a large purple curl resting in the center of her forehead.

"You have a lot of money in your possession. What do you intend to do with it?" asked Mitten.

"That's Abominable business. No concern of yours," replied Gall.

"In Mr. Maxwell's defense, he was about to start an unexpected vacation. The sudden departure rests with Otava," Glimpse interrupted as she stepped from behind her sister.

"The deceased witness she told me about," said Mitten. "Pardon my intrusion, but one can't be too careful these days, especially when my sister is involved. My name is Mitten Masten. Fate has allowed us the opportunity to rid ourselves of two mutual problems. The least I can do is offer you the opportunity to triple that amount." A smile appeared on Gall's face as he finally reached the moment he had plotted for.

"Triple? Just tell me what I have to do!" he replied.

"You can join my underground circuit for fighters," said Mitten. Otava quickly gained Gall's attention as she stepped out of the crowd with her hair draped over her chest.

"I'd be glad to participate. I just need to say good-bye to a couple of friends before I leave," replied Gall.

"We can leave together," said Otava.

"Bullhorns, get the limo," commanded Mitten.

An hour after leaving the club, a purple limo pulled in front of the Styles Corporate Building. Upstairs, Sitoel bombarded Anesidora with questions.

"Akantha said you'd be able to answer my questions. You should summon Hope to do so," pleaded Sitoel.

"It doesn't work like that. Hope will only emerge if the answer needed cures an ailment," replied Anesidora.

"What's that supposed to mean?"

"How could not knowing hurt you? If it's severe enough, Hope will come and give you an answer," explained Banter.

"Banter understands," said Anesidora. Hope is familiar with all the evils, toils, and sicknesses of humankind. Through them she can surface and bear you gifts."

A cold chill crept over Anesidora's shoulder as Gall entered the office.

"Gall?" Banter nervously blurted.

"He suffers from Pandora's prolonged death. Don't worry Gall, Hope has the anchors," said Anesidora.

"I don't know what spell you put over them, but when Hope arrives, I'll tie those anchors around your ankles and throw you off the nearest bridge," replied Gall.

"He thinks she's Pandora," uttered Sitoel.

Banter jumped off the couch to contain Gall as Otava entered the office. Two Bushmaster Carbon 15 pistols were holstered on her shoulders.

"I heard shouting in the hallway. Do we have a problem here?" she asked.

"Yes, and I'm about to tend to it!" Gall answered in a tone that carried a hiss.

"Sitoel, get Hope out of here!" shouted Banter.

"You're Sitoel? *Outta here!*" shouted Otava. A purple aura climbed Otava's frame, and fiery wings erupted from her back as she drew her pistols.

In response, Sitoel snatched Anesidora off the couch with the strength and speed of Victory. A barrage of gunfire followed as Otava's pistols fired three rounds at a time. The bullets rampantly crept across the walls like a trail of salamander feet and shattered the office window. The debris from the window fell onto the roof of the limo and alerted the passengers inside. Mitten and Glimpse stepped out of the passenger doors with a purple aura. Their fears increased when they saw the muzzle flashes of Otava's pistols. It increased the purple luster of their frames as their bodyguards stepped out of the vehicle and loaded their Carbon 15 rifles.

A war party raced for the lobby as Detective Rodriguez and Telly Montross arrived on the scene.

"Great meatloaves of Bethlehem, Otava is having a war party. We can sneak up on them from behind," said Montross.

"Are you out of your mind? We don't have the firepower to face them. We have to call for backup," replied Detective Rodriguez.

"And give that killer another opportunity to escape? No way!" shouted Montross. He jumped out of the vehicle in pursuit while Detective Rodriguez made the call. When he was done, he stepped out of the vehicle, and a voice held him at bay.

"It's not your time" rang in his ear. In response, Detective Rodriguez collapsed on the ground and fell into a deep sleep.

Inside the Styles Corporate Building, the footage from a security camera alerted the lobby guards to form a barricade. Another group raced upstairs to Banter's defense.

"Gall, call off your tramp!" demanded Sitoel. She struggled as she maneuvered around the office with Anesidora.

"Tramp? Why don't you stand still and say that!" shouted Otava. Her pupils reflected a purple flame, and a pair of fangs pressed into her bottom lip as she paused to reload.

"A Fury!" blurted Anesidora. Banter's guards stormed the floor and forced Otava to exit as they aimed their guns. She quickly snatched Gall by the collar and jumped out the window to escape. The flame of her wings melted the projectiles that followed. Otava landed by the limo, and caught sight of Montross aiming his handgun at Mitten.

"This one's for you, buddy!" shouted Montross. He fired a shot and Mitten fell from the impact.

"He shot her in the back!" cried Otava. The sight of the fallen Fury provoked tears of blood from the eyes of Glimpse and Otava. Their war party chanted to mountain spirits as they opened fire and pounded rounds into the lobby like, *The Drums of Thunder*.

Mitten fed off the chants and opened her eyes. She returned to her feet and unsheathed the sickle fastened on her back. She brushed off a flat bullet that pressed against the blade and angrily stared in the direction of Montross. He ran behind a large oak tree for cover as a pair of fiery wings erupted from Mitten's back. She took flight in a purple flame and hurled the sickle through the air. It increased to a size befitting a Titan as it boomeranged through the area. It sliced through half the block and slid through the oak tree like a thin piece of fabric. The sickle returned to a size befitting a mortal as Mitten snatched it from the air. In the debris lay the torn carcass of Telly Montross.

"Now he's only half the man you are," joked Glimpse. Mitten responded with a nod as she landed by the limo.

"I hope this little display doesn't discourage you from joining the circuit?" said Otava.

"After what happened tonight, I find myself in the mood to make new friends," answered Gall. He disappointedly looked at the group standing in the window of Banter's office and boarded the limo.

As the car pulled away, Sitoel grabbed Banter by the collar and raised him to the ceiling. "Who is she?" she asked in a tone that carried a hiss.

"Why are you asking me? I never saw that creature before Gall brought her here!" replied Banter. Sitoel released her hold on Banter and watched the limo while he indignantly pulled the wrinkles from his suit.

"What got into you?"

"The way she said my name … *It sounded like Hel!*"

In Hades, Enemy and Rottenvein patiently waited in the blood-stained fields of Existere's stronghold for Kaleb. A small army of lycans camouflaged in the forest rested just a few feet behind.

"We have been waiting for some time. How difficult can it be to sneak inside and open a gate? He looked just like these lizard men" complained Rottenvein.

"You cannot rush a master at work," boasted Enemy. "My brother is a master of illusion. His disguises have eluded bounty hunters sent by Odin. A horde of giants with a taste for flesh—and they were led by Gilgamesh. He eluded pursuits and raids on the seas to escape Ivar the Boneless. His most notable work was stealing the identity of a bloodthirsty buccaneer. During that time, our beloved Lord Treachery was attacked by an army of Spaniards. He cleverly escaped by covering himself with the blood and remains of the crew."

"No one can attest to that. How can one be certain? For all we know, he could have murdered everyone on board to satisfy his own bloodlust," said Rottenvein.

"He successfully ran your region as sheriff!" snapped Enemy.

An ominous silence smothered the field as the doors to the stronghold opened.

"I might have misjudged the lycan after all," whispered Rottenvein. They waited for a signal from the shadowy figure that walked out before a string of torches sparked behind her.

"Hel!" shouted Enemy. A band of archers dragged Lord Treachery out in chains. Rottenvein quickly grabbed Enemy and wrestled him to the ground to keep him from charging.

"Nosey and Eavesdropping, you may come to me now!" commanded Hel. Two lycans in the field collapsed as Hel's servants raced back to their master like trained dogs.

An Abominable general made his way to the frontline. His skin had shed into the camouflaged forest and the bloodstained armor of Existence. His eyes captured the fear of his soldiers as they pierced the night and picked up the heat signatures of the lycans. He took his place by Hel's side and pointed out the occupied patch in the forest.

"I have to tend to the preparations of my feast," said Hel. "I'll bestow upon you your new position and title before I leave. You are one of three Abominable generals and commander of my Scythian archers. Now seal our first victory and announce your name to our enemies."

"You can call me Copasetic!" shouted the Abominable. He raised his hand as an army of archers ignited their arrows. The poison on the tips fumed as he signaled them to fire. The arrows made the shape of a fireball as they catapulted into the sky, and it resembled a meteor as it crashed into the forest. The scent of charred flesh blanketed the field, as did Copasetic's laughter.

"Bring me any survivors—if there are any survivors," he commanded.

The following day, Detective Rodriguez woke up to a nurse propping his pillow and the Captain at the foot of his bed.

"It's about time you woke up. Your guest has been sitting here all night," said the nurse. The Captain gave Detective Rodriguez a cold stare and kept silent until she left the room.

"What happened out there?" he asked.

"The last thing I remember is Montross jumping out of the car," answered Detective Rodriguez.

"If that's it, you'd better return to your unconscious state!" shouted the captain. "I woke up this morning to the mayor's cries for the weapon of mass destruction no one told him about. Half a city block is buried in rubble. We also found half of Montross propped on that pile like a cherry on a sundae. The Styles Corporate lobby and executive office looks like a wood shack plagued by termites, and that's all you can remember?"

"The guards didn't give a statement? They have surveillance equipment that can pick up a pin drop on that block," replied Detective Rodriguez.

"You of all people know better by now. Every brick in that building holds a cold case file. You knew that when you joined the Homicide Division. They all say the same thing, 'The cameras weren't functioning properly, It all happened so fast, and I didn't see anything because I was hiding.' The death of Montross isn't going to go over well when word gets back to his base of operations. He knew a lot of important people. They'll want answers, and I have to prepare for the one they'll send to replace him."

"Who will they send?" asked Detective Rodriguez.

"Tabasco King" uttered the Captain.

"What does he look like?"

"You wouldn't know him if you stared him in the face. By that time it would be too late. Facta non verba. Deeds, not words, Detective."

Detective Rodriguez briefly turned away from the Captain to prop his pillow, and suddenly found himself in an empty room. He stared at the window, filled with doubt until Akantha entered.

"Can you explain to me how you managed to allow Gall to fall into the hands of Furies?" asked Akantha.

"You want an explanation?" answered Detective Rodriguez. "Nothing is ever simple with Gall! First I find the witness you gave me shot by a colonial rifle, Banter's lobby and office tells the tale of an old western shooting gallery, a member of an elite unit gets torn in half while I'm assigned as his escort, and after passing out, I have to validate a report that won't put me in a rubber room!" Det. Rodriguez jumped out of bed and started to get dressed.

"What can you tell me about the women he was with?" asked Akantha.

"The man I was escorting was running a criminal investigation on them. He said they ran an underground circuit for fighters. He knew they would offer Gall an invitation, so we tailed them for an arrest. He was killed before we could make one."

"Gall will find himself in great danger if he partakes in their gladiatorial games," said Akantha.

"You're worried about Gall? I saw him grip a giant turtle and hog tie it to the brink of extinction. I think Gall can handle himself."

"Gall will face greater challenges than a Kappa. He will face the notorious Nosferatu, known to your people as Vlad the Impaler. He will also face the blood-driven king of a yeti tribe. If he finds a way to overcome those obstacles, he'll fight a devious dark elf known to many as the Corpse Candle. Last will be the Furies, who wield the sickle of their Titan father. I say there's plenty to worry about. We have to gather the other Fates for Gall to survive."

"I was just on my way to speak to Banter," replied Detective Rodriguez.

Before leaving, the phone rang, and Detective Rodriguez paused to answer it.

"You finally woke up!" said the Captain. "I have an entire amusement park lined up for the beauty rest you took. The mayor and several of Telly's friends want answers, so you'd better have a good one. Get down here ASAP!"

*"Captain?"*

"Are you still enduring the effects of some medication? Who else would it be?"

Detective Rodriguez hung up the phone and dialed Risk Fenton's cell phone. When he didn't get an answer, he turned to Akantha.

"Who is Tabasco King?" he asked.

"An assassin, feared by your people and mine," answered Akantha.

"Can you identify him?" asked Detective Rodriguez.

"No, Tabasco King is whatever and whoever he wants to be. There are rumors of him being a doppelganger, and some say he's a shapeshifter. The one truth everyone can agree on is his knack for hunting. The blade he wields is small, but it can sever the head of an elephant. The Sacred Order of the Dragon sends him when there's a need for complete silence. If he's entered the field of play, we'll definitely need the assistance of the Fates. I wouldn't trust anyone or anything until then."

Detective Rodriguez nodded in agreement as they raced out of the room.

In the city harbor, a purple explorer yacht slowly sailed for the Atlantic Ocean. Gall inhaled the fresh sea air like a Lycan buccaneer as he looked over the rail. Otava crept from behind with a warning as she cleaned her nails with a pocket knife.

"You should be resting," advised Otava.

"That sounds like I don't stand a chance," said Gall.

"Take the advice given to you. My sister handpicked these fighters for the same reason she chose the name Gutter Ash. They recreate tales that are appropriate for one's demise. It also depicts their weakness. If you are fortunate enough, you will discover it before you die," explained Otava.

"What is the tragic tale of the first opponent?" asked Gall.

Otava stared into the clouds to watch the full moon rising. Her chest pulsated as she visualized the midnight setting of Poenari Castle.

"The story begins with Cupid, Apollo, and Daphne. Apollo believed the bow and arrow belonged in the arsenal for war. He insulted Cupid for brandishing one. Cupid retaliated with two arrows. A gold arrow that harbored love, and a lead arrow that harbored hate. He shot Apollo with the gold arrow, and shot the daughter of a river god with the arrow of hate. Apollo fell in love, and Daphne couldn't stand to be with him. She knew it would only be a matter of time before Apollo subdued her, so she begged her father to turn her into a tree. This foolish act didn't stop Apollo.

"He dug up the tree and cared for it while searching for a way to break the spell. He finally discovered a clue that said he had to obtain Cupid's bow. Apollo devised several plots to snatch it from Cupid, but Cupid always managed to stay ahead of his schemes. Fearing that one day his luck would run out, Cupid cleverly placed it where Apollo would never find it. He hid the bow on the lips of mortals. They passed it on with every loving kiss.

"When Apollo discovered the plot, he immediately sought an agent with a hatred for love. One that had seen it wither from his or her hands time and time again—a creature that wouldn't betray him when it was obtained."

"The Keres!" interrupted Gall.

"Her days were numbered in this realm. Plagued by the pursuits of witch hunters, angry villagers and assassins employed by the Sacred Order of the Dragon, she struck a deal to change her identity. She would relentlessly track the bow for a cure that would end her bloodlust and change her appearance. She assumed it was a simple task until she found the bow.

"After she turned the mortal into a vampire, he kissed her. She fell in love and tried to conceal the act from Apollo. When Apollo discovered her betrayal, he journeyed to earth with an arrow made from Daphne's tree. In the darkness of night, he shot her while she stood in her window. She landed in the river below the castle, where it imprisoned her for an eternity. Night after night, our fighter cries on the banks, filled with a hate that has cursed the surrounding area," explained Otava.

"So who is this poor soul?"

"Lord Dracula, known to our circuit as Vlad the Impaler."

Overwhelmed by her emotions, Otava quickly turned away as blood streamed from her eyes.

Gall noticed the trail of droplets as they floated with a purple aura, and he attempted to lighten the mood. "So how many opponents have you defeated below deck?" he joked.

"I don't know a soul that ever survived the night," boasted Otava. Gall stood dazed as she gave him a playful shove and walked away. His attention returned to the sea as a small whirlpool stirred the blood to the depths and caused a stream of black smoke to erupt. It poured over the deck with a roar that mimicked the revving of a chopper motorcycle engine.

"I hate to interrupt your little tryst, but blood should be leaking from the eldest sister by now. We had a deal!" shouted Iblis.

"Nothing in our agreement covered spending the night in jail," replied Gall. "The authorities didn't have a case, but they'll be watching every move I make because of a dead witness. The circus you asked me to join shot up Banter's building, and I missed a golden opportunity to toss Pandora over a bridge with anchors tied to her ankles."

"A man like Gall would want to kill Hope," boasted Iblis.

"*Hope?*"

"Your crew of Marid Djinns eliminated Pandora. What remained merged into Anesidora to harbor Hope. Akantha intends to align you with her."

"Why?"

"To keep you from doing what you do best!"

Iblis's eyes brightened as he manifested a hooded black robe. "Time is running out for your brothers," he mumbled.

"We had a deal!" snapped Gall.

"That was before your brother became Copasetic and incinerated a small army of lycans," replied Iblis. "Enemy and Rottenvein barely escaped alive. Lord Treachery is once again Hel's prisoner."

"Where's Enemy now?" asked Gall.

"Sulking over the matter with several barrels of mead. When he reaches his limit, he'll summon the pack for retaliation. In order for me to keep the peace, you'll have to bring me the weapons of all your opponents."

"You'll have them if you can keep Enemy off the Abominables long enough for me to obtain them. Just keep in mind that no realm or world will be safe for you if you cross me," warned Gall.

Iblis slowly floated off deck and hovered over the whirlpool. "Do you think you're menacing because you've slain a few gods? Hold your tongue until you've faced a being that has fallen from grace. William the Blacksmith is the closest you'll ever get. His gift for welding is exceptional, but he was shunned by his community for being a tyrannical prankster."

"I'm quaking in my boots," mumbled Gall.

"You'll soon learn how the combination of the two can make a lethal opponent. When Saint Peter discovered it, he offered William a chance to enter the gates of heaven. All he had to do was abandon his evil ways. William turned away with laughter and was cursed with a soul that would know no eternal peace. For his defiance, I offered him a piece of coal and pointed him in the direction of the nearest dark elf community. While he was there, he mastered the recipe for *"It pierces the heart and clings to the soul."* He fused it with molding clay stolen from Hephaestus and made the Corpse Candle. "A piece of coal is the most lethal weapon in his arsenal," explained Iblis.

"Why would a piece of coal be menacing?"

*"I gave it to him!"*

As Iblis dived into the sea, Akantha and Detective Rodriguez arrived at the Styles Estate. Anesidora frantically paced around the den with Gall's murderous eyes stained in her thoughts. When she finally settled down, she asked Banter and Sitoel for an explanation.

"He would have enjoyed my endless suffering. What did Pandora do to him?" asked Anesidora. Before they could answer, Bella entered the den with Akantha and Detective Rodriguez.

"Your fear and grief match those of a mother concerned for her child. Hope will bring you gifts," said Anesidora. She closed her eyes and opened them with an expression that familiarized a friend.

"Hello, Akantha, caretaker to the household of Zeus," greeted Hope.

"Hello, old friend. May you join the Graces and walk with Trust again in this realm," replied Akantha.

"That is the purpose I wish to serve. I see the responsibilities of a caretaker have dragged you into a path botched with schemes. I wish I was here to help with Zeus," said Hope.

"What's done is done. There is another in need of your abilities. I had hoped to align you with Gall, but he fell into the company of Furies. They will use him for their gladiatorial games. I must hurry before they realize they can exact revenge for his past crimes. I blame myself for his misguidance. I left him as a child to tend to another. Please give me the opportunity to correct the mistake. There is still enough good in Gall to change a world of suffering," pleaded Akantha.

Hope closed her eyes and entered a stage of deep thought. "Your Gall will face Vlad the Impaler. There is little hope in this situation," she uttered.

"Dracula? Gall is going to fight Dracula!" interrupted Banter. Sitoel's eyes began to luster.

"What do you see?" asked Banter.

"Death! The field is filled with blood and hate. The animal packs feed off of it. They dissect us before we reach Vlad," answered Sitoel.

"There is hope if you break the curse of the land and remain inconspicuous to the packs," said Hope.

"What packs? What curse?" asked Banter.

"Vlad leads three packs of nosophoros creatures before an opponent faces him," explained Hope. "An opponent is chased through the field by the wolves, lynx, and bats that inhabit the area. Each makes an attempt to draw blood. The more blood they draw, the better they serve their master. Vlad solidifies his win when his opponent reaches the river. There he savors the blood he collected to learn their strengths and weaknesses. He knows every move they make and waits to deliver a fatal blow that will impale his opponent. After the battle is won, he hangs them over the river and feeds his bride their blood. She is the source of the curse."

Hope closed her eyes to go deeper in thought. "Apollo's war with Cupid imprisoned her in the river. Cupid cleverly placed his bow on the lips of a warrior that belonged to the Sacred Order of the Dragon. Vlad the Impaler unknowingly kept it in the family until the Keres arrived. A disguise gained Vlad the Impaler's affections, but she underestimated the power of the bow. She kept it and became Vlad's wife. When Apollo discovered Cupid had won another battle, he sought Hephaestus for his net of invisibility and carved an arrow from Daphne's tree for revenge. Apollo journeyed to Earth in the middle of the night and shot the unsuspecting victim as she stood in her window. As she fell into the river, he snared her in the net and summoned Daphne's father to seal her fate. When the river god discovered the arrow made from his daughter, he extended the roots to keep her in a coffin. It's unbreakable, and the hate causes branches to protrude through the thickets that grow on the field. They also scrape and scar opponents to collect blood for Vlad. An opportunity to defeat him has never existed," explained Akantha.

"There is hope! You must obtain the helm of invisibility," advised Hope. Banter and Sitoel cringed as Hel came to mind.

Sitoel frantically searched for an alternative method. Her eyes widened, and paced as if she were speed reading a horror story under the beam of a flashlight.

"Please tell us another way," pleaded Banter.

"If the land and packs don't get us, the Furies will. We need the helm of invisibility to save Gall. So you'd better man up for a date and a lot of lustrous talk," answered Sitoel.

"You'll need more than that," interrupted Hope.

"What now?" blurted Banter.

"Cupid's curse on the bow! You must remember his fight with Apollo. You'll have to humble yourself if you want to escape a dreadful fate. This makes Sitoel the better candidate," advised Hope.

Banter tumbled to the floor with laughter and heckled between breaths, "So you better man up for your date."

"You have no idea what you're asking of me. What she'll put me through!" complained Sitoel.

"That's why you're the best candidate. I'll go with you to ease you through your fears," said Akantha. She slowly approached Sitoel with an extended hand.

"Don't do it. I won't do it. You can't make me!" Sitoel protested as she backed into a corner.

Akantha gently placed her hand on Sitoel's shoulder and commanded, "Go to Hel!"

In Hades, two armies led by Existere's brothers enjoyed a festival that catered to their desires. Hel campaigned her cause to Gathyos and Gelonos while Bully served plates with two meats for the course.

When Copasetic arrived, Hel excused herself to join him. "Have you succeeded in your task?" she asked.

"Lord Treachery and his army of lycans are dead," answered Copasetic. "Enemy dug an underground tunnel to escape. I sent a patrol to track him down and found their bodies laced with a brain germ. He's still on our list of problems."

"I have two generals in the dining hall and two Abominables waiting for new vessels. I have no room for a list of problems!" snapped Hel.

Her servant Sneaky brought two small jars into the room. Hel removed the lids so Copasetic could hear the souls that rested inside.

"I hope Gall got away. I never expected a hit like that. I can't rest until I know," uttered Paul.

"How foolish of me!" cried Matthew. "Kaleb needs me to tend to Abominable affairs, and I allowed myself to get killed. I have to find some way to warn him."

Hel grabbed the jars and threatened to throw them on the ground.

"Stop! I made a mistake and underestimated them. It won't happen again," pleaded Copasetic.

"It better not," warned Hel. "These soldiers will not follow failure. They're led by acts of greatness and legends. Existere's mother was a serpentine queen. She possessed the poison to slay many creatures and gods. She also wielded the bow that belonged to Heracles. Her victories in battle echoed on the tongues of the underworld. We'll have to do the same to gain their respect and loyalty. I'm in the process of getting Gram. Now tend to the task I've assigned you. Locate Thor's armor, and do not fail me again!"

As Copasetic set out on his mission, Nosey and Eavesdropping raced to her side. "My Hel queen, Sitoel has returned to our realm with Akantha!" they simultaneously shouted. A thin stream of smoke funneled from Hel's nostrils as Bully grew to a height that shattered the roof.

"Every time they come around we lose a roof!" mumbled Complaints. Bully picked up Hel and placed her outside the walls, where Sitoel stood. Existere's brothers raced with Hel's army to investigate the disturbance and found the Fate that had slain their sister. Akantha approached Hel and knelt before her.

"May we have an audience with the Hel queen?" requested Akantha.

"Your intrusion can be overlooked for the time you spared during my childhood, but this dung beetle faces a range of sanctions," replied Hel.

"I can't do this sober!" cried Sitoel. She reached over to a neighboring table and grabbed a mug of mead as Hel's eyes darkened.

"How unfortunate to see you still among the living. I had hoped a Fury would have better aim," sneered Hel.

Sitoel tossed her drink on the ground and crushed the mug. "I knew you were behind that attack!" she shouted in a tone that carried a hiss.

"I also gave you a warning about returning to my realm. Let me remind you again in case you've forgotten," said Hel.

Instigator parted the crowd with a disco ball and circled Sitoel. "She'll pin your vocal cords to a disco ball if you ever enter this realm again. What are you going to do about it?" he instigated. Akantha jumped to her feet and stood in Hel's path.

"You are aware of the bond between the Marid Djinns. In order to assist Gall, Banter and Sitoel must obtain the helm of invisibility. Please spare us your rage and grant our request," pleaded Akantha.

"So my love requests my assistance," replied Hel. "I also have a stake in Banter's welfare. I prepared a great feast in preparation for it. He should have joined me instead of sending his pet. I may overlook the intrusion if the dung beetle kneels before me and asks."

Existere's brothers chatted amongst each other and took advantage of an opportunity. "Hel queen, you arranged a great feast and asked for our allegiance," said Gathyos. "We will grant this to you if you defeat the Fate that has slain our sister."

"A foolish request. Sitoel has anchors and cannot be slain in my realm without consequence," replied Hel.

"A victory in battle will suffice," said Gelonos.

Hel removed the pins in her hair to reveal the blades hidden within. Both adversaries stared at each other with eyes that lustered hate, and muscles that hardened as they clenched their fists.

"I challenge the dung beetle to combat. She can have any weapon of her choice," challenged Hel.

"I accept the challenge. Escrima sticks will be my weapon," answered Sitoel. The announcement of the fight became a highlight for the feast and provided Hel the support she needed for her campaign. An army roared while the fighters prepared themselves for the fight.

Sitoel tore a piece of cloth from the belly of her T-shirt to mask her face, but Akantha snatched it away.

"You must remember the curse!" advised Akantha. "You have to humble yourself. This means no Marid Djinn, no Echo, and no Victory."

Sitoel bellowed in agony while her insides wailed away a win.

Bully suddenly gained everyone's attention as he silenced the crowd with steps that shook the ground, and buckled the knees of every soldier. Hel followed with the ostentatious flash of a boxer approaching the ring for a championship bout. Her hands were wrapped with a white cloth. A hooded black robe covered her frame while she shadowboxed with Cheater. When Hel reached the center of the courtyard, she removed her robe to brandish a physique that highlighted a dragon in red war paint.

"What weapon will the Hel queen use?" shouted Gelonos.

"The world!" answered Hel.

The world serpent suddenly appeared and circled overhead. Jormungandr briefly paused to open his mouth and displayed Hel's army in his belly. Several ropes extended from his insides as both fighters approached each other without introduction. Sitoel quickly made a defensive stance as she focused on three servants sliding down the ropes like pole dancers. She cautiously watched the movements of Deceit, Lies, and Forgetful as the shadow of a Monstrous wolf crept from behind. Within seconds, the wolf entered her body and Sitoel fell victim to severe hunger pains. She dropped her escrima sticks and cradled her belly as she fell to her knees.

"What you feel now is similar to what I felt the day you and Banter left my realm on the back of that Monstrous wolf" said Hel. She charged at Sitoel with a running kick that pushed her into the crowd. The soldiers shoved Sitoel back into the courtyard with a roar.

Sitoel scrambled to her feet and picked up her escrima sticks. She nervously focused on Jormungandr while peeking at Hel from the corner of her eye.

"I believe your parting word was Presto" said Hel. At that

moment, Hunger left Sitoel's body and allowed Careless to enter. Sitoel dropped her escrima sticks and guard. Hel grabbed Sitoel by the collar and flipped her over her shoulder. She faced the cheers of the crowd as the ground echoed the impact of Sitoel's landing. It unleashed an echo of karma that sounded like blows in a pillow fight. The echoes rippled over the world serpent and made Sitoel aware of her surroundings.

Echo cut Lies and Deceit from the ropes, to unmask Decoy and Entice. A smirk appeared on Hel's face as a flame amassed around the frame of her dragon. She blew a kiss in Sitoel's direction as she staggered to her feet. A fist-shaped fireball raced through the air and crossed over Sitoel's face like a mask. The impact knocked her to the ground and caused her to bite the inside of her cheek.

"I yield!" cried Sitoel. The surrender ignited another roar from the crowd as Sitoel spat out blood.

Cheater placed Hel's robe back on her shoulders as a new army knelt before her. Entice retrieved the helm of invisibility and handed it to Hel.

"Now prepare our generals for their new vessels. I will name them Time and Chance to commemorate my victory," commanded Hel. She approached Akantha as she struggled to raise Sitoel to her feet.

"Give Banter my love, and warn him not to make the mistake of sending his pet again. I'll open more than a wound next time," warned Hel. She walked away while Instigator circled Sitoel with a disco ball.

"What are you going to do about it?" he instigated. Sitoel's eyes darkened as her Marid Djinn returned.

"Don't spoil it now. You lost the battle but won the war. Save your petty grievances for another time," advised Akantha.

"My grievances are far from petty. Gall has a huge debt to repay," replied Sitoel.

"He will owe you his life," said Akantha. She handed Sitoel the torn piece of cloth to wipe the blood from the corner of her lips. Then, Akantha opened a portal to Poenari Castle.

On a ridge that shadowed the corner of the courtyard, a Lycan buccaneer discreetly watched the events through a telescope.

"Iblis will not be pleased when he hears Hel defeated Sitoel in combat, and gained the alliance of Existeres' armies," said Malicious Merck.

"Do not be troubled. Her army is fierce, but they have yet to face the chemistry of a lycan, viking, and buccaneer—the main reason Iblis commanded Enemy to stay behind. I sailed with both brothers long enough to know the road paved before us. Lord Treachery can resolve a matter like this with low casualties and a slit throat over the table. Enemy, on the other hand—let's just say we'll have to double our protective vests on that day," explained Prison Levelfield. Malicious Merck looked to Rottenvein as he removed a knife from the belt of the archer they had taken prisoner. They chuckled as he used the blade to carve words on the chest of his victim.

"Why do you torture him? He has already given us all the information we need to know?" asked Malicious Merck.

"Copasetic incinerated an entire forest. I escaped with my life because of Enemy. In return, he requested I leave a message for Copasetic, the man that captured his brother," answered Rottenvein.

His brain germ took hold while Malicious Merck read, *"What opposed you!"*

While the underworld realms prepared for another war, Detective Rodriguez arrived at the Todou's plane hangar with Banter and Anesidora. Tobias stepped out to greet them with a cross and Bible in hand.

"Poenari Castle in Romania! Don't you know vampires and werewolves don't mix? What type of monster mash did you get yourself into this time?" asked Tobias.

"You mean Keres and werewolves don't mix," corrected Banter.

"Tomato, *tomahto* it all ends the same when you guys get together," said Tobias. "Speaking of werewolves, where's Gall?" He pocketed his cross and Bible as Banter dragged a trunk out of the van.

"He decided to travel with different company," answered Banter.

"He's not the only one," whispered Tobias. He stopped to admire Anesidora's flawless features as he grabbed the trunk.

Detective Rodriguez stepped out of the van and looked toward the office. A man dressed in black fatigues walked out with a Calico M960 holstered on his shoulder.

"He's armed?" mumbled Detective Rodriguez. He reached for his sidearm and Tobias grabbed his hand.

"I don't know a cop that isn't," said Tobias.

"I've never seen him before today. What precinct is he from?" asked the detective.

"He's not from here. He's a member of a JTF2 unit in Canada. I flew a party of three this morning. He stuck around to book a trip to the Himalayas, but I had to refuse. The Abominables and Styles Corporate always have first priority with us," explained Tobias. He continued to drag the trunk to the plane, while Anesidora looked over the man. Then, Hope unexpectedly emerged.

"That man is greatly troubled, but there is hope for him," advised Hope. "All you have to do is inform him of your whereabouts. Spare his heart from excessive strain." Detective Rodriguez cautiously looked over the man as he rolled his sleeves up past the extent of his tattoo. It displayed the sacred order's cross and dragon.

"I'm afraid he'll have to bear the pain a little longer," answered Detective Rodriguez. He rubbed his hand around his throat as everyone boarded the plane. "Hurry up and get us out of here," he whispered.

Tobias hauled the trunk on board and mumbled under his

breath, "Police running from the police? Now I know we're in trouble!"

The Furies' yacht arrived in Romania the following evening. Glimpse supervised the crew as they mapped out a road that led to the river beneath Poenari Castle. Several miniature cameras and microphones were placed on the path to the river. Mitten and Otava took flight in their helicopter to monitor the fight from the air. They watched over Glimpse as she introduced Vlad the Impaler's first opponent. A centaur boldly stepped out of the shadows of the surrounding brush with a broadsword fastened to his back. He curiously looked in Gall's direction as he added another string to the bow he carried.

Gall quickly pulled John Bullhorns to the side as he passed with a camera. "I thought I'd be the first fighter?" asked Gall.

"*You?* An average man is served to Vlad the Impaler as a thirst quencher. We have to make the sport a show. So we arranged a more formidable opponent with some type of supernatural ability. Just be patient and enjoy the fight before you die," answered John Bullhorns.

Gall carefully looked over the field as the cameras focused on Glimpse. She pinned her hair in a ponytail and introduced the centaur while Mitten streamed the event.

"Supernatural beings of the underworld, you may now place your bets on your favorite fighter. Our first brave contestant is an outlaw well known in Hades—a centaur that has escaped Ares' hunts and outwitted Existere's patrols. Now Vogek wages his life to battle Vlad the Impaler—a money fight, or a sacrifice? We will know by the end of the night. I now give you Vlad the Impaler!" announced Glimpse.

The cameras focused on Poenari Castle as the full moon stirred a thick fog. It overflowed from the decrepit windows and torn fixtures like a waterfall into the valley below. It crept over the terrain, and transformed the surrounding area back through time as the river increased in size. Trees grew and took the shape of large pikes. The leaves and branches shadowed victims Vlad had impaled. The thickets on the ground extended and attacked the life that inhabited the field. Waterbugs, spiders, and roaches were impaled on thorns by a ghost that wielded hate.

The sound of a wolf pack howling at the moonlight ignited Vogek's boldness, and he raced down the path. He fired his arrows when he heard the sound of paws kicking up dirt behind him. Vogek was able to fire three arrows at a time without looking at a target. The sound of a whimper piqued his curiosity, and he turned to look at the pack. His eyes widened in fear as he caught the stare of the alpha. His bright red pupils took hold of Vogek while two wolves in the pack sank their fangs into his calves. Vogek quickly kicked them off. He gained speed as another pack prepared an ambush. The bright red pupils that pursued him suddenly appeared in the branches ahead. Vogek looked dumbfounded as the creature descended the trunk in the form of a lynx. Several rained from the branches as Vogek passed. They landed on his back and ripped into his hide with their claws. The thickets on the ground extended and opened more wounds.

The pain forced Vogek to toss his bow and draw his sword. He managed to bat off the predators before reaching the river, but the loss of blood was now a factor. Vogek looked to the sky as a swarm of bats raced across the field to leech on his wounds. He swung his sword with precision, but the fight seemed senseless without a fixed target. The bats picked at Vogek, and returned to the sky as he helplessly swung his sword. Vogek followed them to the bank of the river. He cautiously watched as they circled over the head of an old man in armor. His helmet had two bull horns carved to look like pikes. His gloves were shaped like small wooden pikes that catered to the hate on the field. The cold black color of his armor changed as the bats spewed the blood they funneled from Vogek. After he received the blood of his opponent, the helmet of the armor tilted back. The bats swirled into a black fog and dived into the mouth of the old man. A transformation followed the digestion, and brought forth the warrior known as Vlad the Impaler.

Vlad's muscles grew, and creaked in the armor while veins opened faucets of blood. The digestion aided in the outline of his opponent's weakness.

"I hate to dine on animals, but the beast is your better half," quipped Vlad. "Your hooves have increased their speed to avoid death in Hades. They're also strong enough to kick after your death and increase the flow of blood from your heart." He scraped the wood pikes on his gloves to taunt Vogek to charge, and the centaur responded.

Vogek boldly kicked up his hind legs and charged his target. He leapt through the air and dived toward Vlad with the tip of his sword pointed at the center of Vlad's helmet.

Vlad deflected the sword with his right hand in anticipation. He placed the audience in a state of awe as he impaled Vogek on the pike of his left glove. Vogek's hind legs kicked as the wood sprouted hate and extended through the carcass. Vlad dined on the blood that poured from Vogek's midsection. When he was done, he fed the lady of the river. The cameras switched back to the starting line for Glimpse to announce the winner.

"Vogek runs the floor to score with no timeouts or huddles. He rebounds and goes for the shot with five seconds on the clock. *The silence of the crowd … and the heart stops!* I give you the winner of tonight's event—Vlad the Impaler!" announced Glimpse. Glimpse removed a piece of lint from her suit and looked in Gall's direction. "A brief intermission before the next match," she added.

Gall shrugged as he approached the starting line. "Keres with guerilla tactics. I'm not impressed," said Gall.

"You don't have to be. Just make sure your legs are strong enough to pump blood the way Vlad wants. That's how we pay him," replied Glimpse. She left Gall to check on the earnings they had gained from the fight and the footage Mitten had downloaded from the helicopter.

"Is the money coming in like we expected?" asked Mitten.

"The first match is a success. The numbers are unbelievable. I'm streaming your footage on the private site as we speak," answered Glimpse.

"What about Gall's numbers?"

"I told everyone what you told me to say. A Fate will be fighting in the event, but to them he's just one Fate. They said there's no sport without the other two."

Mitten's eyes gained a purple luster as she landed the helicopter.

"Do you still want us to stream the event?" asked Glimpse. Mitten paused to look at Otava while she debated the bond the Fates shared.

"Yes, and increase the guard. I want eyes on every movement on the field," commanded Mitten.

"Consider it done," replied Glimpse.

Within an hour, the event was back online. Glimpse tightened her ponytail and pulled a small thorn from her suit as the cameras focused on her. "Ladies and gentlemen of the underworld, I bring to you the entertainment of gladiatorial combat. Man against beast, beast against monster, and Fate against the gods of the arena! Some of you may know Gall the Abominable enforcer. His abominable frame weaves death, but Vlad the Impaler is also familiar with that realm. Who will come out victorious—the bone breaker or the blood drinker? The departing or departed? Place your bets!"

The cameras focused on Gall at the starting line. He raised his head as he recited the final verse to "A Warrior's Creed." In anticipation of the bout, Mitten flew her helicopter over the starting line. Her eyes widened with amazement as Gall ripped off his shirt. He kicked off his boots to transform into a monstrous wolf state.

"He's also a werewolf?" blurted Otava. Glimpse looked at her laptop as it displayed a sudden increase in numbers. Clients were suddenly calling to place bets. The howling from a pack of wolves came to an abrupt stop as Gall unleashed a howl of reckoning. His nostrils flared in the air as he picked up the peculiar scent of Hel and Victory.

"I know you're here. Why can't I see you?" he asked.

"I have the helm of invisibility. Just follow my lead, and Banter will cover the rear," instructed Sitoel. A devious grin crossed Gall's face as they raced down the path.

Within seconds, the wolf pack had gained ground. Gall and Sitoel's speed had kept them ahead of the pack, while Banter fired rounds that pierced the heart and clung to the soul. The carcasses of the wolves were pushed back from the impact, and they disintegrated on the ground. The alpha dodged a round as he jumped into the shadows to take on the form of a lynx. When Gall saw the luster of red pupils resting on the branch of a tree, he transformed into his lycan state and stood in the center of the path.

"Why are you stopping?" asked Sitoel.

"I want you to use your guns. Fire them in the direction I throw a punch," replied Gall. Bloodthirsty predators descended the trees, and Sitoel fired her guns as Gall threw punches in their direction.

The muzzle flashes made it appear as if he had the ability to shoot bullets from his paws. They soaked up the blood faster than the thickets. When it was over, the leader of the pack stepped into the shadows to take on the form of a bat. Gall and Sitoel continued to the bank of the river with ease as a swarm of bats circled over Vlad the Impaler. They charged at the duo under the cover of night and met a grisly demise. Sitoel's aim and speed made her victorious in battle. Headshots echoed through the field as Gall continued to shadowbox for amusement.

When it was over, only the bat with bright red eyes remained. He flew to Vlad the Impaler and dived into his mouth as a small strand of smoke.

"Nothing! I know nothing about you!" Vlad angrily shouted.

"I am Gall. Embrace me!" replied Gall. The response infuriated Vlad the Impaler. He raced to Vogek's carcass to drain what little blood remained for the unexpected battle. The desperate surge provoked another transformation. Vlad the Impaler suddenly took on the form of the Keres. The wings of a bat extended from his back, and he used his claws to rip off his armor. A pair of fangs overlapped his lip as his nostrils shaped like bats. They flared and caught the faint scent of Sitoel's bleeding cheek.

"So that is the secret of your shield. You are truly a deceptive creature, but you fail to realize I can still smell blood!" shouted Vlad the Impaler. He raced to Sitoel's position, and she dived into the river to escape. "How fortunate, you chose the currents of an angry river god to deliver your fate. You also left your companion without a shield," said Vlad the Impaler. He disappointedly watched the dive as Sitoel removed the helm of invisibility. She safely placed it in a pouch fastened to her waistline. While Gall discreetly charged from behind to take advantage of the distraction.

"I don't need a shield," boasted Gall. Vlad quickly turned and felt a hard blow to the head. Inches from falling into the river, Vlad regained his senses and took flight into the air.

"Let's bring the battle to a higher level!" shouted Vlad. He flew to Poenari Castle as a Marid Djinn emerged to weave a fate of classic horror cinema.

Gall relentlessly pursued Vlad with the speed of a Monstrous wolf, and Mitten followed in her helicopter. When he had reached the castle, Gall returned to his lycan state to scale the decrepit foundation. Vlad flew through the castle to gather objects to throw and unknowingly stumbled into the range of Banter's hiding place. A barrage of automatic fire pierced Vlad's leg as he struggled to take flight.

"There's three of them!" uttered Vlad. Gall raced to Vlad's position while Sitoel fought the currents of a angry river god. She reached the coffin with the strength and speed of Victory. A small open patch revealed the cold stare that belonged to the lady of the river.

The frame of her cold corpse captured the image of a buried jewel on the lips. A lizard-like tongue waved from her mouth for the taste of more blood. The sight provoked a string of curses from Sitoel as she leaned in for a kiss. The impact blew her out of the water as the lady of the lake rose from her grave. She took flight and dropped the net of invisibility at Sitoel's feet. Sitoel suspiciously watched as she licked her fangs and flew to the castle. Centuries of hate fueled her hunger.

After Gall picked up Banter's scent, he used his gunfire for another round of shadowboxing. Otava focused her camera on Gall as two jabs from the right hand followed two rounds. The rounds penetrated Vlad's right wing, and he spiraled out of control. Gall jumped on the body as it sank past the cliff. He steered Vlad with the intention of impaling him on a tree, but the lady of the river interfered. She impaled Vlad's heart with the arrow of hate that imprisoned her.

Gall jumped back to the cliff, and watched as the arrow anchored Vlad into a coffin that fell into the river. He curiously scaled the terrain back to the bank where the lady of the river landed.

"Why did you do it?" he asked.

"I was sent on a mission to find love, and Apollo punished me for it," she answered. "Vlad added to my torment after he discovered my betrayal. He would purposely spill blood to awaken me from a cursed sleep. A swallow kept me awake for years, and the cries of a river god followed. Do I have to explain my actions any further?"

"No, but where is Cupid's bow?"

Shortly after asking the question, an invisible Sitoel threw a punch into Gall's midsection. He dropped to his knees in shock as she unleashed her frustrations.

"You have no idea what I've been through," Sitoel complained in a tone that carried a hiss. "First I had to bow down to Hel. Then, I had to run through a field filled with hate and fight Dracula. He chased me into a river, where this thing tongue-kissed me!"

"You sound like Tobias," joked Gall.

"You sound like you're hurt," replied Sitoel.

Gall nodded as he staggered to his feet.

"I haven't seen you throw a punch like that since Banter strapped liquid nitrogen to your neck. It feels like old times," replied Gall.

"Now you can let me explain the difference between Pandora and Hope," said Sitoel.

"There's no need for you to explain. I found out from Iblis. Now, you have to leave before the Furies get suspicious."

Sitoel looked toward the sky as Mitten approached in her helicopter. She quickly placed the net of invisibility in a pouch fastened to her waistline and discreetly made an exit seconds before Glimpse arrived with her war party.

They aimed their rifles as the lady of the river took flight.

"Let her go, we have the one we want!" shouted Glimpse.

"I guess I was worried about the wrong pair of legs," said Glimpse. "What happened out there? A signal jammed our cameras after Vlad fell into the river?"

"Maybe a paranormal occurrence disrupted the electrical currents," replied Gall. "I've been known to have that effect. I'll take this for payment." He walked to where Vlad's gloves lay and embraced them like a trophy.

"We'll finish this conversation back on the yacht," replied Glimpse.

While the Furies prepared for the next event, the Lycan buccaneers stormed Existere's stronghold. Several explosive charges placed by Prison Levelfield cleared a path for entry. The bloodshed from battle accumulated as coronary arteries piled up from the use of their punch technique. Rottenvein struggled to keep pace as they fought their way to the prison beneath. They decorated the pathways with blood and torn limbs until they found Lord Treachery. Rottenvein squirmed through the crowded doorway as they carried him out of an open cell.

"I haven't seen one done this badly since Calico Jack," whispered

Bopo Lava. Rottenvein looked over the battered body as Timber Orslope and Unchained Gauge gently placed him on the ground. The chest was torn open, and poison still fizzed around a broken rib cage.

Rottenvein ran to a corner of the room and vomited from the sight of organs functioning without skin.

"I'm surprised something like this would make you sick," said Bopo Lava.

"Only my brain germs move after death. How could he still be alive?" asked Rottenvein. The roar of a revving chopper motorcycle engine gained everyone's attention. Iblis emerged from the smoke of the surrounding torches to answer.

"He's alive because he made a pact with me!" shouted Iblis. The Lycan buccaneers gathered around Iblis as he stood over the body.

"The pact was signed and sealed on the night he was attacked in Campeche," explained Iblis. "Damphirs disguised as Spanish soldiers were about to act out their orders when Lord Treachery called out to me. He was willing to barter anything to return to his brother and exact revenge for his father. We struck a deal, and no one can break it but me."

"I knew there was a catch to Enemy's story," mumbled Rottenvein. He slowly made his way back to the body. He watched the chest close as Lord Treachery screamed the last word before his death.

"Copasetic!"

His eyes widened, and gray hairs filled with poison stained his fur. The patches shed from his skin as Unchained Gauge raised him to his feet. Bones snapping back in place helped replace the claws torn out by heated pincers. A new pair extended as Lord Treachery became whole again. The Lycan buccaneers cheered as he unleashed a devious growl.

"I will have my day," said Lord Treachery. "The fools thought it was safe to talk after my staged death. Copesetic plans to return to Lake Champlain to retrieve Thor's armor. He needs it to wield Existere's bow."

"Who did you leave in charge while you were tending to my affairs in this realm?" asked Iblis.

"Destroyer," Lord Treachery blurted before passing out.

"His body is still feeling the effects of the poison. Return him to his lair in the Adirondacks," commanded Iblis.

Timber Orslope obediently compiled and carried Lord Treachery to safety.

When he was gone, Iblis gave Rottenvein instructions for a surprise attack. "Hel looking for weapons and armor is a threat to my plans. I want you to return with them, and inform Enemy of the events that have taken place. Tell him to drink long and hard while he sails the *Deaf Dum Dead*. Nothing is to be left behind when he reverses the act committed here."

"Reverses the act?" asked Rottenvein.

A sinister laugh crept from under Iblis's hood as the Lycan buccaneers simultaneously shouted, "THE BLOOD EAGLE!"

The following day, Iblis discreetly made his way through an open porthole on the Furies' explorer yacht. A thick fog of smoke transformed into the shadow of a hooded figure as Gall placed Vlad the Impaler's gloves on the bed.

"You were victorious in battle. Now give me my reward," said Iblis.

"I have the gloves that belonged to Vlad the Impaler. The wood pikes are filled with hate and will extend to impale a victim in your grasp," replied Gall.

"Excellent. My sources tell me Sitoel possesses Cupid's bow. She also has the net and helm of invisibility. My Marid Djinns have fulfilled my expectations. It grieves me to say the Abominables have become a disappointing concern. Copasetic tortured and killed Lord Treachery. He only survived the ordeal because of a pact he made with me. Unfortunately for Copasetic, the experience of a chest being ripped open and claws removed by heated pincers remained," said Iblis.

"It doesn't change the deal!" shouted Gall.

Iblis walked to the open porthole and waved his hand over it. It cast a vision of the Lycan buccaneers' lair.

"I'm going to tell you a secret that was kept between two brothers. Treachery and Enemy vowed to avenge their father's murder. They slowly discovered how difficult the task would be after narrow escapes and countless battles. The bounty on their heads was getting higher. Survival only guaranteed more enemies. They were forced to bring another lycan into their circle in case they failed. This lycan had to learn their bond. He also had to compete with their brutality and bloodlust. They found such a being and made him a Lycan buccaneer. To enhance this chemistry, they killed three of the most ruthless buccaneers and stole their identities. This is the finished product," explained Iblis.

Gall approached the porthole for a closer look. He saw Unchained Gauge escorting Rottenvein aboard a ship. He leaned in closer to overhear the conversation.

"What type of atrocity is this?" complained Rottenvein. "There are no weapons on this ship. The builder only constructed masts. How am I to fire my brain germs?"

"The sight of the masts on this ship will strike more fear in the enemy than any cannon. I introduce to you the Destroyer," replied Unchained Gauge. Rottenvein stepped aside as a Lycan buccaneer with a protective vest climbed the deck. A pouch filled with nails and a hammer was strapped to his waist.

Rottenvein suspiciously watched as the Destroyer pulled a chain with five Scythian archers bound to it.

"The scouts are a welcome home present for my brothers," boasted the Destroyer. He tied his prisoners to a mast as Enemy climbed the deck with one under his claw.

"Let the party begin!" shouted the Destroyer. He extended a claw and swiped through the midsection of one of his prisoners. He reached inside the incision and grabbed the intestine. He pulled, and he pinned it to a mast just a few feet away. The Destroyer cut the bindings to the sound of laughter. Everyone cheered as the organ

pulled the prisoner to the opposite mast. After taking a few steps, the
Destroyer dug a claw into his back and repeatedly tapped the spine.

"Dance!" he shouted. The prisoner unwillingly complied until
his insides poured out. The Destroyer continued down the line for
the amusement of the Lycan buccaneers. After the death of his prisoners, he placed five scratches on his vest.

"I will quadruple that amount when I sail the Deaf Dum Dead
tonight," challenged Enemy.

Enemy extended a claw and placed a scratch on his vest. He
kicked the legs from under his prisoner as Lord Treachery climbed
the deck in his Monstrous wolf form. In preparation for the Blood
Eagle, Enemy cut the bindings of his prisoner and made use of his
infrasound. The blood curdling growl halted the thought of escape
as Enemy exercised his jaws. His prisoner looked for a route to run,
but another threatening growl hid behind every mast Lord Treachery
curled around. The Destroyer joined in, and the sounds sickened
the prisoner with fear. He struggled to get to his feet and discovered
his skin was peeled from his back. A slow fade to darkness followed
the sting of his ribs being torn from his spinal column. A puddle
of blood stained his knees. He suddenly realized he had taken his
eyes off Enemy for too long. He was paralyzed with fear from the
moment Enemy carved out the eagle.

Enemy severed the lung and gave the prisoner his only hope for
escape.

"That's record time," complimented the Destroyer.

"I want his body hanging from the main mast. After tonight,
I want enough skin to make flags and sail Lake Champlain," commanded Enemy.

"Aye!" shouted the Lycan buccaneers. The vision quickly faded
away as Gall turned to Iblis.

"I can tell you everything is going to be alright, but I'm afraid
you'll see right through me," heckled Iblis.

"You'll never complete your collection of weapons if one hair is
harmed on his head," warned Gall.

Iblis released a sigh of grief from under his hood. He snatched the gloves from Gall and buried them in the inner pocket of his robe. "I guess I can sneak them away from the pack. I'll have to lie about a private torture in my domain, but you'll have to fulfill your promise. Every weapon you win in battle, or your death!" A thick mist of smoke smothered Iblis frame.

"Wait, you said them'?" asked Gall.

"The Abominables are whole again. Their new names are Time and Chance," answered Iblis. The thick mist funneled through the porthole and dived into a small whirlpool with the revving sound of a chopper motorcycle engine.

Shortly afterwards, Gall heard footsteps approaching the rails above him. He used his lycan ears to eavesdrop on the conversation. On deck, Glimpse approached Mitten with news of the upcoming match.

"Our spies in the Himalayas have detected a problem. The Sacred Order of the Dragon sent Tabasco King to look for us," said Glimpse.

"If Tabasco King is there, an order of complete silence has been issued. Why don't you tell them the truth? William murdered their friend," replied Otava.

"William did it after we told them who he was," explained Mitten. "We are just as much to blame. I knew the Corpse Candle would become a problem. It's grown too powerful over the years. You can't keep a weapon like that a secret from the Sacred Order of the Dragon."

"You can't keep that kind of power a secret from anyone. Hel expects us to extract Gram from it. This event may prove to be our last one yet," said Glimpse.

Mitten's facial expression changed from a concerned frown to a cunning smirk.

"If this is going to be our last event, let's go out with a bang," suggested Otava.

"My thoughts exactly," said Mitten. She walked to the rails of the deck and gazed at the full moon.

"We're going to make our next match a *Substance* match. All our fighters will take part. Inform the yeti tribe and all of our clients," instructed Mitten.

"Excellent choice," replied Glimpse. "The arena is both contained and secluded. I'll make the necessary arrangements. The loss of Vlad the Impaler ended the doubts of Gall's abilities. We should have an increase in income this time around."

"Gall's abilities?" said John Bullhorns. "Traces of a high-powered rifle and tracks of an attack on the ground weakened Vlad the Impaler. Gall's friends were involved in his victory."

Otava joined Mitten by the ship's rail and released tears of blood.

"There should be no interference in this match. We have to have a plan in place, just in case they're lucky enough to find the location," said Otava.

"Lucky? Gaining entry into the yetis' forbidden arena surpasses luck. Only the yeti king and his second in command can do so. They would have to find and fight the entire tribe to get their key. If they happen to leap over that obstacle, they'll find a Titan, the Corpse Candle, and the Kangchenjunga Demon on the field. The terrain is also against them. Tracks can easily be made and detected in the snow. I'd say the odds are heavily stacked in our favor. In fact, I'm going to announce the fight like an old country song. *Even the road ran out on me!*" explained Glimpse.

Gall looked at the sea as a purple aura accumulated from Otava's tears.

"I know you care about him, but our lives and everything we've built is at stake," said Mitten.

"We never had a match with all of our fighters in one ring. It's more of an execution than a passage to atonement," said Otava.

"Don't fool yourself, every battle fought has been an execution," advised Mitten. "Our fighters became gladiators because they were too powerful for us to defeat. Fate has changed that for us. Vlad the Impaler has been defeated, and the others will be in a weakened state after the match. We can take what we want from whoever is left standing. If you want Gall to achieve atonement, keep a close eye on him until we reach the Himalayas. It will keep his friends away and increase our chances as well."

Shortly after the Furies' meeting, Gall heard a knock on his door. He opened it and fell into the lure of purple eyes.

"I knew it was only a matter of time before my charms worked on you," boasted Gall.

"A thousand curses for your charms," replied Otava. "They separated me from a goose feather mattress. I have to keep a close eye on you until we reach the Himalayas. We can take time to study this footage before our next match."

Gall stepped aside and gestured for Otava to enter.

"You mentioned our next match. Will I be fighting Gutter Ash?" Gall coyly asked. A frown crossed Otava's face in response. She removed a disc from the pocket of her sweatsuit and inserted it into the disc player.

"The next match is going to be a *Substance* match. All of our fighters will face off in Zemu Glacier," answered Otava. She pushed play and walked to the bed. "There's no footage on Gutter Ash, or the Titan," she added as she kicked off her boots and lay back on the bed.

"That's okay, I saw the Furies and the sickle in action already. I just need to satisfy my curiosity with the other fighters," replied Gall. He sat down beside her to watch the footage that involved the Kangchenjunga Demon.

"The yeti tribe forbade anyone from entering their sanctuary," said Otava. "They transform into Asian black bears to help keep their identity a secret. We used to strap a camera to the back of a bear to get footage of the kill, but that was in the past. The old king, Mirka, was replaced by his second in command. He cares little for the laws of their land and boldly walks in his yeti form. He is known as the Kangchenjunga Demon. After he revolted against Mirka, he

raided one of the sacred repositories of the Himalayas. He stole a
tree branch that was heavily guarded in their vault."

Gall watched the footage of a yeti entering an arena surrounded
by snow and ice. In a pouch fastened to his back was a large tree
branch.

"What's so special about the tree branch?" asked Gall.

"Shiva wanted to make room for a dance. So he swept it through
a lake and drained it of its water," answered Otava. Gall continued
to watch the footage as Glimpse introduced his opponent—a giant
with an eye solely for murder, still snacking on flesh that hung from
the spikes on his club—Rimpeck, the cyclops. At first it seemed as
though the battle would be won by brute strength. Rimpeck towered
over the Kangchenjunga Demon and tumbled over with laughter as
the demon transformed into an Asian black bear.

"I would rather you stay that way until I make a rug out of your
hide," threatened Rimpeck.

The Kangchenjunga Demon charged at Rimpeck and dodged
the fatal blows of a spiked club. He used his hind claws to skate on
the ice, while his arms scratched and clawed Rimpeck's legs.

"Did you think a couple of scratches would finish me? Charge at
me again, and I'll have the hide I'm promised!" shouted Rimpeck.
The Kangchenjunga Demon returned to his yeti form. He removed
the tree branch holstered on his back and locked it between his jaws.

The Kangchenjunga Demon returned to the form of an Asian
black bear and charged at Rimpeck. Rimpeck tightly gripped his
club and prepared a final blow. He made a batting stance and nearly
slipped on a puddle of blood. The scratches were deeper than he
thought. He looked up as the Kangchenjunga Demon skated past
his legs and brushed the branch against his wounds. Within seconds,
the leaves had latched to the flesh, causing the wounds on Rimpeck's
body to exsanguinate.

"Pay close attention to this part," said Otava.

The tribe began to chant mantras, and the Kangchenjunga
Demon fed off the vibe. He pulled the branch with increased

strength, and Rimpeck tumbled forward. The Kangchenjunga
Demon returned to his yeti form, walked to Rimpeck's eye and tore
it from the socket. He held it up to the camera as Mitten flew by
and shouted, "Praetorian!"

The footage ended with the Kangchenjunga Demon pounding
the pupil into a disc of matter as thin as a rug.

"They have a rejuvenation pool beneath the arena. The king
bathes before a match and gains strength from the tribe as they
chant mantras for healing. If Rimpeck had been lucky enough to hit
him with the club, he still would've survived the attack," explained
Otava. She pointed to the screen as it introduced the next opponent.
"Religious fanatics across the globe pay top dollar to see what fate
befalls William. He turned his back on Saint Peter after he offered
passage into heaven. A few days after that, he found a community of
dark elves and increased his skill in forging. He invented the Corpse
Candle, and a sword named Gram is a part of it. It has the ability to
cut through anything. He uses it to attack and defend. It also helps
him drill through terrain. It has made him the deadliest opponent
in our circuit."

Gall watched as a man in black fatigues walked into a warehouse
armed with a Calico M960. Shortly afterwards, a flying object that
resembled the flame of a candle followed him inside. Gall turned up
the volume after he heard gunfire.

"Why isn't there any footage from inside?" he asked.

"Just keep watching," replied Otava.

Gall waited and saw the flame of a candle exit the main door.
The man it followed inside unexpectedly walked out in a dazed state.
He followed the flame for miles. When he had reached a marsh, a
heavily armed hydrofoil with a cross and dragon on the hull came
to his rescue.

Gall carefully watched as a surprise attack tore the hull in half.
The four passengers swam and huddled around each other while
firing in every direction. Small waves slowly separated them and
pulled them under one by one. The torn carcasses floated back to

the surface as the Corpse Candle muffled the underwater gunfight. Only the soldier that stood on the bank of the marsh remained. The flame slowly began to dim as the Corpse Candle leapt from the marsh. On the back of his cape was the outline of a sword. It waved through the air as though it wasn't affected by the water. The candle lit flame returned to his helmet as a piece of coal. He extended his hand, and It glowed with a silver lining as he waved it through the soldier. When he was done, he dragged the torn carcass into the depths of the marsh.

"He kept that one? Does he like to collect trophies?" asked Gall.

"No, he just wanted to send a message"

"I guess we have our hands full"

"*You* have *your* hands full. Especially if you think you can defeat us with what you saw. Nothing is what it appears to be. You can lose your head before the attack. We all depend on something. If you're lucky, you'll find out what it is before you die," advised Otava.

On the south end of Lake Champlain, Copasetic lined up a small army of Scythian archers on the bridge. Time stood by his side, while Chance anchored a boat in the lake with a crew of soldiers.

"All our scouts and three infantry divisions have failed to return. It's fair to say that we've been discovered," said Time.

"Other people's plasma! If you want to hunt in the wolf's den, you have to learn the pack," replied Copasetic. Chance aided two divers as they brought up the last piece of Thor's armor.

"We have what we came for. Hurry and climb aboard. I'm starting to get a bad feeling about this," said Chance.

The ship docked at Crown Point Lighthouse to unload the armor. The shadow of a large bird stepped from behind the structure in anticipation of its cargo.

"Decoy is here. Fasten the crate to his leg so he can be on his way," commanded Chance. The soldiers did as they were told. When they were done, Decoy took flight to Mount Defiance to deliver the crate. As the soldiers prepared to leave, a thick fog unexpectedly crept over the area. It blanketed the lake and smothered the shore like a tidal wave. It provided the perfect cover for an attack. The Lycan buccaneers crept in the center to surround the lighthouse and cover both ends of the bridge.

The moonlight focused on the lake, and provided a terrifying sight as the Deaf Dum Dead sailed with a small ship under tow. It stirred an insurmountable amount of tension as it displayed soldiers with their insides loose. A string of corpses hung from the top mast with the skin of their backs sewn to make a sail. Chance looked to the bridge for cover as a pack attacked his crew. They quickly slain his men as Collard Legends gripped the collar of Chance's armor and threw him onto the deck of the ship. Copasetic signaled his archers, and they lit the tips of their arrows in response.

"Make sure your aim is accurate. They will not give you a second chance," advised Time. The archers prepared to fire on the Deaf Dum Dead. They waited for Copasetic's signal, but the infrasound from the pack on the bridge interrupted.

A chorus of growls and snarls echoed from the fog. The fear of sticking a hand out and having it bitten suddenly took hold of the archers. The paws of two vengeful Monstrous wolves quickly took advantage of the moment. They snuffed out the light of a fireball as they attacked from opposite ends. Enemy raced across the bridge and swiped his claws across every vital organ that stood in his way. Lord Treachery pounced on the back of Time during the skirmish.

"Surrender or he dies now!" shouted Lord Treachery. He locked his jaws on Time's neck to express the seriousness of his words.

Copasetic turned to his men, and saw Enemy's aftermath as he placed a claw to his neck. Enemy extended the claw on his free paw and placed twenty scratches on a vest that now resembled a scratching post. The Abominable generals were dragged to the rails of the bridge and saw their Chance bound to a mast on the Deaf Dum Dead.

"What obnoxious cost brings you here today, after what you inflicted on my captain yesterday. Now we laugh at what you borrowed, you won't get to use it tomorrow,'" recited Obnoxious Koss.

The Lycan buccaneers tossed the Abominable generals off the bridge. They landed on the deck of the Deaf Dum Dead as it passed underneath, and fell into the clutches of the Destroyer.

"Iblis requested that nothing be left behind to tell a tale. Clean up the mess and be back in time for the party," instructed Enemy.

"Aye!" shouted the Lycan buccaneers.

The next morning, the Abominable generals were dragged and tied to the masts of the Destroyer's ship. In preparation for the party, he removed their armor and nailed the pieces to the opposite mast.

"You'll be chasing after your own armor when I nail the end of your intestine to it," joked the Destroyer. The Lycan buccaneers tumbled over with laughter before the roar of a revving chopper motorcycle engine interrupted. Iblis emerged from a thick fog of smoke and settled into a hooded cloak to oversee the execution. He joined Lord Treachery and Enemy on deck as the Destroyer swiped a claw across Time's abdomen. The Abominable generals responded with laughter. Removing the intestine only tickled Time.

The Destroyer nailed it to the opposite mast and cut the bindings. He buried a claw in Time's spine and tapped it to his amusement. "Dance!" he shouted. The laughter of the Abominable generals drowned out the cheers of the Lycan buccaneers. Time collapsed and rolled with laughter while his organs pooled on the deck.

Rottenvein ran to the rails and vomited overboard. "What sordid pact did this one make?" he asked. He returned to look over the body while Iblis investigated the scene.

"It's not the Abominable generals!" snapped Iblis. The Lycan buccaneers extended their claws in defense as Iblis pried open Time's mouth. He pulled Entice out by the tongue.

"Hel's servants are the answer to this mystery," explained Iblis. He released Entice, and she fled back to Helheim without hesitation. Iblis pried open the mouth of Chance and Copasetic. To everyone's surprise, he pulled Lies and Deceit out by the tongue. They kicked and screamed while he dragged them back to Lord Treachery.

"Curse that Hel queen. She has robbed us of our revenge!" shouted Enemy.

"Take every lycan you have to track Decoy. I saw him land in Mount Defiance before the battle!" commanded Iblis. Enemy responded with a nod as every Lycan buccaneer in the lair raced to that location. Iblis held back Lord Treachery until the lair was empty.

"What am I to do?" asked Lord Treachery.

"I want you to be Rottenvein," replied Iblis. "Hel and the Abominable generals believe they've outsmarted us. They've forgotten that when it comes to Lies and Deceit, I fathered them all"

While flying over the Himalayas, Tobias pointed out several sacred places to Detective Rodriguez.

"Are you thinking about converting?" asked Tobias.

"No, I struggle with faith. The majority usually becomes the norm when I'm at work. Being in spiritual environments of high regard helps me connect with my soul," answered Detective Rodriguez. Banter watched Akantha until she finished her phone call. She folded her cell phone and looked out the window with tears in her eyes. Banter turned to Anesidora and saw another troubled expression. Anesidora looked out the window as though it was the last time she'd see those sights.

"I keep waiting for Hope to surface with that encouraging phrase of hers," said Banter.

Anesidora turned to Akantha and waited for her explanation.

"My friends tell me the next match will be a Substance match," said Akantha. "All the fighters will face off in one arena. No form of life has ever entered it without the yeti's permission. Gall will fight the Kangchenjunga Demon, the Corpse Candle, and a Titan in Zemu Glacier. If he wins, he'll have to face the Furies."

"So that's why it's taking Hope so long to surface. She's struggling to find some," replied Banter.

"It's worse than you think," explained Anesidora. "This battle will eventually become a war for all kinds. If the yeti king wins, he'll assemble an army to conquer the world. The disorder of hierarchy will spill into the realms of those that have survived the first war of the heavens. They had hoped to replenish their ranks for another war, but the punishment for their actions took the immortality given at birth. Their life expectancy was higher than that of mortal beings, but death was now certain." She turned to look out the window as a ray of sunshine entered.

"Tribes were formed and scattered across the globe—also the realms beneath. Some decided to harvest souls through vegetation. Three groups that harvested ambrosia, peaches, and apples were successful. Other groups experimented with armor and weaponry. It was the only vessel suitable enough for their mightiest warriors. Eventually the idea to experiment with another vessel surfaced. It stirred disorder because it dealt with creation. Very few mortals could serve as vessels. Some developed beast-like appearances and characteristics. Others became cannibalistic in nature. It caused great harm to themselves and others. This practice was eventually banned, but others continued to experiment secretly to serve their needs. You've faced this enemy twice before with Pandora and Quinton Blaine"

"Gall said there was something strange about Quinton. He was the only one to survive the attack," said Banter.

Anesidora nervously fiddled with her fingers as though she had never known how to feel or touch.

"They were made from the same clay as me," explained Anesidora. "He outlived his usefulness when he couldn't control the soul. Since that time, his master has developed better chemistry. That is how the Corpse Candle came to be. Iblis sent a mortal to a community of dark elves. He joined and endured the transformation to become one. While he was there, he increased his skill and forged the Corpse Candle. The clay of Hephaestus, and the alchemy of their forbidden metals birthed a vessel that can hold up to six souls at a time—a helmet fused to a piece of burning coal, a hooded cape, and four sleeves. They cover the arms and legs. His creation has shifted in power since the bond of the Marid Djinns. Now there is a sleeve with the lightning staff of Zeus, the trident of Poseidon, the olive club of Heracles, and the Mjollnir. There's no doubt in my mind that Iblis will find a way to add the helm and net of invisibility."

"You said Mjollnir? It's Mjölnir," corrected Banter.

"A lot of them make that mistake, especially when they try to pronounce certain names. I'm betting Akantha used to, but she's gotten better at hiding it. I know because I'm dating a soldier that lost in the first war. It's a helpful clue when you're trying to distinguish them from us," interrupted Detective Rodriguez.

"For the record, my reading and writing still suffers in certain areas. I can't tell you why without judgment from my peers."

"I know, I get the same thing at home. They lost the war and kept their pride. After this trip, she'll run home to better herself"

Sitoel gave Anesidora a pleading look of desperation.

"I was sent to get Hope so she could explain. She has to surface and give me my answers! I've seen the death that waits for us in the arena. If she doesn't surface with a way to beat them, then she should surface for my reasons—so I can know before I die!" Anesidora closed her eyes, and Hope opened them with a smile as bright as a ray of sunshine.

"There is hope, Sitoel," greeted Hope.

"I want to know who I really belong to," replied Sitoel. "After hearing Anesidora, I'm starting to speculate if I'm even human."

"You are not made like Anesidora. Here is where you belong, and your family is about to get bigger. You feel the same as when you first bonded with the ones that stir inside Banter and Gall. It's only natural to feel the same way when you face the fourth Marid Djinn," said Hope.

"The *fourth* Marid Djinn?" interrupted Banter.

"There is another one connected to you. He is the weaver of your fates," answered Hope. She turned to Akantha, who nodded her head in approval. "The first great war of the heavens benefited no one but Iblis. During that time, he pickpocketed a key from the Archangels. It had the power to open realms in the heavens and abyss. It can also pass through time. Iblis learned of the key and had it forged during his imprisonment. He enlisted the help of one of the Eight Immortals. Lu Dongbin's sword contained a special ink that helped forge his drawings into existence. Iblis manipulated Lu Dongbin into using that gift so he could return the original key. Lu Dongbin agreed, and an evil occurrence took place. He copied the key and the engraved writing in detail. To his surprise, the silhouette of a small child surfaced instead. Iblis pulled the child from the pit, and created three Marid Djinns to serve as its protector. Similar to a mortal child, the fourth Marid Djinn ran erratic with its ability to explore everything. It discreetly emerged in gods and demigods for secrets. He also inhabited animals and mythological beasts for their strengths and weaknesses."

Hope briefly looked in the direction of Detective Rodriguez. "It also emerged in the vessels of mortals. Especially those familiar with war. He would frequently practice military tactics, combat maneuvers, and hand-to-hand fighting skills. Unfortunately, his erratic jumps through time made it difficult to keep up with him. His mortal vessel was assassinated before the Marid Djinns were able to emerge in the Praetorian Guard."

*"My* Praetorian?" asked Detective Rodriguez.

"Yes, the fourth Marid Djinn served as a Roman emperor. He also served as a president and soldier of war. An angel discovered his presence while he was out collecting souls in the winter of Valley Forge," answered Hope.

*"Washington!* That thing was inside George Washington and they didn't vanquish it!" interrupted Detective Rodriguez.

"It was more of an interrogation. He was able to communicate with George Washington and discovered the intentions of the fourth Marid Djinn without disturbing the timeline," answered Hope.

Detective Rodriguez gripped the handle of his sidearm with anger. "Don't give me no crap about timelines. I still carry the scars that thing gave me. The angels should've looked past an interrogation and remembered how Washington attacked on Christmas!" he snapped.

"I looked to you because I know those wounds still ail you. Do not be a troubled detective, there is hope. Your hatred and battles with the fourth Marid Djinn keeps the Sacred Order of the Dragon from disposing of you. There was a time when they considered making you a member. You just had the misfortune of making an alliance with the other three Marid Djinns before they could bring you in."

"Are you implying that I should be grateful?"

"Yes, it makes you the perfect bait. It also gives us an opportunity to avoid a war the world is not ready for."

Detective Rodriguez disappointedly turned away and leaned back in his seat to ponder on Hope's point.

"Do not be troubled with your situation," said Hope. "You have the assistance of three Marid Djinns, and they have a net and helm of invisibility."

"What good are weapons when I see our death in the arena? I can win a battle, but I'll lose the war. They can't see you, but they can track your footprints and pick up your scent," said Sitoel.

"There's a way to walk safely among them. You must free Mirka," advised Hope.

"Who is he?" asked Sitoel.

"He is the yeti king by birthright," answered Hope. "The Kangchenjunga Demon plotted his capture while he was in the form of a black bear. He now resides in a cage located in Kangchenjunga's National Park. You should also know he hates humans."

Sitoel and Banter looked at each other with uncertainty.

"Does Hope have to explain everything?" snapped Akantha.

"Yes, when it comes to asking a yeti that hates humans for an escort into his sanctuary!" replied Banter.

"Sitoel already possesses the power and skills to do so," said Hope. "She can utilize Cupid's bow, but remember Victory is in your blood. An echo of karma also follows. You need only whisper love or hate before blowing a kiss to fire an arrow."

"Now I can devise a plan," said Banter.

Hope sunk back into the deep thoughts of Anesidora. She left a hint about Akantha before leaving.

Everyone's ears suddenly perked to an unexpected argument between them. They tried not to stare while overhearing a conversation in babel.

"There are no secrets between Hope and me," said Anesidora. "You are one of the ones that meddled with creation. The vessels of the Marid Djinns were not made of clay. You exercised other means. That practice was also banned, and how long before the detective finds out he's like me. You mothered them all!"

"I was assigned to care for the fourth Marid Djinn after the death of the emperor," replied Akantha. "I had to find ways to get them together and avoid another death. I beg you not to judge me, or place me in a situation to become an assassin to keep my secret." Akantha made the subtle tone of babel put everyone at ease. While Anesidora nervously nodded her head in agreement.

In Helheim, Copasetic reunited Existere's vision with the arrogance of her bow, and her poisoned bone arrows. Soldiers cheered and knelt as he performed trick shots in the midst of a snowstorm.

When the display was over, Copasetic returned to the throne room. "I've earned their recognition," he said.

"Yes, but you nearly cost me an entire army," complained Hel. "The casualties in the Adirondacks are unacceptable."

"Other people's plasma! You could've sent a fearless general in after you tortured and murdered their captain. I guarantee he'd have the same results. As well as his own death."

"If strategy is your defense, then you'll have no problem on your next mission," said Hel. "My spies tell me the Furies will be hosting a *Substance* match. All of their fighters will battle in an arena in Zemu Glacier. I have a lot invested in this event. I chose to increase the

Furies' chances. I want you to take as many soldiers as you need. You must infiltrate the rejuvenation chamber beneath Zemu Glacier."

"What do I do when I get inside?"

"A new ally has joined our ranks. You will watch over him while he infests the pool with brain germ."

Copasetic turned to the entrance of the throne room as Lord Treachery entered in the disguise of Rottenvein. In response, he quickly loaded a bone arrow into his bow and took aim.

"What makes you think you can trust a turncoat?" shouted Copasetic.

"Lower your weapon," said Hel. "There is no better lie detector than Lies and Deceit. They circle him without repeating his words. He'll taint the waters of the rejuvenation pool to further prove his loyalty."

"My Hel queen has yet to tell me how I could achieve this task. My brain germs will not survive in those conditions," replied Lord Treachery.

"You will retrieve a flame from the pit of Helheim. It will weather the pool until the task is done," answered Hel.

"Am I to serve you my own ashes after I break the frostbite of your storm and reach the flames of your pit? The fire is rumored to be stronger than lava," replied Lord Treachery. He cautiously stepped back as a small stream of smoke funneled from Hel's nose.

"Temper!" she shouted as her servants gathered behind her. Temper jumped out of the crowd and knelt before his queen. "Go to my pit and retrieve a flame. You will use it to weather brain germ in the rejuvenation pool in Zemu Glacier. You will return when the yeti king is done with his bath," explained Hel. Temper dived through the floor of the throne room and landed in the pit of Helheim. He quickly snatched a flame and floated back to the throne. Temper entered Hel's body, and the flame highlighted the dragon tattoo on her frame. She exhaled the smoke while Temper pulled the flame from her mouth. He gained a manlike appearance while he weathered the effects of third degree burns.

"You have everything you need," said Hel. "Now camouflage my archers for the snow of the Himalayas, and bring me Gram"

They raced from the throne room while the Lycan buccaneers gathered around Iblis in their lair. In the center of his palms were the tongues of Lies and Deceit. They repeated Lord Treachery's conversation and whereabouts since his arrival in Helheim.

"You heard the words of your Captain. We must set the sails of the Deaf Dum Dead for the Himalayas. I also have a stake in this event. We will leave Rottenvein here and pick up another ally on the way," commanded Iblis.

Days later, flyers regarding a missing bear were already circling the town when the Furies arrived. The Deaf Dum Dead was anchored a few miles from Zemu Glacier, and Tabasco King was lurking in the vicinity. The midnight breeze sprinkled snow on a black face mask with purple flames as the Furies gathered on deck. Their purple aura highlighted the chainmail behind their breastplates to match the fire in their eyes. Their armor was identical, and Mitten giving orders was the only way Gall could tell them apart.

"John Stormcloud and John Hawk will go to town at sunrise to get supplies. We'll meet at Zemu Glacier after the helicopter is fueled," instructed Mitten. She grabbed the other two members of her war party by the fur collars on their coats and took flight. Otava locked arms with Gall, and Glimpse carried the Titan as they followed a trail of northern lights to Kanchenjunga.

When they had reached their destination, four Asian black bears stood upright to escort the notorious gladiator that had defeated Vlad the Impaler. They dug their paws into the white crescent marks on their chests and peeled back the black fur like reversible jackets. The yeti stood at an abominable height as they greeted John Bear and John Bullhorns with sign language. Gall brushed off the cold frost of travel by transforming into his lycan state and unleashed a howl of recognition.

"Rudra!" the yetis nervously shouted as a small landslide buried their feet. They dug into the snow and removed spears made of ice in defense.

"What are they afraid of?" asked Otava.

"They think Gall is a deity named Rudra. He's known to have a great roar and personifies terror. They think he came to punish them for the theft of the branch," explained John Bear.

Mitten looked over Gall with a smirk. "Show them we have the situation under control. Gall is just a man with supernatural abilities like us," she said. John Bullhorns removed his coat and handed it to Gall.

Gall cautiously watched as he removed a hair braid that held three rounds. He tied it around his neck and pounded his chest three times as he endured his transformation. "You were a sasquatch the whole time!" said Gall. The yetis regained their courage as their cousin fearlessly stood eye-to-eye with Gall.

"I warned you about appearances," Otava replied.

"Do not fear his magic," said Mitten. "He had friends that helped him cheat in the event. You are to keep a constant eye on him while I'm with your king."

"That sounds like I'll be staying somewhere else?" replied Gall.

"Zemu Glacier. I made arrangements," answered Mitten. The yetis pointed their spears and escorted Gall down a path to Zemu Glacier.

A yeti stayed behind to continue a conversation with John Bear. He translated it to Mitten as they headed for their hidden sanctuary.

"He said to forgive them for their fear. They have been unnerved after interrupting the hibernation of the Kangchenjunga Demon. They advised him to tend to the matter in the rejuvenation chamber, but he insisted on waiting until the fight."

"Tell him we are even for the mantras he taught the war party," replied Mitten. She turned to whisper to Otava, "Just our luck to be rid of an annoying lycan and get stuck with a disoriented yeti. We'll have to carry him to the rejuvenation chamber first thing in the morning."

Just a few hours before sunrise, the Lycan buccaneers gathered on the deck of the Deaf Dum Dead. Iblis patiently waited for the ally they had picked up along the way, a dark elf. Their guest climbed from below deck, suited with four sleeves and a helmet. Every piece of his armor had the imprint of a weapon filled with a liquid metal. As he approached Iblis, the liquid drained from the imprints and coated his body in silver. When the imprints of the weapons had turned from silver to black, the helmet ignited a spark. A candle lit flame peeled from the center and flew through the air. It circled Iblis as William pulled the hood over his head.

"Hel plans to give Junior a bath. After Rottenvein completes his task, you will drain the pool and eliminate the Titan. I want his sickle before the end of the day," commanded Iblis.

William responded with a nod as he raced across the plank and dived into the water. He broke the border of land and burrowed to Zemu Glacier with the guidance of the burning coal.

When Gall had reached Zemu Glacier, his nostrils perked to the familiar scent of Hell and Victory. He slowly extended his claws as the yetis nostrils flared through the air. Two of them left the group and raised their spears to investigate. As they approached an invisible Sitoel, she greeted them with a whisper and a kiss.

"*Hate*," whispered Sitoel. She blew a kiss that overwhelmed her attackers and forced them to turn on each other. They relentlessly tore into each other's hides until their spears broke. Sitoel removed the helm and approached Gall as he eliminated the last yeti with the lycans' punch technique.

"You're growing," said Sitoel.

"I was eating snow on the way here," answered Gall.

Gall scooped up more snow as Mirka stepped out of the secret entrance of Zemu Glacier. Several of his loyal tribesmen chanted mantras as he endured the benefits of the rejuvenation pool.

"After teaching me your language, the Kangchenjunga Demon tricked me into thinking I could face the perils beyond our borders on my own," said Mirka. "I foolishly abandoned the love shared between a king and his people to do so. Sitoel has given me a second chance. We will form a barrier between the entrance and the rejuvenation pool. I can't guarantee how long it will hold. My soldiers are few, and the others are too scared to face the Kangchenjunga Demon." Mirka shed gray hairs from his body as another coat surfaced, and Tobias flew overhead.

Everyone looked to the sky while Banter and Detective Rodriguez parachuted from the plane. Banter carried a small crate in his hand that held an inflatable raft.

"What surprise is Banter bringing to the field?" asked Gall.

"A hook with bait. The net of invisibility is lined over the raft. When the Corpse Candle pokes it from underneath, it'll drop over him like a curtain and trap him," explained Sitoel.

"I will show you the way to the arena," said Mirka.

On the Furies' explorer yacht, Tabasco King discreetly made his way on board disguised as John Bear. The steps of a sasquatch rocked the vessel as the hair on his body grew, and overlapped the small blade strapped to his wrist.

"John Bear? What happened to your rounds?" asked John Hawk.

"I'm making them," answered Tabasco King. The flicker from his blade was the last thing John Hawk saw before decapitation. Tabasco King discreetly tossed the body overboard and made his way to John Stormcloud as he fueled the helicopter.

"John Bear? Where are your rounds?" asked John Stormcloud.

"You have mine," answered Tabasco King. The flicker of a blade simultaneously removed John Stormcloud's head and braid wrap in one swipe. A devious grin appeared on Tabasco King's face as he tied a necklace with one round around his neck and took the identity John Stormcloud.

He took flight in the helicopter and went over a scheme that involved the removal of the Furies' heads. He felt the plan would be successful until he reached Zemu Glacier. His instincts for hunting immediately picked up the dangers in the area like a radar. He flew over a small group of elite archers led by the warmth of Hel's Temper. On the opposite end, Gall punched through the ceiling of the arena to make room for his fight with a Titan. Behind him, a flame from Iblis guided the Corpse Candle beneath the glacier. In the middle, the Furies and a small army escorted the Kangchenjunga Demon down a path a mile away. The Kanchenjunga Demon's personal guard carried him on their shoulders, while Otava pulled the leash that was fastened to the Titan's neck.

Tabasco King landed the helicopter in a clearing and patiently waited for the Furies to approach. The purple flames in Mitten's eyes warned him of her mood as he gave news of rebels.

"I flew over a large ice barrier and a small army of rebels before I landed. We will have to find another entrance into the glacier," said Tabasco King.

"There is no other entrance!" snapped Mitten. She removed the sickle fastened on her back and signaled the army to prepare for battle.

"The show must go on" shouted Glimpse. She removed a film camera from a backpack and handed it to Tabasco King.

Otava dropped the leash of the Titan and checked her pistols before jumping into the pilot seat of the helicopter.

"Keep the camera off the entrance while broadcasting. I don't want to worry our clientele. I'll meet you inside after I deal with the rebels," said Mitten. Otava responded with a nod while Glimpse pulled Tabasco King into the helicopter to broadcast her introduction to, *"Even the Road Ran Out on Me."*

Shortly after takeoff, Otava discovered the same sights as Tabasco King. Her eyes widened with amazement as she flew around Gall's

new height and appearance. A quick glance of a charcoal flame that
disappeared beneath the glacier also made her aware of the Corpse
Candle.

"We don't have to work our way into the arena," said Glimpse.
"Gall has proven to be more useful than we expected. Circle around
him so I can get footage and hype the introduction for the fight."
Tabasco King focused the camera lens on Gall as Otava circled in
the helicopter. She locked eyes with Gall as he unleashed a howl of
reckoning.

"Good morning, members of the underworld. Today will go
down in history as the biggest gladiatorial event ever orchestrated
by Furies—a *Substance* match we titled, *"Even the Road Ran Out on
Me."* With that, she made her introduction:

Where rain doesn't make it to the other side of the mountain,
like the sickle of a Titan when he's poutin',
the road ran out on me!
Where the roar of a lycan can stir avalanches and mudslides,
and extend a claw to place you in a grave knee-high,
the road ran out on me!
Where the Kangchenjunga Demon sweeps the flesh off the bone
like dust off your clothes,
the road ran out on me!
Where the flicker of the devil's flame
forces you to change lanes,
the Corpse Candle makes his claim.
The road runs out on me!

Otava continued to circle Gall while the bets placed increased.
At the base of Zemu Glacier, Temper began to burrow through to
the rejuvenation pool. Copasetic stood by the entrance of the hole
he made and gestured for Lord Treachery to enter. After he climbed
inside, Copasetic gave the archers a signal to leave.

"You're going to leave him after the tongue-lashing Hel gave you?" asked Time.

"We did our job. The package was safely delivered to Zemu Glacier," answered Copasetic.

"What do we tell her when we return without him?" asked Chance.

"A cold chill crept over me when our new friend entered the throne room," mumbled Copasetic. "I looked him over with new eyes and saw a heart that could beat a lie detector test. No fear or doubt from a turncoat that knows we tortured and murdered their Captain?" He slowly walked away while Time and Chance looked dumbfounded. They removed the hunting knives from their pouches and stabbed the roof of Temper's tunnel until it collapsed.

"Other people's plasma!" they blurted.

As the Abominable generals made their way back to Helheim, Mitten boldly approached Mirka's barrier. Mirka's soldiers cautiously watched as she took flight and hurled her sickle in the direction of their blockade. They quickly threw spears as it increased in size, and the sound of twigs breaking riddled the area as ice shards fell back to the ground. The sickle boomeranged off the blockade and returned to Mitten's hands. The impact stirred a barrage of ice shards that exploded into Mirka's army.

Mitten thought she had the battle won before Mirka appeared on the front line. His muscles grew while his personal guard chanted mantras. He mustered the strength to pick up a large block of ice and catapulted it at the opposing yetis. The impact crushed their front line as Mitten signaled a charge. Mirka took the reins as the best warrior on the field, but the sight of the Kangchenjunga Demon kept the rebels at bay. He slowly regained his senses as he woke from his nap. His eyelids fluttered from the blurred specs that fell on the battlefield. His nostrils flared at the scent of spilt blood, and his glands began to salivate for battle. The Kangchenjunga Demon licked his lips as he consumed the field with a scheme. Mitten waited with anticipation as the environment revived the current king. She landed by his side and commanded, "Move the king to the front line and charge!"

The army obeyed and pushed the rebels back through the shattered barrier. Mirka also took precaution as the Kangchenjunga Demon removed the branch of Shiva harnessed on his back.

"It's over now, my people cannot protect you any further. I need the survivors to rebuild," said Mirka.

"Your tribe will never be the same again if we can't keep him from the rejuvenation chamber. You have to stay and fight!" demanded Banter.

"He's right, they did all they could. It's up to us ... *me,*" said Detective Rodriguez.

"What's that supposed to mean?"

"What would you say to a Roman emperor that was betrayed and slain?"

Banter took a minute to ponder on the question as the Kangchenjunga Demon approached. "*Beware the Ides of March!*" he answered.

Detective Rodriguez ran to the shattered entrance of the blockade to confront the ghost of his past. The Kangchenjunga Demon stopped to make out the blur that boldly stood just a few feet away. He tilted his head to the ground to make use of his other senses as Detective Rodriguez uttered the words "*Beware the Ides of March!*"

The warning ignited an uncontrollable rage in the Kangchenjunga Demon. The twitching of his eyelids stopped, and the muscles in his jaws stretched to formulate words. His pupils turned black as Junior gripped his soul and surfaced on a raised tone. "*Praetorian!*"

Junior plowed through Mirka's army in pursuit, and Mitten grabbed her cell phone from her pocket. She dialed Otava to inform her of the news. "Junior just entered the field," she said. "Keep the camera on the arena entrance, the Kangchenjunga Demon is about to make a bloody introduction."

Detective Rodriguez raced into the maze of the glacier. At the opposite end, Temper and Lord Treachery entered the rejuvenation chamber. Temper ran to the pool and dived in like a traveler stranded in the desert. A thick cloud of steam filled the chamber as he adjusted the temperature of his body. Lord Treachery entered the chamber and cautiously waited to see who followed as he withdrew a small vial from his pocket. When no one else appeared, he feared his disguise was discovered.

"Hurry, the match is about to start. They'll be making an entrance any second!" shouted Temper.

Lord Treachery quickly emptied the contents of the vial into the water. Temper swam to the bottom and stirred a small whirlpool to keep the germ alive. Lord Treachery patiently waited before a candle lit flame unexpectedly burrowed into the rejuvenation chamber. The Corpse Candle followed and broke the ice beneath Lord Treachery's feet. William surfaced through the opening and picked Lord Treachery off the floor with laughter.

"Did I startle you, cousin? I expected the dark elf that endured his transformation with me would be more alert," said William.

"Speak in whispers, a servant of Hel swims in the pool," replied Lord Treachery.

"I thought you followed the pack. I looked for you on the ship, but no one cared to speak of your whereabouts. I guess now I have my answer," replied William.

"I still serve Iblis. I'm on a mission of high importance. I had to contribute a vial of brain germ to please Hel," explained Lord Treachery.

"That puts the fun back into things."

"This is not the time for pranks or jokes."

William took off the helmet of the Corpse Candle and faced Lord Treachery with a stony expression. "This suit has granted me a life as cold as a well digger's feet," he explained. "I hoped it would solidify the rank of general in Iblis's army, but the spot is reserved for three Marid Djinns. Iblis spared no expense for Junior's safety. The sleeves and helmet were forged with the same ingenuity that crafted the Skidbladnir. One size can fit all, and it will accommodate Gall when he wants to increase in height. Only one can wear the helmet, but there's a vault that harbors several sleeves if assistance is needed in weaving a fate."

"I fail to see how the invention of such a weapon can cost you the rank of a general?"

"Ask Iblis that question, and he'll tell you the story of a man that fell into his service after turning away from the heavens. The position and title are reserved only for three Marid Djinns."

"So he welcomed you to hell. As odd as it may seem, I can relate."

William slammed his fist on the edge of the rejuvenation pool. "Meanwhile, my list of enemies grows with every search. I fear the Tuatha De Danann more than the others. Their people have known war since time began in this realm."

"What brought that fight about?" asked Lord Treachery.

"It started when Iblis handed me the arm and sword of King Nuada. I discovered that the arm that never relinquished the sword did not harness a soul. Instead, I found a map and key that led to the underground dwellings of the Tuatha De Danann. After I informed Iblis, he sent me on a mission to retrieve Fragarach from their treasure vault. I did as I was commanded and saw unforgettable riches. I also saw a sacred orchard of apples, and modes of transportation with weapons as advanced as ours. I also found Excalibur."

"Excalibur? Iblis has been searching the high seas forever for that sword."

"Manannan Mac Lir found it."

William paused and gave another stony expression. Lord Treachery cautiously looked over the pool to make sure Temper was still at work, while William reflected on the past experience.

"Before I could grab Excalibur, a beautiful maiden entered the treasure vault," explained William. "She was like the fairies that once graced our woods. I put the tip of Fragarach to her throat to test the special ability of truth and learned how Excalibur came into their possession. Manannan Mac Lir interrupted the conversation and accidentally forced my sword. She fell into his arms, and I used Gram to dive underground before a fight. I managed to escape with Fragarach, but Excalibur was left behind. Later I discovered the maiden was the wife of Manannan Mac Lir. She fell to the sword's second special ability—an incurable sting. It left her paralyzed, and a bounty was placed on my head. Manannan Mac Lir is offering Excalibur for the reward."

Lord Treachery pondered on a solution, and was suddenly thankful he had not revealed his identity to William.

"You need reassurance to keep you from falling into the hands of our enemies," said Lord Treachery.

"Do you know of any?"

"The rejuvenation pool!"

William dipped his hand into the pool and carefully looked over the puddle centered in his palm.

"You expect me to swim in a pool after you put brain germ in it?" he asked.

"I did not put a brain germ into the rejuvenation pool. I merely placed a placebo to disguise my infiltration into Hel's ranks."

"I will have to remove the Corpse Candle," replied William.

"Who will guard it better than the one you endured your transformation with?" said Lord Treachery.

"I will bathe in the pool, but I am also on a mission," replied William. "I'm supposed to drain the pool after you place the brain germ."

"What better way to get rid of Temper. I will wear the Corpse Candle and complete your task. When I'm done, we can both return to the ship," suggested Lord Treachery.

"I will explain the mechanics of the Corpse Candle, and return you to the ship when I collect the sickle from the Titan. That is also a part of my mission," replied William.

While William explained the mechanics of the Corpse Candle, Junior closed in on Detective Rodriguez. The halls of the glacier were cold to humans. They were lined with snow and ice. It provided comfort for a yeti but caked around the detective's calves like mud. Every step was heavy, and carried the weight of his fears while a name echoed through the passages.

"Praetorian!" shouted Junior. He strode through the pathways with ease. He fanned the branch of Shiva to tease its thirst for blood. The detective began to weigh his chances of making it out alive, and the odds were not in his favor.

Outside the rejuvenation chamber, the sun rose and reflected a light through the hole Gall made in the arena. It gave the detective hope, but the stretch between him and the opening was nearly a mile. The detective peeked at his rear and quickly dodged a swipe from a paw. It was at that moment, he cried out to a supernatural force that gave better odds than a bookie.

"He who stands at the left hand of God!" cried Detective Rodriguez. He quickly jumped to his feet and sprinted for the opening. Junior paced with amusement while he sharpened his claws on the ice wall. He gained ground and made another swipe that clawed through the detective's jacket.

"He who presides over every suffering and the wound of the sons of man!" cried Detective Rodriguez. He removed his coat to lighten his weight, and tossed it at the branch that waved through the air.

The detective raced through the opening and slid on a large patch of ice. It carried him to the center of the arena, where an inflatable raft was anchored. The sight of Gall provoked another cry for help as the Kangchenjunga Demon stepped out of the doorway.

"He who watches over thunder and terror!" cried Detective Rodriguez.

"Praetorian!" shouted the Kangchenjunga Demon. He stepped out of the doorway, and Gall extended a claw that pierced his skull and body. The Kangchenjunga Demon collapsed on the ground, and the branch blanketed his bloody frame. His eyes slowly returned to a gray color as Junior left the body.

Emotions propelled through the arena as Otava and Glimpse circled in the helicopter.

"Gall just eliminated the Kangchenjunga Demon!" complained Glimpse. Her cries of disappointment were quickly interrupted by a series of beeps from her laptop. The flow of bets for the fights to come was increasing. Gall unleashed another howl of reckoning while the sleeves of the Corpse Candle adjusted to Lord Treachery's frame.

William dived into the rejuvenation pool like a kid on a hot summer day. The broad smile on his face tossed his troubles and fears away. He dived underwater to lure Temper with a crooked wink, and Temper followed to investigate. William swam back to the surface to signal Lord Treachery to drain the pool.

"You must hurry! Temper is chasing me," explained William. "The sleeves on your arms hold Gram and Fragarach. Just point your finger at the ice and guide the piercing of forbidden metals through the barrier like I showed you," instructed William. Lord Treachery stood still and gave no response. William jumped out of the pool and suspiciously approached to see why. He looked closely into the eye shields on the helmet as Lord Treachery's eyelids fluttered. His pupils turned jet black as Junior gripped his soul and surfaced.

*"Praetorian!"* he shouted. He unleashed the Corpse Candle's small flame to cast a deadly illusion for Detective Rodriguez.

Outside the glacier, the detective crawled into the inflatable raft centered in the arena. He trembled from cold and fear as an invisible Sitoel pulled him in.

"You can catch a cold running around here without a jacket," said Sitoel.

"What good is a jacket if you don't have skin. I barely escaped that thing," replied the detective. He watched as the branch of Shiva drained the blood from the Kangchenjunga Demon, and started to pull flesh from bone.

The light of a candle lit flame suddenly gained his attention as it exited the side of the glacier. It stopped just a few feet from the detective to place him in a hypnotic state. It burst into small colorful specks that scattered throughout the area to create a surrealistic illusion of his homeland.

"Rome?" blurted Detective Rodriguez. Sitoel struggled to keep the detective from stepping out of the raft. The helm of invisibility fell from her head during the struggle and caught Otava's attention.

"Outta here!" she shouted as the helicopter flew over them.

"Grab the steering stick when I swing around again!" she commanded. Glimpse handed Tabasco King the camera to comply.

Otava withdrew her guns as the Corpse Candle made an unexpected entrance.

"Praetorian!" Junior shouted as he exited the glacier. The Corpse Candle crashed into the propellers on the helicopter and forced it to spin out of control. Gall snatched the detective and Sitoel from the raft as Junior fell from the sky. The Corpse Candle pierced the center of the raft and it deflated. The net of invisibility locked his movements as he sunk into the ice. The Furies' helicopter continued to spin out of control. Tabasco King jumped from his seat and slid down the side of the glacier to escape. He landed next to a hole where the entrance collapsed and fell unconscious. Glimpse grabbed her laptop and extended her wings to escape. She landed next to Mitten and realized Otava was still trapped inside the helicopter. Otava cried out to Gall when she couldn't unfasten her seat belt.

Gall gently placed the detective and Sitoel in the arena. He snatched the helicopter from the sky as it circled his head.

"This doesn't make us even. I'll have my day," she barked at Gall. Otava extended her wings to burn through the seat belt and took flight. Her eyes lustered as her anger grew from the missed opportunity.

"Sitoel was on her way outta here! I had her in my sights before Junior messed up my shot," shouted Otava. She landed next to Mitten as she plunged the sickle into the corpse of a yeti. Mitten carried the blood-soaked weapon to the Titan and waved it in front of him.

"Are you crazy!" protested Glimpse. "Junior's running through the field with a vendetta. We can't control him if he picks the Titan!"

"Do not disturb me while I'm preparing my fighter," replied Mitten. "Do something useful like getting the camera out of the helicopter. We're about to film our main event." She then whispered into the Titan's ear, "Do someone proud." She handed him the sickle, and the feel of the weapon smothered with blood overwhelmed Forgetful. Hel's servant fell from the Titan's body as it grew in height. Glimpse retrieved the camera, and focused the lens to capture the surge. He sharpened his sickle on the side of Zemu Glacier as he continued to grow in height. When he overshadowed the peak, both fighters became worthy for a fight that would crown him a king of monsters. The Titan raised his sickle with bloodlust and prepared a fatal blow, while Gall's snarl turned into a growl.

Everyone patiently waited for Junior as he gripped the soul, and unexpectedly surfaced with an infrasound. Gall's eyelids fluttered, and his pupils lustered a jet black color. The infrasound paused the attack long enough for a direct blow over the Titans' heart. When the heart stopped beating, the Titan collapsed on the glacier, and Junior proceeded with the Blood Eagle. The tearing of flesh and bone in ample time broke the record of his Enemy. Junior turned the glacier another color as blood gushed from the Titan. When his masterpiece of horror was done, Junior extended a claw into the arena and dug out Lord Treachery. He returned the Captain, helm, and net of invisibility to the deck of the Deaf Dum Dead. A sinister grin appeared on the face of the lycan when Junior returned to the arena.

"Praetorian!" he shouted.

Everyone stood frozen in fear as he unleashed another wave of his infrasound. The impending danger provoked another cry for help as he approached the detective.

"Between heaven and earth is Azriel with blade in hand, and he is destruction of all!" shouted Detective Rodriguez. The lycan stumbled back, and Junior fell from his body as the glacier began to crack. Iblis unexpectedly appeared and skated across the ice to cradle Junior's fall. The silhouette of a toddler fell into his embrace before they disappeared. The branch of Shiva latched onto the glacier to quench its thirst for blood, and the suction forced a structural deformation.

Mirka and his soldiers raced to the rejuvenation pool to save the glacier. The collapsing of the ice shattered the door, and Temper raced from the pool to the hole he made. William was forced to follow as Mirka stormed into the room with his soldiers. They quickly jumped into the pool and began to chant mantras. The chanting moved shards of ice and funneled the water through the glacier like a sewage system. It quickly cleansed the structure and the branch of Shiva. In a matter of seconds, the color of the glacier returned with caps of snow smothered over the top.

Temper burned through the ice that blocked his tunnel. The water poured over Tabasco King, and he regained consciousness. He suspiciously watched Temper as he walked away and mumbled excuses for his failure. A steady flow of curses from William's mouth also gained his attention. He crawled out of the hole and saw a face that belonged to Otava's war party. "I'm too cold to ask why you are here or which John you are. Just take me to Mitten's sanctuary so I can figure out a way to get the Corpse Candle back," he demanded. A broad smile appeared on the face of Tabasco King as his blade discreetly slid down his sleeve.

"Why are you so happy?" asked William.

Tabasco King responded with a swipe across William's neck. William's head rolled to his feet, and Tabasco King happily collected it. He tossed the body over his shoulder to complete the mission. At the base of Zemu Glacier, the Furies gathered around the Titan and extended their wings to give him a proper burial. Their purple flames grew and disintegrated the carcass. The sickle he wielded returned to a size befitting a mortal. Mitten snatched it off the ground and delivered it to Banter. He cautiously raised his rifle as she approached with her sisters.

"If you're looking to finish your fight with Gall, he's on the other side of the glacier," warned Banter.

"We already fought Gall. Each fighter represented one of us," replied Mitten.

"Their stories reflected one we've become familiar with. When you explain it to Gall, tell him we got the idea from *Reign or Rain?* He'll know what it means," added Otava.

Mitten held up the sickle, and the Furies spat a purple flame on the blade. "Give him this. We gave it fire as part of his atonement. When it grows, it'll spark the flame and increase the capability of the weapon."

"You should give it to him yourself?" replied Banter.

"We're pressed for time and fugitives to the Sacred Order of the Dragon. You'll have to do it," replied Mitten. She handed Banter the sickle and took flight. Glimpse gave Banter a wink before she followed with a laptop in hand.

"Outta here!" blurted Otava.

In Helheim, Hel introduced her Abominable generals to her private bodyguards. The children of Styx and Zeus's personal guard were now in her service. All but Victory. Sitoel had snatched it from her grasp. Hel decided to mull over the loss with a torture session.

"You are already familiar with Bully, now I'll introduce you to Gravity and Devastation." Hel's servants gathered around her throne as Bia responded to her new name. She waved her hands, and the gravitational pull forced the Abominable generals to their knees. Another wave from her hand pushed their bodies to the floor. The force of Gravity anchored their bones and organs. They bellowed in pain as Temper entered the throne room.

"Temper, what took you so long to return?" asked Bully. Temper looked over the Abominable generals as blood dripped from the nose and mouth.

"I know Hel's temper after failure. I had to cool down first," he answered.

He approached the throne as Kratos stepped out of the crowd to exercise the name Devastation. In his hands, he gripped the necks of Lies and Deceit. Temper nervously watched as he squeezed their throats. The facial expressions of shock and grief funneled through their emotions.

"Is the water in the rejuvenation pool tainted or not?" asked Hel.

"I don't believe it is. I saw a dark elf swimming through it before the glacier started to collapse," answered Temper. Eavesdropping and Nosey rushed to Hel's side.

"The dark elf was William. He gave Rottenvein the Corpse Candle and left when Junior took control," explained Nosey.

"Now Iblis has the Corpse Candle, the invisible net, and the helm of invisibility. Blackmarket Ginyel is forging them into one on the Deaf Dum Dead as we speak," added Eavesdropping.

"Iblis has taken from me too many times. We will all learn a lesson from this!" shouted Hel.

Hel walked over to Copasetic and removed two bone arrows from the pouch on his back. She held the sharp blade tip to the light as Devastation brought Lies and Deceit to her. He continued to squeeze their necks until their mouths opened wide. They squirmed in pain as Hel forced the arrows into their mouths and through the hands of Devastation. After she set the arrows in place, a flame outlined the tattoo of her dragon. Hel leaned over their mouths and spewed a flame to forge a new tongue.

"Now your words will cut and poison when you speak!" shouted Hel.

That same night, the Furies left the yeti sanctuary under the cover of darkness. Mitten unraveled an escape plan while they boarded the yacht.

"John Bullhorns tells me there's a storm brewing on the seas," she said. "We'll sink the yacht and return to the hidden sanctuary the yetis prepared for us."

"No one's going to believe we drowned at sea," replied Glimpse.

"It'll buy us time. Whoever searches for our yacht in the dock will make several assumptions. One will be that we didn't return. My only concern now is where to find two members of our war party," said Otava. John Bullhorns and John Bear worriedly watched the shore. They allowed a few minutes to pass before setting sail.

The question remained unanswered as Mitten made her way below deck. She picked up the faint scent of blood before reaching her door. Her fears increased as she entered the room. She quickly discovered the blood wasn't human. The headless corpse of a dark elf lay on her bed. In the corner chair, a yeti sat with the head propped on his lap.

"Tabasco King?" uttered Mitten.

"Yes, and I find your escape plan insulting. You know you can't escape the Sacred Order, especially at a time when your services are still needed. The Corpse Candle is now in the possession of the Marid Djinns. So, it can get really cold in here ... or we can enjoy a peaceful ride together?"

"What's the catch for a peaceful ride?" asked Mitten. "Do I get to keep my head for another day? I'm also missing two members of my war party. Did you offer them the same deal?"

"You can consider us even for Montross and his unit. Those two and the head on my lap can give you an opportunity to keep your head on your shoulders permanently. The Furies can return to their ranks in the Sacred Order of the Dragon."

A second chance at life won over the need for an argument.

"Otava won't be pleased with the loss of two of our members, but another shot at Sitoel might help settle her down," said Mitten. "So where are we going?"

"You are aware of our alliance with the Tuatha De Danann. Before you interrupted, Manannan Mac Lir was preparing a path to return me to our post beneath Bannerman Castle."

"Manannan Mac Lir is behind the storm?"

"We arranged to make an exchange."

Tabasco King stood from the chair and gently placed the head on the bed. "I was assigned to run operations in the castle after the death of Sound. You would be wise to hide any jewelry or shiny items. I retained the services of Myte Pocket and his Redcap goblin gang."

The following day, the Marid Djinns gathered around a fireplace in a Kangchenjunga guest house. Gall enjoyed his first cup of masala chai. It settled his stomach after Akantha's cure to return him to normal. Banter looked over the sickle and relayed the message the Furies gave to Gall. Sitoel and Detective Rodriguez also filled him in on the conversation Hope shared before the event. After docking his plane, Tobias joined them in the guesthouse. Akantha opened the door before he could knock and welcomed him in.

"It's hard to believe that baby shadow could cause so much trouble. It's just a baby!" said Sitoel.

"That thing is no baby! It's a stone cold killer. It took the life of my partner and gave me several near misses. I swore to bring an end to his reign every chance I got," replied Detective Rodriguez.

Tobias entered the room and expected a warm greeting, but Junior was the only topic for discussion.

"Who were you calling out to?" asked Gall.

"Archangels, they've been hanging around me ever since that thing came into my life," replied Detective Rodriguez.

"I could see them on the field while Junior was with me. I felt his fear when the one in the black hood came," said Gall.

"Who is he?" asked Sitoel.

"Azriel," blurted Detective Rodriguez.

"The angel of death? The Archangel that was sent to claim the lives of Egypt's firstborn? That kid has to be dangerous if they're chasing him," said Banter.

"And he's a part of us?" mumbled Gall.

"Why me? All I ever wanted was a simple life," uttered Tobias. "People in my church warned me. This is what happens when you rub shoulders with people related to the antichrist. How long do we have?"

Gall tumbled off his chair with laughter while Akantha consoled him. "You don't have to worry," said Akantha. "The fourth Marid Djinn is far away from here by now."

A knock on the door startled her. Akantha turned to answer it and found three Lycan buccaneers standing outside.

"Salutations to you all," greeted Lord Treachery.

"How did you get past my senses?" asked Akantha.

"One might say Junior left a trail of challenges to be accomplished. By now you should have told the Marid Djinns that he is the weaver of their fates," answered Lord Treachery. Enemy and Unchained Gauge followed him inside with a chest, while Detective Rodriguez discreetly entered a neighboring room. He hid behind the door as the Lycan buccaneers made their way to the fireplace. The chest aroused the suspicion of everyone in the room as Enemy opened it.

"We were hoping someone could further explain the weaver of our fates before you interrupted," said Banter.

Enemy displayed jewels with no imperfections. The color, clarity, cut, and carat weight were flawless.

"When you see a shadow that outlines a fate that took place, it becomes a sign to a path Junior has laid out for you," explained Lord Treachery.

"I saw a shadow around two fates that took place at the same time—twins that were bound together, and lips of fire," said Sitoel.

"Now you are bound to an echo of karma and possess Cupid's bow," explained Lord Treachery.

"I saw the shadow of an eagle ripping the eye out of a skull during a fate," said Banter.

"After we retrieve our map, we'll retain your services for capturing the eye of Ra and Horus," explained Lord Treachery.

Everyone in the room turned to Gall. They patiently waited to hear an experience of an outlined fate.

"Are you serious? More than half my fates took place in the shadows. Do you honestly expect me to keep track of them all?" replied Gall.

Sitoel approached the chest to admire the contents. "Is this for our fee and services?" she asked.

"The jewels serve a different purpose," answered Lord Treachery. "There are two ways to deal with the Redcap goblins. One can use jewels or quote a verse from the Bible. Religious symbols also hold weight. We use jewels because we have no tongue for the other."

"What is a Redcap goblin?" asked Sitoel.

"If you're lucky enough to look into their eyes, you'll find a devilish and soulless creature," explained Lord Treachery. "They're small, but they can deliver fatal blows with ease. The mechanism of their bodies operates like a machine. The blood stored in their caps drains and ignites a need for more. They'll chase you until they replace it. The drive sparks the bloodlust in their eyes and ignites the magic of their iron boots. Enemy couldn't outrun them, and he was forced to give up the map on every attempt. They keep it in a cave, and everything inside has a jewel embedded in it. That is why they are always in need of them. Enemy's failures provoked me to come up with a plot. I was successful in making two deliveries to their lair in the disguise of a Redcap goblin. So I can sneak one person inside."

Enemy grabbed a jewel from the chest and held it up for everyone to see. "My speed helped me in battle, but the Redcaps always won the war. Only Victory can beat their speed."

"Redcap goblins in Egypt? I thought they only inhabited castles where evil deeds took place, not pyramids," said Banter.

"Allow me to explain from the beginning," replied Lord Treachery. "Some time ago, the Sacred Order of the Dragon had an alliance with your father. They used his resources and vaults to harbor the artifacts they lost in the first war. That deal soured when Morgan met Iblis. When the search for artifacts changed to weapons, the Sacred Order of the Dragon was forced to send agents to oversee Morgan's transactions. During this time, Enemy and I were still fugitives. Hoping to kill two birds with one stone, the Sacred Order of the Dragon reconstructed a post to spy on us and deal with Styles Corporate. Bannerman Castle harbored the reinforcements for the task. Sound was in charge at the time, and she kept Redcap goblins for guards. Since that time, we have made several attempts to infiltrate and retrieve the map. It looks like a ship manifest."

Banter approached Lord Treachery at the fireplace with his head hung low. "I remember those days. I tried to bury them with Morgan. Wait a minute, Sound showed me a ship manifest when she hired us to help capture you. Nothing about it resembled a map."

"To the untrained eye, it looks like a ship manifest, but it's a map. The description of the ship and the names assigned to the packs have meaning and serve as symbols for direction. I will only need one of you for this mission."

"I'll go. I'm faster than Enemy, and I have a stronger healing ability," said Gall.

"No, a lycan is sure to fail. I only go in disguise," replied Lord Treachery.

"I'll go, I'm more than qualified with Victory in my blood and

Cupid's bow. I also have an echo that follows me wherever I go," interrupted Sitoel.

"We respect your gifts, but I'm afraid another opportunity has presented itself," replied Lord Treachery. Lord Treachery turned to Banter with the expectation of his approval.

"Me? I thought you wanted your map back," said Banter. "It's a suicide mission if I go. What chance would I have against Redcap goblins?"

"That is why Iblis is extending the services of the Corpse Candle. I hate to rush you, but your training will be brief. We must retrieve the map before an alignment of stars over the pyramids."

"The Corpse Candle is a powerful weapon. It makes a big difference now that you've offered it to me. I will assist you on your mission."

"Excellent. Your training will start at midnight. Iblis is currently waiting for Blackmarket Ginyel to arm it with the helm and net of invisibility. He will deliver it as soon as it is done."

Everyone followed the Lycan buccaneers as they made their way out the door. When there were no more sounds of conversation, Detective Rodriguez returned to the room. He walked over to Banter and placed his hand on his shoulder.

"I can finally return the favor and offer you some help for once," said the detective.

"How?"

"'Do you not know that in a race all the runners run, but only one gets the prize? Run in such a way as to get the prize.'"[1]

A confused expression appeared on Banter's face before he remembered Detective Rodriguez's girlfriend. "Your girlfriend has been to Bannerman Castle?" asked Banter.

"She brought me there once while working on a case. That Bible verse can be your ace in the hole. No Redcap goblin came near us when she recited it. I still haven't figured out the secret about the

---

[1] 1 Corinthians 9:24 (NIV).

jewels. She wore a lot of them, and she refused to give them to the Redcaps because they spoke to her."

"They spoke to her?"

"Like a chorus in a song."

Everyone returned to the den and gathered around the fireplace.

"That Bible verse may be all I need," mumbled Banter.

"Don't be foolish," warned Akantha. "You may have knowledge of myths and legends, but you lack faith in those words. You can't just roll them off your tongue. The words have purpose, and no one knows what surprises tomorrow brings. You should prepare to be alone." Banter responded with a nod.

At midnight Lord Treachery arrived on schedule. He escorted Banter to an open field where Morbid Medley, Enemy, and Iblis awaited. As Banter made his way to them, Gall pulled Lord Treachery aside for a heartfelt conversation.

"I heard what happened between you and my brother," said Gall. "If I could change things, I would."

"No need to trouble yourself with grief," replied Lord Treachery. "I understand the bond between brothers more than you know. The Lycan buccaneers still consider you as part of the pack. You should also be aware that Copasetic is just a shell. When I catch up with him, I'll free your brother from that shell so that his soul can finally find peace."

When Banter had reached Iblis, he found Enemy wearing Vlad the Impaler's gloves. Morbid Medley held a roll of sheep gut around his shoulder, and Obnoxious Koss carted a large cage with two Harpy eagles that matched his height.

"What type of training session is this going to be?" asked Banter.

"You can call it survival," answered Enemy. He stepped forward and planted the pikes on the gloves into the ground.

"Bring me blood to tell the story of the Corpse Candle," commanded Enemy. Within seconds, the pikes extended roots that filled the field with a maze of hate.

"No peeking," blurted Morbid Medley. He raced through

the maze and fastened strings of sheep gut between random tree branches. He made the knots tight enough to sever a head or limb if they snapped.

"The Redcap goblins are extremely swift," explained Enemy. "Every light in the castle goes out when you steal from their cave. You won't see the blows from their axes, but you'll feel them. You must learn how to maneuver through that field."

"What are the Harpy eagles for?" asked Banter.

Obnoxious Koss opened the cage, and they flew through the entrance of the maze.

"They are possessed by two of the harpies the Marid Djinns slayed," replied Iblis. "The pursuit for the gem I give you will be relentless. You must keep it in your possession like the map. You have to make it through the field without losing it. You can begin when you're ready."

"There were three harpies. What happened to the third?" asked Banter.

"An obnoxious cost!" answered Obnoxious Koss. "Her sisters told me the third has joined the ranks of Hel. The best of the three snatchers has been given a name that has stirred battles and wars throughout history. Hel calls her *Mine!*"

Enemy dug into the center of his vest and handed Banter a green gem. It possessed a luster that could not be hidden by the dark of night.

"I think you forgot something?" hinted Banter.

"If you're referring to the Corpse Candle, I did not forget. It is for you to decide what souls you'll need to make it through the field," explained Iblis.

Banter reflected on the weapons the Marid Djinns collected during their struggles. He turned to Iblis when he couldn't make up his mind. "What do you suggest?"

"Gram and Fragarach are exceptional pieces when paired to-gether," advised Iblis. "I wouldn't use them for digging. The castle is surrounded by water. You don't want to flood any passages. So I would use them for defense. They were once two swords that could cut through anything. In turn, they can provide you with an impenetrable armor. Fragarach also possesses the incurable sting, and what you grip is forced to tell you the truth—a handy tool if you can't find what you seek. The cloak has been adjusted to provide you with invisibility, and a pocket was woven inside to hold the invisible net. I would also recommend the might of Mjölnir. It will provide your armor with superhuman strength. Last, I would choose Lightning. It can provide a quick teleportation should you find yourself in a jam. The helmet of the Corpse Candle holds the most cunning weapon you'll know. I gave William a piece of coal that could project a map of where he needed to go. William fused it to the sword of Gwyn Ap Nudd. Now it projects a path that leads to the home of its victim. While under a hypnotic trance, they obey the command to follow an illusion that ends in the graveyard. William was a prankster and always found that amusing."

"I'll take everything you've recommended."

"I shall return!" Iblis disappeared and returned within the blink of an eye. In his arms were a cloak, four sleeves, and a helmet.

"Now you must become familiar with the souls you possess," said Iblis. Banter put on the Corpse Candle, and quickly discovered what Iblis meant by those words. He adjusted the helmet and saw the faces of six monsters staring back at him—the souls of soldiers that fought in the first war. Their eyes opened as the liquid drained from the sleeves. "You must synchronize with the souls and the alchemy of the elements. After they become familiar with your fighting style and movements, you'll be invulnerable."

"How do I synchronize with them?" asked Banter.

Iblis snickered as he turned and whispered to Enemy, "He thinks I'm talking to him."

At that moment, a Marid Djinn emerged for the average walk through the park. Banter was pushed back into the farthest corner of his mind. He was now on the outside looking in. He became familiar with the time when he first bonded with his Marid Djinn. The

Marid Djinn pulled the hood of the cloak over his head and entered the maze with invisibility. He removed the net from the inner pocket and placed the gem inside. He tossed it over his shoulder and raced through the maze with the lure of its shine. The armor of the Corpse Candle hardened as Gram surfaced for his role. The tree branches that lined the walls of the passages suddenly attacked with hate. They speared the armor and snapped like twigs on impact. The Marid Djinn proceeded as the maze sprouted pikes to impale an unsuspecting victim. It also extended vines to strangle him to death. The Corpse Candle grew in height and gained a broad muscular tone as the Mjölnir surfaced for its role. It ripped the vines from their roots and punched its way through the field with ease. When Banter heard the sound of Harpy eagles piping overhead, he gripped the net and extended his arm.

The Harpy eagles nosedived from the sky and targeted the gem with their talons. The attempt to claw through the net failed. They used their beaks and claws to pull it from the Corpse Candle, but the grip was too strong. In desperation, they made an attempt to snatch the entire body. They dragged the Corpse Candle several feet before Fragarach surfaced for his role. The Corpse Candle grabbed one of the harpies by its throat and asked, "What happened to your sister?"

To his amusement, the harpy truthfully piped the name, "Mine!"

"No" answered Banter.

A sudden touch from a finger that held an incurable sting ended the pursuit. The harpy hit the ground, and a spark ignited from the helmet. A candle lit flame grabbed the attention of the remaining harpy. It separated into several colorful spects to create the illusion of the Suicide Trees in Tartarus. The harpy flew to the illusion in a hypnotic state and triggered the traps left by Morbid Medley. Several lashes from the sheep gut riddled the body of the harpy. The attack sent the severed limbs back in the direction of the Corpse Candle. The blood from the carcass spilled, and the roots funneled the stream back to Enemy.

A puddle formed around his feet while a chorus of sheep gut

continued to whistle through the air. At the end, the Corpse Candle exited the maze of hate without a blemish.

"Tell Lord Treachery to prepare the Deaf Dum Dead for immediate departure. We have two weeks before the alignment of the stars," instructed Iblis. Enemy responded with a nod as the Corpse Candle returned the gem.

The next morning, the Deaf Dum Dead anchored miles from Bannerman Castle. Enemy spent the day on a reconnaissance mission and returned at nightfall.

"There's something afoot at Bannerman Castle. There are tracks of Redcap goblins patrolling in the daylight. I can't get close without risking detection," reported Enemy.

"They must be expecting a delivery. We can't wait for it to arrive. We have to proceed as planned," replied Lord Treachery. He used his Lycan transformation to shift his bones into the frame of a Redcap goblin. He pulled a bloodstained cap over his head to complete the disguise, while Banter armed himself with the Corpse Candle.

When they were done, Banter pulled the hooded cloak over his head and embraced invisibility. He crept off the deck, and followed Lord Treachery to a hidden entrance.

"Halt! Who goes there?" shouted Myte Pocket.

"A fellow Redcap from the seas of Scotland knocks at your door with gems once more," answered Lord Treachery.

"I know that voice. If it belongs to a Redcap named Reaper Status. You can proceed further down the road," instructed Myte Pocket. Lord Treachery proceeded toward the hidden entrance with the treasure chest on his shoulders. He placed it on the ground and opened it as Myte Pocket stepped out of a camouflaged door.

"You were never this cautious before? What brings all this about?" asked Lord Treachery.

"We're expecting a delivery," answered Myte Pocket.

"How fortunate, my jewels are needed."

"Both fortunate and unfortunate for you. The lair is under lock and key until we secure the delivery. I cannot pay you before that happens."

"Who are you expecting?"

Myte Pocket looked to the waters surrounding Bannerman Castle. A large wave suddenly brought the Furies' explorer yacht to shore. "Tabasco King. We are to make an exchange for William's head."

"William of Soules?" asked Lord Treachery.

"Is that the only William you know? The William I speak of owned the Corpse Candle," replied Myte Pocket.

"That's impossible!" blurted Lord Treachery.

"You sound as if it could never be done? I assure you, Tabasco King is delivering the head as we speak. Drop your delivery down the shaft and return tomorrow for payment. You can spend your free time enjoying the festivities within our borders." Banter and Lord Treachery cautiously watched as he jumped through another door. The sound of iron boots racing underground followed his exit.

Lord Treachery carried the chest to the shaft and emptied its contents.

"Why did you sound surprised when Myte Pocket told you William's head was being delivered?" asked Banter.

"I was one of the last people to see William alive," advised Lord Treachery. "I encouraged him to swim through the rejuvenation pool to avoid such a lethal attack. If he was beheaded, it would not last for long. You have to take extra precaution. He's the previous owner and inventor of the Corpse Candle—two good reasons why we should cancel this mission now. So I need you to get the map and get out of there fast." Lord Treachery waited for a response, but heard only the sound of Banter sliding down the shaft. "Scallywag!" he blurted.

On the shore of Bannerman Castle, a large wave shipwrecked the Furies' explorer yacht. Manannan Mac Lir stepped out of the shadows of a decrepit structure to greet its passengers. His facial features displayed signs of him still mourning a loss. Revenge kept him awake and driven. The bags around his eyes weighed under his pupils. He reeked of the sea like alcohol on a habitual drunk, and fastened on his shoulders was Excalibur. He unsheathed the sword as doors opened and ejected a gang of Redcap goblins.

"There's no need to be alarmed. We are only here to safeguard the prize," said Myte Pocket.

"No one touches the sword before I collect William's head," warned Manannan Mac Lir. He lowered the tip of Excalibur to Myte Pocket's chest to back up his words. A few feet away, Tabasco King approached in the form of a Redcap goblin.

The Furies followed with two Sasquatches from their war party. One held out William's head, and the other carried his body.

Myte Pocket eagerly pushed the sword aside to greet them. "You have truly outdone yourself, Tabasco King. You convinced the Furies to return to the ranks of the Sacred Order of the Dragon. William's head will also be added to your collection."

"Prepare a coffin for William," commanded Tabasco King.

"There will be no proper burial rites for this animal," demanded Manannan Mac Lir. "He stole from my land. Before he left her paralyzed, he tortured and raped my wife. His remains will know no peace. I want him to feel my grief in the afterlife." He sheathed Excalibur and reached for William's head.

"I'm afraid you misunderstood," explained Tabasco King. "A coffin isn't a casket. It's a term we use when we want to collect samples like blood and tissue. We also have to check the authenticity of Excalibur. Please hand the sword to Myte Pocket."

Manannan Mac Lir grabbed William's head and pried open his eyelids. "These are the eyes I've seen in battle. They bested me when I stopped to hear her last words. Be swift with your findings. My patience to bring him home is wearing thin."

Manannan Mac Lir disappointedly handed the head and sword

to Myte Pocket. Just a few feet away, Banter crawled out of an open door.

"I want your best Redcap guarding Excalibur while William is on the slab," commanded Tabasco King. "Tomorrow! No one, and nothing can outrun Tomorrow," replied Myte Pocket. The sound of heavy iron boots approached as a slightly bigger and more muscular Redcap stepped out of the shadows. His eyes were squinted to the point where a blink rendered him blind. A small pouch of pebbles was fastened to his waist, and two large pikes were strapped on his back.

Manannan Mac Lir angrily watched as he spoke in sign language before collecting William's carcass.

"This is your best guard? He's nearly blind and deaf!" said Manannan Mac Lir.

"No one, and nothing can outrun Tomorrow!" assured Myte Pocket.

Tomorrow pushed everyone aside and jumped through an open door.

"Lay your worries aside, old friend. We have much to discuss," said Tabasco King. He escorted Manannan Mac Lir to a hidden elevator inside the ruins of Bannerman Castle. The Furies waited outside for it to return.

Banter discreetly followed a Redcap goblin through a trapdoor. He cautiously observed his surroundings as he crept through several passages cluttered with more doors. The structure of the underground castle strangely resembled the original. It was as if it had been flipped upside down. The sight took Banter back in time before reaching an entrance that was divided into a cave. Near the entrance was the elevator door. It opened to a conversation that immediately grabbed Banter's attention.

"I spoke to the elders of the council about offering your wife your plate of immortality," said Tabasco King. "They wanted me to ask you about your secrecy of the stem. They want to know how much information your wife revealed before her attack."

Banter stopped following the Redcap and pursued Tabasco King. He followed them into a den that served as an office.

Manannan Mac Lir walked to the fireplace and nervously picked up a fire iron. He poked the logs in the flame as if Iblis were hiding behind them.

"I know this is hard for you, but you must tell me if the secret of the stem is safe," pleaded Tabasco King.

"Hard for me? The barriers of my land are as broken as our language. Every cry my people made returned unanswered or too late," complained Manannan Mac Lir.

"Your cry was not unanswered. We found her killer, and I'm giving you his head."

"That is true, but could the attack have been prevented? I was present the day Thor fell to a placid fate. Odin summoned us to witness Thor's promotion to general. The battle was to serve as a proud boast. I secretly held my position in the waters with King Nuada. Zeus hid in the clouds with Heracles. Zeus was so infatuated with stature that he struck down the lycans that attempted to climb over Thor on the bridge. He failed to see the problem that was stirring beneath. We all did, until Thor met his demise."

"His sacrifice will not be forgotten. We all agreed to provide champions to serve as generals for the next war. The reward was immortality, and you were to be served a plate that contained leaves from the stem. I understand the terms of our alliance."

"Do you?" replied Manannan Mac Lir.

"I swear I do."

Manannan Mac Lir continued to rant while he recklessly waved the iron poker. "I'm the only one left! What does that tell you?"

"We are aware of Iblis's plot," replied Tabasco King. "Who do you think collected the remains from the Blaine lighthouse killing?

We covered that spill, and we prefer to keep the secret of immortality as well. So what did your wife reveal about the stem?"

"She knew Gilgamesh found the stem of immortality. She also knew that the sea serpent that took it didn't belong to my sea or the other sea gods."

"You told her it was Jormungandr!" shouted Tabasco King.

"That was all she knew. Will it affect my request to serve her my plate?" asked Manannan Mac Lir.

"I'll have to check with my superiors."

"Let them know that if they don't comply, I'll feel betrayed and I'll act accordingly. I also speak for the Tuatha De Danann."

Tabasco King responded with a nod and gestured for Manannan Mac Lir to follow him out of the room. Banter patiently waited for them to leave and returned to the entrance of the cave. At the entrance, another conversation piqued Banter's interest. It was a discussion between the Furies.

"I can't believe you sided with Tabasco King. He murdered two members of our war party," complained Otava.

"In case you've forgotten, we were scheduled for a beheading," explained Mitten. "Tabasco King would've picked us off one by one while pretending to be one of us. Even if we managed to escape, the Sacred Order of the Dragon would've attacked with full force. How long do you think the battle would've lasted without the sickle? This is a blessing in disguise."

"How could this prison possibly work in our favor?" asked Glimpse.

"Do you know a better place to find a new weapon?" answered Mitten.

The Furies stopped at the entrance of the cave. Otava and Glimpse fearfully stepped behind Mitten as she cleared her throat to recite a verse from the Bible.

*"Do you not know that in a race all the runners run, but only one gets the prize? Run in such a way as to get the prize,"* said Mitten. She repeated her words as she made her way through a passage lined

with doors. Banter cautiously followed, and could hear the annoyed chatter of Redcaps as they peeked from behind the flickering shine of their pikes. At the end, Myte Pocket boldly stood in the doorway.

"What do you seek, Fury? Speak swiftly before I unleash Tomorrow upon you," demanded Myte Pocket.

"I am a soldier to the Sacred Order of the Dragon. I am entitled to choose a weapon for battle against our enemies. You can complain to Tabasco King if you have a problem," answered Mitten.

Mitten pushed Myte Pocket aside and entered a cavern divided into two sections. Next to a room filled with treasures was a lab. Inside the lab, the Redcaps performed their coffins. The Furies curiously watched as two Redcaps placed William's head back on his shoulders.

"What weapon do you seek?" asked Myte Pocket.

"I heard a rumor about the Four Winds being here," answered Mitten.

"A chain pendant holds Boreas and the cold breath of winter," boasted Myte Pocket. "A bracelet holds Zephyrus and his message of a spring breeze. A ring encases Notus and his summer rainstorms. Eurus rests in a navel ring, creating whirlwinds from the leaves he collected with the East wind. They make a lovely jewelry set." He escorted the Furies to the area where the Four Winds rested. There he removed a jewelry box from a hole in the wall, and the lights blinked. Chatter from Redcap goblins hidden in the exterior walls riddled the area.

"Hurry up, this place is starting to give me the creeps!" begged Glimpse.

"I'll show you the way out," said Myte Pocket.

They passed the lab, and Mitten stopped at the entrance. She took one last look at William while two Redcap goblins carefully stitched his head back on his shoulders.

Another Redcap goblin entered the lab with Excalibur. A gem was now embedded between the chimeras.

"Farewell, my favorite gladiator," said Mitten. "Your soul will never find peace in this prison, but it's better than what Manannan Mac Lir has planned for you."

The Furies left the Redcap lair repeating the same verse they had recited upon entering. Inside, Myte Pocket approached William's slab with a sinister grin.

"We'll collect more than blood samples and tissue to prepare your coffin. We'll need your soul!" heckled Myte Pocket. "Fortunately for us, you came with your own cell. Excalibur will be your new home."

Banter cautiously watched as Myte Pocket held up Excalibur. Redcap goblins circled the slab and passionately chanted, "Are you ready for Tomorrow? There's gold in those pot stills. They match the gold in my bones. Nothing outshines the souls in my stones. I speak to the heart to turn it cold. Gems, rubies, diamonds I hold!"

The chanting was supposed to take hold of the soul, but another unnatural occurrence took place. William's organs began to rejuvenate. Banter entered the neighboring cave while the Redcaps performed the ritual. He found the map conveniently placed by the door. It had a ruby embedded in the top right corner. Banter reached for the map, and a familiar voice gained his attention.

"Banter Styles! Your thoughts are still fresh in my mind. Your bond with her matches mine and Eon's," said Sound.

Banter looked into the center of the ruby and found Sound staring back at him. "They imprisoned you here? I thought you were a member?"

"This was a personal request before my demise. I knew there had to be some importance for this manifest. Those mangy hounds were always trying to steal it. I thwarted every attempt, but I can't take all the credit. My link with Eon has helped me as well. Allow me to introduce you to his vessel. *Tomorrow, are you ready!*"

Tomorrow stepped out of a door that shadowed the entrance. He pulled on a chain from which dangled an emerald pendant that was tucked under his shirt.

"I am here," answered Eon. "When he leaves the cave, I'll make it a swift death."

In the neighboring cave, the sound of chaos flooded the cavern as a rejuvenated dark elf came to life. William snatched Excalibur and extended the flames to make a diversion for his escape. Banter also took the opportunity to snatch the map. He followed the flames of Excalibur as the lights turned off, and sounded the alarm. William skillfully dodged the blows delivered from the doors that cluttered the passageway. When he reached the end, Tomorrow swept him off his feet with a pike.

William fell to the ground and saw another Redcap goblin standing at the opposite end of the passageway. He raised Excalibur to provide more light and discovered Manannan Mac Lir's head resting in his palms.

"William!" Tabasco King angrily shouted. William quickly regained his bearings and raced up a ramp with Excalibur. Tabasco King extended the blade hidden in his sleeve and pursued. Tomorrow looked down the passageway as blood drained from his cap. His eyelids smothered his pupils as his boots boosted his frame to chase Banter.

At that moment, a Marid Djinn emerged into a different kind of animal. A candle lit flame ignited on the helmet of the Corpse Candle. It raced down the passageway, painting the illusion of a graveyard. A tombstone with the symbol of a cross appeared in front of every door. It kept the Redcap goblins at bay while the Corpse Candle boldly walked the path. His armor hardened with Gram as it gained the strength of Mjölnir. He tore the doors off the hinges and pulled out the Redcaps that hid behind them. He shattered the bones in their legs and tossed them into the illusion of an open grave. Some perished in the flames left behind by Excalibur. Others screamed for Tomorrow as he blindly entered the field of battle.

When the last scream was muffled by death, the sound of two pikes stabbing into the armor of the Corpse Candle became clear. The armor broke the metal tips and shattered the wooden handles on impact. The Corpse Candle reached for Tomorrow's legs, but the Redcap became a grim apparition that slipped through his fingers.

He left blotches of blood on the armor from the bites and claw marks of his escape. The loss of teeth and nails seemed foolish before Tomorrow flared his nostrils through the air. He used the scent of his blood to follow the Corpse Candle as he blindly maneuvered through the crosses that littered the path.

"Don't let him escape!" barked Sound.

The Corpse Candle proceeded up the ramp as Tomorrow made use of his other abilities. He removed the pebbles from his pouch and threw them. They rained on the armor like bullets fired from an automatic gun and fell with the flare of falling stars. The Corpse Candle brushed off the attempt as he continued up the ramps. He suddenly fell in line with the battle between William and Tabasco King. William turned to face his pursuer and felt the precise swipe from his blade. It was close enough to loosen the stitching across his throat.

Tabasco's eyes widened with uncertainty when the wound quickly closed after two coughs. William gave a devious grin and retaliated. He cut off the hand that held Tabasco's blade and jumped through a door. Tabasco's hand slid off the ramp as the Corpse Candle approached from behind. Tabasco could hear the steps of the Corpse Candle, but only saw Tomorrow charging from behind. Tomorrow leapt through the air and curled himself into a ball.

The impact from his cannonball attack pushed everyone out the door. They crashed through the debris and landed at the feet of the Furies. Tomorrow slid off the back of the Corpse Candle, dazed and confused.

"No one outruns Tomorrow!' he mumbled. He rose to his feet and pulled back the hood of the Corpse Candle before he fell unconscious. Two Sasquatches circled William, and faded memories forced him to take a defensive stance.

"William?" blurted Mitten.

"If he's over there, who's using the Corpse Candle?" asked Glimpse.

"It has to be one of the Marid Djinns. The day our elders feared has just fallen at our feet. The capture will bring the reward of a high seat in the Sacred Order of the Dragon," replied Mitten.

Inside the Corpse Candle, Banter regained his bearings and groggily returned to his feet.

"He's too thin to be Gall. So it's got to be one of the other two," said Mitten.

"Outta here!" blurted Otava. The Furies extended their wings and took flight into the air. Otava withdrew her pistols, while Mitten handed Glimpse two pieces of jewelry. Mitten put on the chain pendant and slid the ring onto her finger.

"Boreas, breathe into the rainstorm of Notus to give me hail!" commanded Mitten. Boreas unleashed the cold breath of winter. Notus unleashed a small rainstorm with the force of a monsoon. They stirred up a chemistry that created hail the size of softballs. The Sasquatches left William to chance and joined the attack on the Corpse Candle.

Gram and Fragarach surfaced to shield Banter from the hailstorm. It pushed him into the deadly blows of the Sasquatches. They stopped to pick up debris to make a bigger impact and allowed Glimpse to attack.

She slid on a bracelet and locked her navel ring in place. "Eurus, unleash the autumn leaves you've collected and aid Zephyrus with my fire!"

Eurus fired a stream of autumn leaves from Glimpse's navel ring. Otava fired her pistols into the stream, and the muzzle flashes started a fire. Glimpse aimed her bracelet as Zephyrus increased the blaze with the breath of a spring breeze. The large flames circled Banter and kept him contained. The broken pieces of ice and snow woke Tabasco King. He frantically waved his hand and shouted to gain the Furies' attention.

In that brief moment, the Corpse Candle burrowed underground to escape. The Furies angrily landed near Tabasco King and demanded an explanation.

"We had the Corpse Candle contained. I prepared to make a fatal blow!" snapped Mitten.

"William was the primary target! He assassinated Manannan Mac Lir during his escape. Now we have to explain his death and the loss of Excalibur to the Tuatha De Danann," explained Tabasco King. He covered his injury with his free hand to stop the bleeding.

The crystal sparkle around the wound caught Glimpse's attention. "We know how to help you heal," she said.

"You know nothing about me. How could you possibly know how to heal my hand?"

"I can recognize the signs of the rejuvenation pool. The Furies were invited to the glacier a century ago. The yetis are kin to our war party. Whether you know it or not, you've been affected by it."

A broad smile appeared on Tabasco King's face as he led the Furies to another underground door. The melted ice and burnt leaves quickly extinguished the battle that took place. Shouts from Sound woke Eon and Tomorrow. He flared his nostrils, and it led him to a patch in the ground. He faintly turned into a grim apparition to follow the trail, while Banter surfaced a mile from the Deaf Dum Dead. He could hear the crew cheer and laugh as he walked down the path. The laughter was brought to an abrupt stop when William unexpectedly appeared. He leapt from the branches of a neighboring tree with Excalibur in hand.

Banter stood motionless while William looked over him with hungry eyes. He didn't know what to expect before William handed him Excalibur.

"Why don't you keep it?" asked Banter.

"What makes you think I won't?" said William. "Iblis will give it to my apprentice. Blackmarket Ginyel will make it a sleeve. It will become part of a collection that I intend to see again someday. You can also deliver a message to Iblis for me. Tell him Manannan Mac Lir's head was collected by Tabasco King. I'm an escaped prisoner, and it's best not to seek me out." He raced back into the woods as the sun began to rise.

Banter continued down the path and made another abrupt stop.

"No one outruns Tomorrow!" shouted Tomorrow.

Tomorrow knelt on the road like an Olympian at the start of a race. Banter prepared himself for another cannonball attack before a Lycan buccaneer took advantage of the opportunity. His punch technique ended Tomorrow from behind as if he were yesterday. Lord Treachery tossed the coronary artery from his claws with contempt.

"You should choose your words more carefully. Tomorrow could be Today. Henceforth, the name Reaper Status emerges to serve its purpose," replied Lord Treachery. He gestured for Banter to hand him Excalibur, and he extended the flames to make ashes of the corpse. Sound screamed in horror while her soulmate endured the flames.

"You have killed me several times over. I'm done with my suffering. I beg you to break the gem," pleaded Sound.

"You can save your cries for mercy for ears that care. Your love and the Redcap he molded will return once more. We'll discuss the terms of these conditions when Iblis arrives," replied Lord Treachery.

"I'm trying to fight the feeling that I was used as bait," said Banter.

"'Bait is such an ugly word when you're protected by an impenetrable armor," replied Lord Treachery. "You can take these past events with a grain of salt after Junior's quick exit. It only takes one assassination to rattle his nerves."

The Lycan buccaneers raced to their location, and Gall followed with Sitoel. Lord Treachery gathered the cap and boots from Tomorrow's corpse.

"You know it's bad luck to take the hat and shoes of a dead man," joked Enemy.

"You speak of bad luck as if I never experienced any after my pact with Iblis," replied Lord Treachery.

"The Corpse Candle is becoming uglier by the day. Why does Iblis insist on adding this sordid creature to it?" asked Enemy.

"Speak of the devil," interrupted Unchained Gauge. He pointed out a small whirlpool that elevated Iblis to the surface. He jumped from the center with the roar of a revving chopper motorcycle engine. The Lycan buccaneers cleared a path as he approached with Cerberus by his side.

A few feet away, Lord Treachery laid out the cap and boots that belonged to Tomorrow. Cerberus circled and sniffed the objects until he caught a scent.

"Bring him to me!" commanded Iblis. A flash of lightning sent Cerberus to purgatory to fetch Tomorrow. Iblis removed the sleeve that held Lightning and handed it to Sitoel. Then, he removed the sleeve that held Trident from his arm and handed it to Gall.

"Excalibur will be yours when it is finished," said Iblis. Banter responded with a nod. "The Marid Djinns will use these gifts to bring me the eyes of Ra and Horus," he added. Iblis reached into his robe and removed another sleeve that bore the symbol of a sword.

"Hey, I know that sword. It belonged to Lu Dongbin," said Gall.

"It used to belong to Lu Dongbin. It now belongs to me. I chose to make it part of the Corpse Candle. Watch closely and I'll teach you how to forge one of my greatest creations," said Iblis.

Iblis slid on the sleeve and reached into his robe. He removed the gloves of Vlad the Impaler to make a connection. Iblis dug the pikes into the ground, and the liquid drained from the symbol. The act of creation was so sinister it turned the color of the liquid black. The alchemy intertwined with the hate-filled roots sprouted into the form of a Redcap goblin.

"Another Tomorrow!" uttered the Lycan buccaneers.

*"A better Tomorrow!"* corrected Lord Treachery.

The liquid in the Redcap goblin also fed off the sleeves that were being worn, and Banter could feel it connecting to Tomorrow.

"You'll need more than roots and branches to contain my love," warned Sound.

"An obnoxious cost to make them as one!" complained Obnoxious Koss.

The Lycan buccaneers turned to Iblis as he tore away from the roots.

"A bloodstone can contain Tomorrow," answered Iblis.

"No gem can contain Tomorrow. It'll take you forever to find one," replied Sound.

"The one I speak of has significance," explained Iblis. "It belonged to a tribe of gypsies, molded over time by battles and competition between other tribes. Now it rests in the safe of an Abominable."

"How did you know that?" asked Gall.

"One might say it's because I'm the devil, and I know all your heart's desires. Or, I can tell you I saw it in your safe when you attempted to elude the police," answered Iblis.

"My ring?" blurted Sitoel.

Iblis responded with a nod as Sitoel shook her head in disbelief.

"So *Sit-o-Well* the gypsy was good for something after all," heckled Sound.

"Hold your tongue witch, unless you forgot what happened the last time I corrected that mispronunciation," threatened Sitoel.

Suddenly Tomorrow's cap began to move on its own.

"Cerberus has found him! You must hurry. Use the sleeve to transport Gall to his estate and return with the bloodstone," instructed Iblis.

"I will be swift!" Sitoel angrily replied in a tone that carried a hiss. She slid on the sleeve and cast a lightning bolt that took her and Gall away.

Within seconds, they arrived at the Abominable Estate. A swift punch to Gall's abdomen followed. He dropped to his knees gasping for breath as Sitoel removed her escrima sticks.

"You knew how much that ring meant to me! Now we have to fork it over to Iblis," snapped Sitoel.

"Give me a chance to explain," said Gall. "I kept it because Lu Dongbin warned me of the events that would take place before his death. I thought it would be safer in my safe, and if Iblis turned

against us, we could use it against him." He staggered to his feet
and walked to the safe.

"Why would you think such a thing? It's just an ordinary gem?"
asked Sitoel.

"It's not an ordinary gem. It's rumored to be the same stone that
Christ bled upon when he was stabbed during the crucifixion," replied Gall. He opened the safe and removed the bloodstone. "I can't
explain now. You'll just have to trust me. Technically, the bloodstone
will still be in our possession. Iblis will give the sleeve to one of us."

"It better be me!" shouted Sitoel. She cast another lightning bolt
to transport them back to Iblis.

When they returned, they saw Tomorrow's cap and boots standing on their own. The objects shook in fear as Cerberus backed
Tomorrow and Eons' soul into a corner in purgatory.

"Now hand me the gem!" demanded Iblis. Gall held out the
gem, and Iblis snatched it from his hand. He approached the cap and
gripped a few inches below it to grasp the soul. Iblis pulled it from
purgatory by the throat and cast it into the bloodstone. Tomorrow
regained his form, and to everyone's surprise, Eon was bonded to
him. Iblis centered the bloodstone in his creation. The branches
sprouted vines that held it in place of the coronary artery. Everyone
watched in awe as Iblis recited the verse. "Tomorrow, are you ready?"

When he was done, a pair of eyes sprouted and reflected the
luster of the bloodstone. Iblis walked over to Gall and handed him
the sleeve and gloves.

"Me? Why me?" asked Gall.

"The alignment of stars at the pyramid is only the display of
a gate," answered Iblis. "You have to unlock it, and to do so you'll
need a key."

"Praetorian!" interrupted Junior. The shout from Tomorrow's
vessel caught everyone but Iblis off guard.

"He's grown attached to you," said Iblis. The fourth Marid
Djinn stretched the roots of hate to a height that matched Gall's.

He also changed the facial features to resemble a black Venetian bauta mask.

"It's not safe out in the open. Let's return to the ship and set sail for Egypt," instructed Lord Treachery.

The crew of the Deaf Dum Dead returned and hoisted the sails for Egypt. Excalibur was handed to Blackmarket Ginyel to make a sleeve. He raced below deck to begin work as Enemy presented another problem to Iblis.

"We need more vests! There wasn't any time to mold any," complained Enemy.

"Blackmarket Ginyel will not be done with the sleeve if he tends to the task. What are we to do?" asked Unchained Gauge.

"Do not be troubled when you have a Redcap goblin on board. Tomorrow's enhanced craftsmanship is at your service," answered Iblis.

"An excellent idea!" replied Enemy.

"You may also take the opportunity to brief our passengers on the dangers we'll face while on this mission," advised Iblis.

Enemy gestured for the Marid Djinns to follow him below deck as he began to explain. "There's a reason why I refer to our vests as being *protective.*"

The group made their way below deck, and the clatter of a blacksmith at work aided the conversation. Enemy pointed out a door to Tomorrow and escorted the Marid Djinns through another door on the opposite side.

"They were made from spider webs," said Enemy.

Banter tumbled over with laughter at the idea. "I've heard of spiders making silk, but vests?"

Enemy walked to the corner of the room where a pile of objects was covered with a blanket. "Why should that be so hard to believe? A common spider web possesses a sixth of the density of steel."

"Yeah, but you'll need a lot more than a spider's web to make a vest," said Banter.

Enemy pulled back the blanket and removed a vest from a crate.

"This one saved my life. To show my appreciation, I've decided to give them hell every time we meet." Enemy held up the vest and displayed the tooth of a megalodon wedged in the center.

"Dinosaurs? We're going up against dinosaurs!" shouted Banter.

"I knew this display would put an end to your heckling, scallywag. These vests have been put to the test. The only time I saw one torn apart was when Zeus called upon Lightning. Fortunately for us, he's now on our side."

"How did Horus get dinosaurs for protection?"

"We have Isis to thank for that problem. Remember the story I told you about Grit and Muzzle Blast?"

"Yeah, it pertained to the concerns of a dying mother—how the accumulation of grief and fear can summon a guardian angel for the child."

"Well, now you don't have to imagine the magnitude of fear and grief accumulated by a goddess," answered Enemy. Enemy gently placed the vest on the crate, and patted the tooth in a manner that showed appreciation to the mother that had spun the web. "When the life of Horus was threatened, Isis hid him in the marshlands of the Nile River. Horus eventually learned how to communicate with these creatures. He told them his story, and they became servants in his court for kingship. This gift is also backed by the powers of Ra. Isis created a snake and laid it in Ra's path to obtain it. It poisoned him, and forced him to reveal his real name to her. The bold act granted her a shared power that Isis gave to Horus. This power can turn the average predator into a dinosaur. We will face as many as six in a pack." Enemy walked over to a barrel of mead and punched a hole in the top. "We always had to replenish our ranks after a trip like this." He lifted the barrel and drowned his face in the overflow. He emptied the contents and shattered the barrel with his punch technique. "I advise you to double your vest. Another hunt begins!"

Follow the transformation of the three Marid Djinns in comics and graphic novels:

Three Marid Djinns in the Eye of Ra and Horus

The Vaults in Styles Corporate Building: An Angel with No Borders

The Lycan Buccaneers: Attempt Capture in Vain! Wanted Dead!

# About the Author

J uan Berry has been a fan of supernatural stories since his child-hood, an interest that eventually moved on to films. One of the reasons he decided to create characters of his own and write books is that he someday intends to adapt his stories into movies.

Printed in the United States
by Baker & Taylor Publisher Services